PRAISE FOR

THE OLD ROMANTIC

"Remarkably astute . . . Dean has perfect pitch [and] she sneaks in just enough grace to give her characters a chance to prove Thomas Wolfe wrong: As long as you don't expect anyone to get out the good china, you can go home again."　　　　*—The Washington Post*

"A highly entertaining, vivid evocation of love and marriage in various forms . . . Dean's characters have the rough edges and surprising grace of real people, and her fierce humanism animates every page."　　　　*—The New York Times Book Review*

"Dean's characters, like ensemble actors, explore the light and dark sides of relationships, memory, death, and the deep pull of family love."　　　　*—People*

"Dean's narrative gifts are a delight. All the characters, whatever their age or degree of separation from the main route of the plot, are as individually rounded and polished as pearls on a string."　　　　*—The Boston Globe*

"Dean's razor-sharp observations, coupled with her very real affection for her characters, make the pages fly."　　　　*—Entertainment Weekly*

"Vividly imagined and surprisingly funny . . . Call it sentimental if you like, but it's also sweet and genuine and universally true."　　　　—Associated Press

"Dark, scurrilous, and richly comic . . . There is so much to treasure in this terrific book."　　　　*—Financial Times*

"[A] sardonic yet sweet tale of an estranged family trying to heal old wounds."　　　　*—The Ladies Home Journal*

"Brilliant . . . [Dean's] insights are dazzling. . . . Characters rake themselves through self-revelations, and the prose leaps with a fervor for the present moment."
—*Minneapolis Star-Tribune*

"Very appealing . . . Dean shows a fondness for her characters while still sending them up mercilessly—and hilariously. . . . Delightful."
—*The Guardian*

"Louise Dean has one of the most original, insightful, and funny voices I've read in contemporary fiction. She seems incapable of writing a dull sentence. The hilarious family drama at the heart of *The Old Romantic* is so terrible, truthful, and touching, and the characters so vivid and alive, I couldn't put the book down."
—Stephen McCauley, author of *The Object of My Affection*

"Thick with complexity—the stuff of real writing. It is about memory and the unstable, selective nature of it. It is about love, as distinct from romance. . . . [it] is about coming home and finding an authentic voice—something [Dean] has certainly done here."
—*The London Telegraph*

"A grimly hilarious family saga . . . leading to a denouement that perfectly balances humor and poignancy. Dean, with her superb ear for language and class nuance, gives readers the essence of contemporary British life in this touching and funny family portrait."
—*Publishers Weekly* (starred review)

"Dean mercilessly sends up the working class to hilarious effect even as she compassionately reveals, in fresh and vivid language, the primal desire to return home."
—*Booklist*

"Tartly sweet . . . A dark yet sometimes rocking comedy . . . Dean's acerbic affection for her characters and her social commentary are both spot-on and surprisingly poignant."
—*Kirkus Reviews*

"This novel's pitch-perfect dialogue, sparkling wit, and sharp observations of life, love, and mortality make it a winner."
—*Library Journal*

THE OLD ROMANTIC

Louise Dean

RIVERHEAD BOOKS

New York

RIVERHEAD BOOKS

Published by the Penguin Group

Penguin Group (USA) Inc., 375 Hudson Street, New York, New York 10014, USA • Penguin
Group (Canada), 90 Eglinton Avenue East, Suite 700, Toronto, Ontario M4P 2Y3, Canada
(a division of Pearson Penguin Canada Inc.) • Penguin Books Ltd., 80 Strand, London WC2R 0RL,
England • Penguin Group Ireland, 25 St. Stephen's Green, Dublin 2, Ireland (a division of Penguin
Books Ltd.) • Penguin Group (Australia), 250 Camberwell Road, Camberwell, Victoria 3124,
Australia (a division of Pearson Australia Group Pty. Ltd.) • Penguin Books India Pvt. Ltd.,
11 Community Centre, Panchsheel Park, New Delhi—110 017, India • Penguin Group (NZ),
67 Apollo Drive, Rosedale, Auckland 0632, New Zealand (a division of Pearson
New Zealand Ltd.) • Penguin Books (South Africa) (Pty.) Ltd., 24 Sturdee Avenue,
Rosebank, Johannesburg 2196, South Africa

Penguin Books Ltd., Registered Offices: 80 Strand, London WC2R 0RL, England

Originally published by Penguin UK: 2010
First Riverhead hardcover edition: February 2011
First Riverhead trade paperback edition: February 2012
Riverhead trade paperback ISBN: 978-1-59448-563-3

The Library of Congress has catalogued the Riverhead hardcover edition as follows:

Dean, Louise.
The old romantic / Louise Dean.
p.   cm.
ISBN 978-1-59448-779-8
1. Working-class families—Great Britain—Fiction.   2. Older men—Fiction.
3. Fathers and sons—Fiction.   I. Title.
PR6104.E24O63   2011   2010036868
823'.92—dc22

PRINTED IN THE UNITED STATES OF AMERICA

10   9   8   7   6   5   4   3   2   1

For Beryl and Tim

The great thing in life is to make some sort of a refuge for oneself. At the end of one's existence, as at the beginning, one's got to be borne by a woman.

François Mauriac, *The Desert of Love*

THE OLD ROMANTIC

1

People seem to tumble down to Hastings and not get up to go home again. It's where they turn up, every Jack and Jill that ever fell out with the family, lost a job, had half an idea, got a bad habit. The town is a huddle of administrative towers and down-at-heel shops with their backs turned on the sea views.

Poor Hastings. The steam train once chuffed proudly into Warrior Square, where the statue of the Empress of India stood with her hooded eyes on the sea. The minor royals played here for a season, the gentry's carriages drew up at the West Hill lift, the bourgeois bought villas in St Leonards. But now the Olympic-sized bathing pool is gone, the model town vandalized and the pier closed. Rock candy congeals in cellophane under blow heaters, and steel udders drop soft whip in souvenir shops. In the tuppenny arcade, on any given day of the week, there'll be an old man feeling for change in the trays.

The seafront west to St Leonards is a parade of four-storeyed Regency guesthouses that display 'For Sale' or 'To Let' signs. In size and colour, they are as uniform as a pack of custard creams and nothing bothers the skyline until the end of the promenade where 'Marine Court' soars—a 1930s fantasy, a block of flats masquerading as a cruise liner.

Where the seafront ends, the buildings kneel, going from three storeys to two, and the twentieth century bobs and jogs along in semis until it's brought up short at the Bo Peep pub. On a blackboard tied to a lamp post, the pub has two bands chalked up for this weekend: Friday night's 'Shameless Behaviour' will be followed on Saturday by 'Dirty Shoes'. From here on is the road to Bexhill, a few miles of terraced houses, lining a corridor through which the traffic is relentless. This is the area known as Bulverhythe; it is where his father lives now.

Nick's shoulders round as he scans the house names. He ducks when they pass under a railway bridge, and slows the Range Rover to a crawl. Those obliged to go round him honk censoriously, all the heavier on the horn because of the car it is.

'A bungalow,' Dave said. 'You'll find it.'

His father's is the only house reduced to a single storey of meanness on this street and it's the worst placed. Two lanes of traffic careen down the steep hill from the right and spill cars outside the old man's place, branching left and right at his very front door. Ken lives slap bang on the junction, and in between the traffic lights.

Nick pulls up onto the pavement without indicating, and the pair of them, he and Astrid, sit tight with the great car rattling and shuddering in the wake of the abuse and hooting of the passing cars.

It is fifteen years since he last saw his father.

2

This is not his town; this is his father's town. This is not coming home. He did that when he moved back to the Weald, where two counties meet in hills and valleys, in a hinterland of hop bine and tractor track, white weatherboard cottage and oast house, fruit field and orchard. That morning when he walked the dog, with woodsmoke forming halos above the dwellings, the country-side of his childhood seemed primitive to him—with no tarmac, no pylon, no telephone mast visible at all. Walking brings back memories. He likes to potter into the past and nip into the future, the way the dog moves, a waggy-tailed waverer on the scent of something good and aware too of other pleasures all about.

When they went over the stile onto the newly ploughed field, the dog ran at its centre and rooks took to the skies vexed and carping and cawing, circling in a posse. It was March, but win-ter presided despite the farmer's efforts to kick-start spring. The field reeked of manure, and Nick had a flashback of his brother, Dave, squatting on the white seat of Nick's new Raleigh bicycle, bought for him for getting the scholarship to private school, as he wheeled him home.

'Don't tell Mum, right? You won't tell Mum, will you?'

And the first thing he'd said, bursting through the kitchen door: 'Dave's shat himself, Mum! He's got it all down his legs!'

All sorts of betrayals, he'd thought sadly, remembering his brother's face, all sorts of betrayals to get ahead. An elder brother is always on the make. His little brother was dismayed, on the other hand, if he got anything at Nick's expense. Whether it was merely a good stout stick or a brand-new toy, Dave would look at it, then look at Nick. 'We could share it,' he'd say, 'or you could just have it.'

Before Christmas, his only contact at all with his mother and father was through his brother.

'They've not spoken in ages. Donkey's years,' Astrid says in company and he lets it pass, nods it on its way, this shorthand, this convenience, and gets in the next round. But there is no nonchalance, never mind the number of years. Poor put-upon Dave has been duty-bound to all parties to pass unkindness back and forth; and he's done so, too good-natured to be good. The hurt is thus still keen.

'God almighty,' Nick says to Astrid now, peeping at his father's house, humorous and rueful, 'I did mention to you that my father was a touch working class, didn't I?'

'Perchance' is the name painted onto a cross section of a log, varnished and tacked to the guttering over the front door of the bungalow. The front garden is concrete. The other houses have

two-foot-high walls for decency's sake but his has been demol-
ished. Weeds have sprung up in the cracks of the forecourt.
There's a lean-to shelter outside the bungalow, with a corrugated
yellow plastic roof and under it is a tall set of shelves stacked with
various plastic bottles, some with their heads cut off: cooking oil,
window cleaner, plant food. There is a decrepit Christmas tree in
a pot, and an old Queen Anne wing-backed chair bearing a large
string bag of onions.

They sit there with the engine running. She turns the bracelets
on her wrist. 'Grim,' she says lightly.

3

The net curtains drop back into place in the window and out of the front door comes the couple: a short woman, no more than five foot, rotund and orange-coated, something like a Russian doll, followed by an old man who is tall and angular. She is red-faced and merry; he is pale and disdainful.

'Oh, shit me, it's the Krankies!' says Astrid, looking at the small stout woman in her mac, support socks and rain bonnet, twisting a plastic carrier bag.

Ken pushes the front door to test that it's locked shut. When he turns round, he does not so much as raise his head. He walks bowed and solemn in stark contrast with his wife, who is waddling ahead eager and open-mouthed. The stubble on his jaw glitters. He bears the weight of a navy-blue raincoat as if it's a tarpaulin. He has the translucent hair of a toddler: a floss in a soft white quiff. There's something about it that begs for a small Cadbury's Flake, Astrid thinks, one side of her mouth curling into a smile.

Nick opens his door, lets in the sea air and the seagulls' screams.

The first phone calls from the old man were silent, but Nick could hear the gulls in the background, just as he can hear them now: a chorus of outrage, remorseless and repetitive, stirring up an age-old ache.

'Love you,' says Astrid.

He turns his collar up and gives her a wink, but his face is dismal when he goes to face his father again.

It would not be your traditional family roast lunch, she thinks, but then it hadn't been your traditional Christmas call that got this particular ball rolling. She'd amused their friends with it all on Boxing Day in the pub.

'I couldn't believe it! I mean, call me old-fashioned but in our family we have turkey and stuffing on Christmas Day and a call from Auntie Jan in Portsmouth. So there we are, paper hats on, about to pour the gravy and the phone goes, and Laura's like, Mum, who's Nick on the phone to? And I'm like, It's his dad, darling, he's just wishing him a merry Christmas. And the next thing you hear from the conservatory is Nick screaming, And you're nothing to me either, you old bastard!'

Nick had stood his ground there at the bar, pint in hand, and smiled with his mouth, attempting a comedic sangfroid, but when they left just before midnight, in the cold night of the car park, he caught hold of Astrid and said, 'You tell me. What kind of a man speaks to his son that way?'

And when she looked into his eyes in the lamplight and heard his breath catch, she saw what he wanted and gave it to him.

'I know,' she'd said. She kissed him on the mouth and held his face and stroked his hair. 'I know. It's terrible.'

4

There was no contact there on the forecourt under the low grey sky. They were two men pulling their coats to, in the wind. They held their faces sideways onto each other. Each seemed to find something in the distance to dismay him. When Nick stuffed his hands into his pockets, his father did the same. When he spoke, he jerked his head. When his father spoke, he jerked his head too. June, Ken's wife, stood between them, gleeful, looking from one to the other. Her mouth was moving and she was nodding at Nick and nodding at Ken, commending one to the other.

When the windows fogged, Astrid used the button to lower the driver's window. She leant across to peer into his wing mirror and observe them. The car seemed suddenly to become part of the scene—huge, black and looming—and she was embarrassed.

Nick's father was wearing pointed shiny shoes. His raincoat was immaculate, his trousers sharp of crease. There was something of the 1950s about him. He was scowling. 'How long does it take from where you live? We've been waiting since midday.'

'Is it Tenterden where you are?' June asked. 'Did you come through Hawkhurst? Is that bus station still there? It's an hour on the bus if you get a good change-over at Hawkhurst.'

'It takes about half an hour in the car,' said Nick.

'You must of drove like a nutter if it took you half an hour.'

'It's only twenty miles, Ken,' put in June, affably. 'And the traffic on a Sunday isn't like on the weekdays.'

'How do you know? You never drove it.'

'And look at this!' said June, bringing the Range Rover into the conversation with her arm. 'It's bigger than our house! I say, Kenneth, did you see the car your son's driving now?'

Astrid sat up in her seat and checked the traffic over her shoulder. It was time to be taken account of. The lights changed and she dropped down out of the car and slid along the side to arrive at the rear in front of them all.

The men had their hands in their pockets. She put her hands in her pockets too. The father sucked in his cheeks and raised his eyebrows, his expression of disapproval of both her and the car as plain as if Nick had produced a hooker from a stretch limousine.

'Hi,' she said.

'All right,' said the old man, more speaking for himself than enquiring after her.

She greeted June with cheek kisses, and it was as if the woman was turned to stone by such a display. In her throat, June made the gurgling noise of a chicken brooding.

'Well, I never did. Well, Ken? You didn't expect to see your own son turn up like this, did you now? With this posh lady too.'

The old man indicated the car to her with an impatient wagging finger. 'Come on, or else we'll be late.'

Nick took June's arm to help her into the rear. There was a small step up and her hard skirt, her bad joints and stout legs conspired with her easily triggered sense of humour to make getting her into the car quite a palaver. She was straining and whooping, in contrition and amusement. Once in, and shifted across to the right side, she sat holding her handbag, panting, a lock of hair over one eye. 'I'm all out of puff, the man said!'

Nick went to take his father's arm. He was shaken off. His father put a hand on the seat and a hand on its headrest and pulled himself inside. Sitting sideways, the old man's legs hung in the door well and, as an afterthought, he at last drew them in.

When Nick pulled out onto the main road, Astrid saw his face was set with concentration as if it were really a difficult thing, this driving business.

'I like to keep my mind active,' June prattled pleasantly. 'Now, I know from the milometer on David's car that it's nine miles to Fairlight. Harley Shute, Hollington. Up Blackman Avenue onto Old Harrow Road, then Sedlescombe Road North past the Tesco's.'

'Oh, she knows where all the shops are. She knows the shops all right,' said Ken.

'Then the Rye Road and past the B&Q down into Guestling, then on down Rosemary Lane. It's a very nice place, Fairlight. When you think about it, it's as pretty as anywhere.'

'How would you know? Where have you ever been?' snapped Ken.

'I've been to Wales.'

'That's all you bin to! Wales!'

'It's a very nice place, Wales.'

'There's nowhere like home.'

'Maybe for you, but this is not *my* home.'

'Thirty years you bin 'ere. You tell me then, where is your home? In the sky, is it?'

'If He'll have me!' she trilled victoriously.

'Just like Wales, is it, up there then?'

'What we deserve comes to each and every one of us in good time, Kenneth.'

'All in good time, she says,' he repeated darkly. 'There's no good time. When He calls you, He calls and that's that. But, oh no, she knows best. She knows better than Him.'

Nick checked the driving mirror, to see the woman's face. There was so much steely goodwill in her that with her mouth closed it came out through her eyes.

'June? Hey. You must have been a saint to put up with this one,' Nick said, catching her eye as they drew up at the lights.

Her eyes twinkled and she reached for Ken's hand, but his father's hand remained crabbish on his knee with hers on top of it. He looked out of the window, his face bitter.

Ken and June met on the promenade outside the White Rock in 1988, just a year after his divorce from Pearl, Nick's mother. Unabashedly, she told him that she was a woman of some means thanks to her late husband. Not more than thirty minutes later, according to Dave's version of events, the pair of them stood up with everything more or less arranged. It was a pragmatic alliance for Ken. Her money bought the next four flats that they developed and added to the company's lettings.

But June had different ideas about the marriage and, according to Dave, she set great store by the fact that Ken had bought her flowers and chocolates during their engagement and that they'd had the odd meal out. She had romantic aspirations.

She was to be disappointed. Although there was the occasional outing to The Italian Way, on the seafront, Ken made sure never to have more than a bowl of soup out and was highly critical of 'people' who were greedier than him in public, such as June.

'Tell 'em what I said on my birthday, June,' Ken said now as they went up the hill of the Old Harrow Road.

June leant forward, pleased to be called to bear witness. She looked like the sort of woman who would enjoy being in court. She looked like the sort of woman who didn't get much in the way of company. 'Seventy-eight years old and he says to me, if you please, the very first thing when he wakes, he says—'

'November the twenty-fifth, it was,' the old man put in.

'He says, June, he says, This is the year I'll die. I said, What a thing to say, Kenneth! Fancy waking up on your birthday and saying that. . . .' She burst into laughter. 'It tickled me! What a thing to say!'

'Same day every year, it is,' Ken grumbled. 'November twenty-fifth.'

At the traffic lights by the Sainsbury's on Sedlescombe Road North, with his arms embracing the steering wheel, and bent over it, Nick looked as if he were climbing it to get as far away from his father as possible. His focus trained on the red light, his eyes blinked like a digital clock.

The light changed.

When the car took off, the seat belts locked and pinned them to their seats.

5

The first call of the New Year was from Dave to tell Nick that
their dad's sister, Auntie Pat, had died. Nick declined to go to the
funeral. Dave called him again a month later, in February, at
work.

'All right, mate.'

'All right, Dave.'

'Know any good hymns?'

'Good hymns? What for?'

'For a funeral.'

'What, Auntie Pat's? I thought that was done and dusted, so to
speak.'

'No, Dad's.'

After a moment's silence, Dave broke out into a throaty chuckle.
'He's what you call a hymn short of a funeral service, our dad.'

Ken had become obsessed with death since Pat's passing, he

said. Talk about maudlin! He'd got himself a book on Victorian services of order and he wanted the whole shebang. He'd called them up at home and got Dave's daughter, Emily, to look through her recorder book for school assemblies and play through this hymn and that hymn, and then he'd said, 'No, that's not the one,' and put the phone down. He'd had Dave's son, Matt, print off from the Internet some sort of order for nonintervention. He was in and out of the undertakers on Norman Road, leafing through funeral plans and making a nuisance of himself.

'Get this, right, he had a bit of maroon-coloured nylon ruffle with him in his coat pocket the other day and he asked Marina what she thought of it. It was only flaming coffin lining.'

'Silly old sod.'

He seemed to have developed a crush on the funeral director on Norman Road, Dave said. 'A woman.'

'That's something.'

'Keeps on about her being a fine woman and such a shame he's met her so late in life. I think he's hoping for a discount or something. He's gone and offered her his services.'

'Christ. Has he got anything left to offer?'

'Helping out, working at the undertakers as a volunteer. Well, he's more or less retired from the business, thank Christ. Got no interest in it anymore. Says property's usury, or something. I don't know. He likes his Bible these days.' He was going to church of a Sunday and talking a storm about the big man in the sky, but in truth, as Dave put it, Ken was clueless. He was like a man in a bar trying to order something he'd had as a child by explaining how it tasted.

He'd really gone downhill lately, Dave said. 'Health-wise, I mean. He's always been a bit bloody nutty, innie? But he's frail with it now.'

He'd had prostate cancer the year before, and he had the beginnings of Parkinson's now and didn't drive. Dave didn't like to ask, but he thought their father was probably having a bit of trouble with the waterworks too.

He came to the point, in his way.

'Look, you know, I mean, I know you're going to say no, and you don't have to and, I mean, why should you, know what I mean? If I was you, I wouldn't, and you could say years have passed—too many, maybe—but, you see, well, I dunno . . .'

'What?'

Would Nick consider a get-together?

'I don't think so, mate.'

Nick put him off, but Dave began to call every week and the calls become more and more burdened.

'Yes. You?'

'Yup. All right.'

'So, what's going on?'

'Nothing.'

'Right.'

'Busy?'

'Yup. You?'

'So-so.'

Pause.

'Well, good talking to you.'

'You too.'

'Bye then.'

'Yup. Bye, mate.'

This was how Dave prevailed upon his elder brother, and the pall of the silences spoke more to Nick's heart than anything Dave could say.

Astrid was as much prurient as compassionate when it came to Nick's family. Very quickly, perhaps even before she'd thought it through, an outfit came to mind. She reasoned, pussy-bow blouse in mind, that they were so happy, nothing could touch them. You should make peace with your past, she said. After all, you've come home, haven't you?

Her eyes sparkled.

Women, he'd said to himself, were the most mysterious of mates. Where a man wants to know what's going to happen next, a woman wants to know what it means.

6

By the time they mounted the hill past Baldslow on the Ridge, there had passed several minutes of silence, punctuated here and there by a thrilled sigh from June as she recalled another part of what her husband had said on his birthday.

'This your wife here, is it then?' said Ken, pointing a finger at Astrid, to make it clear who he meant.

Astrid turned and met his eyes.

'Nope. This is Astrid,' said Nick evenly.

Ken's chin jutted as he moved his head to see through the side window, up past the lodge into the car park of the cemetery and crematorium. 'Nothing doing today then.' He set his eyes on the road, scrutinizing it for potential accidents, grasping the back of Astrid's headrest. '*Astrid?* What's that—Danish, or something? Always has to be a foreigner, dunnit! Cor, that gel saw you coming—what was her name?' He nudged June. 'What was her name?'

'Was it an Angelica who came with you to our wedding?' June began. 'Because after that there was a Lydia, wasn't there, or something? At the christening, wore that—well, I call it mauve—frock. Lydia, that's right, *tall*, or was it Laverne . . . ?'

'Or bleeding Shirley. Give over, woman!'

'Annette! That's right. I knew I'd get there in the end!'

Astrid's fingers went limp on his knee and Nick squeezed them together with his own hand, but failed to catch her eye.

When he saw the sign for his brother's house, he slammed on the brakes, and under-geared, the car lumbered painfully up the potholed track to 'Longwinter Farmhouse'.

'Bleeding long way up this drive, it is,' said Ken. 'You couldn't walk it, could you, June? With your legs.'

'I daresay I couldn't.'

'You wouldn't be able to go walking about in Wales, would you?'

'I daresay I wouldn't.'

'Bit posh for you here, innit, June?' Gripped with sudden delight, Ken's voice quavered.

'I'll manage.'

The old man gave curt instructions to his driver. 'Pull up by the sheds there. That's it. Stop there. Swing it in behind David's car, that's it. Come on! Plenty of space. Get a move on. Our dinner'll be cold by the time you've got us there. Blimey. Take it easy. I say, June—I nearly lost my breakfast there.'

When Nick had helped June down and set her in motion like

a clockwork penguin towards the house, he went round to his
father's door.

Ken lay a hand on each of his shoulders as he got down. Nick
had to steel himself not to flinch from the unwelcome touch.
His father's eyes were a thin blue, paler than Nick recalled. He
spoke in a fervent whisper. 'Remember your mother and me, how
happy we was when you was a nipper? Remember how she used
to have a turn if you caught her singing . . . ? She used to raise her
fists to me when I come up behind her, she was a bit 'andy that
way, wa'n't she? She was what you call an honest woman, though,
wa'n't she? Wa'n't she?'

Nick glanced towards the house and saw June standing on the
doorstep in her triangular coat, holding her bag with two hands,
waiting.

'Just a minute now, give your old man a minute of your time.
I know you want to get in that house and get away from me. But
give your old man a second now. It's bin a long time, 'annit?' He
tightened his grip on Nick's shoulders. 'Listen now, son. I'm going
to die.'

'We're all going to die.'

'Yes, but the odds is getting shorter for me, though, a'n't they?'
He rolled his eyes and tutted. 'Now look, I might not of met my
maker as yet, but I have met *reality*.' He said the word as though
it were holy. He meant a lot by it. He'd always had his favourite
words. His father was not stupid; if he had a good thought, he
hung on to it. 'Do you know what I mean? *Reality*. What I done
wrong. What I bin.'

It was difficult. His father was holding him there, telling him
to stay there, to heed him, and yet all they had between them was

the air they were breathing. He'd long cultivated different tastes and different habits deliberately so as not to resemble him.

'I'm your father. What's in me, is in you. Wherever I'm heading, you're right behind me. You're walking in my footsteps. 'Cause I'm your father and you're my son. And no one can change that.'

Astrid said to him once, with the laundry folded, supper cleared and Laura in bed, when they sat down for a glass of wine, that it's only when you have children yourself that you can really love your parents properly. You see all the little things that took it out of them, the hot-water bottle, the clean sheets, all the things they did even though they were aching to sit down, even though they didn't get thanks for the good things, only the blame for the bad things. They'd laughed at the injustice served by Laura, who, when finding the joke shop by the station had closed down, wailed at her mother: 'That's *your* fault!'

'Kids blame their parents for everything. It's only when you have kids yourself that you stop being a kid,' she'd said, her face the picture of innocence.

'We're blood,' the old man insisted. 'You and me. We're father and son. Like it nor not.'

'All right,' Nick conceded. 'All right, but let's talk about it inside.'

'Thank you,' Ken said, and he patted his son's arm and looked towards the house, his expression both conciliatory and keen.

7

Dave's wife, Marina, was at the door with her arms folded, raising her shoulders and looking at the sky in comment on the miserable weather, and an invitation into the warmth of the farmhouse. She resembled an ostrich with the broad plumage of a big skirt, thin from the waist up in a ribbed polo neck, with a long neck and a beaky nose. The fuzz that burst from the hair clip was a top note of mayhem, Astrid noted, comparing herself favourably and donning a homely smile. Dave popped a tanned bald head out from behind Marina and emerged, hands in jeans pockets, sunny of smile.

With one old-timer running out of clockwork and seizing up at the door, Nick propelled the next one forth. From behind, with his head nodding over the paving, Ken was clearly an old man, doddery and frail as Dave had said. Nick bit his lip. '*You're walking in my footsteps.*'

The old man stalled on the threshold of the farmhouse,

gripping June's arm and preventing her from entering until she had answered his urgent question.

'Ain't that right, June? Ain't that right?'

'If you say so, Ken.'

Marina and Dave exchanged mournful looks at what was taking place and shared the same with Astrid and Nick, who were outside by the welly rack.

'You can only love *one* person in your lifetime. You can only get married, in the eyes of the Lord, *one* time. That's right, though, innit?'

June laughed spiritedly and rolled her eyes. 'Like I said, *If you say so, Kenneth*.'

He released her arm and subsided, looking down at his polished shoes, mulling this over.

'Come on in, Dad,' said Dave. 'Come on, now.'

As Marina embraced June, she rubbed the old woman's back in condolence. 'You wouldn't think it was spring, would you?'

The old boy piped up again from the doorway. 'See, she and I, David, we're just companions really. We was only married in registry anyway.'

'All right, Dad. Come in, now. Let's get Nick and Astrid in and close the door.'

'Did I break your mother's 'eart, do you think?' And before Dave could answer, Ken was nodding miserably, 'I did. I know I did.'

Dave settled both him and June in the two carver chairs at the pine table, facing the length of the kitchen. Astrid gave a bunch of white lilies to Marina and the women exchanged cheek kisses and fell promptly into the self-deprecation that is the stock-in-trade of women who want to play nicely.

'Oh, the wind's wrecked my hair!'

'Don't worry, I look like that on a good day! Sometimes the most I can do is look clean—and sometimes I can't even manage that!'

'Oh, I know!' cried Astrid, fulsome and false. She worked with women day in, day out. Marina was no threat; this was not a woman who'd sell her children to be thinner and younger. So she added for good measure, 'I can't believe how old I look without make-up these days!'

'I don't even bother! It has to be our anniversary for me to shave my legs!'

Astrid gave Nick a triumphant smile. She'd done her part. Let family relations recommence.

But the older couple were not at home and they declined to give their coats. When served a cup of tea, they sat stiffly holding the mugs, looking like a photograph from a bygone era.

June was cowed, perhaps by the large kitchen and its chunky modishness—the Aga, the dresser with its natty chinaware, the table laid in bold colours with candy-striped cutlery and spotted napkin rings—or perhaps by the weight of the pint mug itself, or the hops hanging from the beams. Their dinner plates at home were the size of the side plates here. They drank their tea in Bulverhythe from small fluted cups with saucers. They kept their crockery in the plastic tub in the sink under grey water. They heated pre-packaged burgers in buns in the microwave or boiled water for packet soup. Dominating the display in their kitchen was a great economy-size bottle of yellow washing-up liquid. You didn't sit people in your kitchen! You closed a door on it, in her book.

When Matt sauntered through to help himself to a drink from the fridge, Ken's eyes lit up and he gave June a dig in the ribs.

'That's the future there,' he said. 'In that boy.'

Matt, with asymmetrical dyed black haircut, in a vest and low-slung jeans, leant against the Belfast sink, can at his lips. His eyes didn't show, but the top of his boxer shorts did. There was a silver chain trailing from one pocket of his jeans.

'Nice looking, innie? June? 'An'some. Like old whassisname, done the singing . . .'

'Frank Sinatra.'

'No.'

'Frankie Valli?'

'No. Whassisname? Went round on the red bus with that bird from Worzel Gummidge.'

'Cliff Richard?'

'Thassim!'

Matt's eyes focused on the keyhole of the can as if willing it to take him in.

'Frankie Valli! What's wrong with you? He was American an' ugly as sin.'

Seeing the two women at the range in chat, Dave asked Nick to come and have a look at the carport he'd built. The brothers went out, Dave's hand patting Ken's shoulder as he went.

Ken was giving June one of his funny looks, down the length of his nose. June sat there impervious, bag on lap.

'He keeps asking me if I know Jesus,' Marina murmured out of the side of her mouth to Astrid.

'Who? Ken?'

'Yes.'

'What do you say?'

'No, but I've heard good things.'

'Oh shit!'

'Well, what can you say?'

'I hope he doesn't ask me any trick questions. Nick said he was a bit nutty.'

Matt slunk around the perimeter of the kitchen—his target the door—and, coming up alongside them, ventured a lacklustre enquiry in the old couple's direction. 'All right then, are you, Granddad? Nana June?'

'You're the future, aren't you, sunbeam? Chip off the block. Be running the business in a couple of years.'

'Don't look at me, man,' the thirteen-year-old boy said. His lower lip was a half-sulk. He blew his fringe up for a second to reveal kohl-rimmed eyes.

'What's he say, June?' said Ken, with a sharp grin, leaning in to her to hear.

'I don't know!'

Matt was, according to Marina, an 'emo-boy'. They didn't know what it was, she told Astrid.

She lifted a saucepan lid and dragged a tiny piece of broccoli to her mouth. 'I've no idea what he gets up to on his computer day and night. I wish he'd get into girls; you know, real ones.'

'What did he say, I'm asking you? What did my grandson say?'

Pining for the silent bliss of the virtual world where he was Master and Lord, Matt made a break for the door.

'You want to clean your ears out, Kenneth.' June lifted her brow in supplication and whistled. 'Lord, give me strength.'

It was the women's laughter that did it. Ken folded his arms over his chest and ground his teeth.

'Sounds like you're having fun,' said Dave as they came back in. He shrugged off the cold from outside and clapped his hands.

Ken narrowed his eyes at June. 'You and me, we're going to be parting ways, woman!'

'So you say!'

Astrid looked over the rim of her wineglass at Nick.

'She don't tell me where she keeps the money, you know.'

'And you don't tell me where you keep yours, Kenneth, so we're even.'

'Mine's the business money, though, innit?'

'And mine's my own money, the money that came to me when Brian died. And I'm holding it for the next generation.'

'The next generation! No point in talking to someone who's pig-headed.'

'That's right!' she chimed.

'Who has to get the last word in.'

'True enough!'

David and Marina worked together to get the lunch out of pots and pans and onto plates, with little scraps of meat off the carving board going into his mouth and hers. Dave threw Nick a pleading look over his shoulder, and nodded at the old man.

Nick was, wineglass in hand, to the side of his father's chair. 'Bearing up, are you then?'

'Still alive, in' I?'

Both of them held level gazes into the mid-distance, as if they were at a match.

'Doin' all right on the lettin's front, are you then?'

Astrid was startled by Nick's voice. The words dropped out of the slack mouth, flat and tinny, the 't's had simply disappeared, and there was a belligerence about his lower face which resembled the old man's. He sounded working class!

'Who cares? Lettin's! Who gives a sod about lettin's? It's small beans. A penny 'ere, a penny there. I sold most of them houses at the top of the market. Naargh.' He gave a sneer, pulled at his lapels. 'Naaargh. I'm more or less retired now. Retired! That's a laugh. More like dead. There's nothing to retire for, is there, anymore? People used to 'ave 'obbies. People used to go bowling, din' they? Now they go shoppin'. In and out of that poxy shop, what's its name?'

'Lidl's,' said June, dimpling.

'What?'

'Lidl's. You can get your Heinz soups three for two pound and your Jolly Good Fellows pizzas three for four pound fifty-nine. You only need to pop them in the oven. You can't eat a whole one!'

'See, that's what I mean. That's what I'm saying. This is not the world I was born into. It's gone. Nothing's the same. They keep chopping down the war memorials. No one stands for anything, no one believes in nothing. Pier's closed. Most of the boozers are rough. Full of people drinking.'

'At The Bo Peep they have Stella Artois, Carlsberg, Tennent's, Spitfire, Harveys and Strongbow on tap,' said June, counting them off on her fingers. 'They have six different white wines by the glass. They spent two hundred and fifty thousand pound doing it up. It's five pence a pint more than The Swan, which is just ten yards from it, and that's how they pay for it.'

'Can't you let me finish without you getting your oar in? I was saying how people used to go out together, dressed nice. With hats on. People knew their place. Didn't need to push and shove. You took your turn. You had a family life, and the kids helped out.'

Astrid crossed the room to stand next to Nick. She slipped an arm around his middle briefly, but felt him tense at her touch.

'They still do in the Mediterranean countries,' Nick said.

Dave came across to the table to set the plates down. Shorter than Nick, he was more muscular and, where he wasn't bald, his head was shaved. He had his tongue out while he wiped off each plate with a cloth before laying it. He was as clean as a whistle, in a smart shirt, cuffs rolled back loosely; he smelt of aftershave. On his forearm, underneath the golden curly hair, was a bodged tattoo.

He spotted Nick's glass.

'Top up, Nick? Astrid?' he asked, and went to the fridge to bring the bottle to them. 'All right there, Dad?'

'No, thank you. I'm not a boozer.'

Matt and his younger sister, Emily, slid into seats opposite the old couple, the girl closing her Nintendo DS with a jaded expression, putting it next to her plate. They sat there, listless and beleaguered, arms hanging, present in body only.

Riding on the balls of his feet, the level of Nick's wine was bobbing. 'You'll see families out together in their Sunday best in those countries, and they don't drink to get drunk like we do over here; they might just have an ice cream and a glass of wine.'

'We never drank to get drunk in my day.' Ken rolled his upper lip under his teeth.

'And they thought it would catch on here—café society!' Nick shook his head. 'What a joke. We're off to Sicily on Saturday, as it happens.'

Dave went at the roast joint with the electric carving knife, making a high-pitched sawing noise, which died a little as each slice of meat fell.

'Are you? Wonderful. Whereabouts?' said Marina, sucking the juice off her thumb as she put some meat down onto Matt's plate.

'Syracuse. It's in the south-east.' His voice was back to its normal articulate elocution, every consonant in play. Astrid held his arm and squeezed it. 'Well, properly, Ortygia, that's the Old Town. An ancient site of mythological importance.'

'Fancy that,' said Marina, giving the salt cellar a tap with her fingernail. 'Is it a nice hotel you're staying in? I always like the way they fold an arrow into the toilet paper. Emily did it for a while, bless her; it used to make me smile when I sat down on the lavatory and saw it.'

'No, I didn't!' Emily's mouth fell open and her eyes reddened. 'I did not!'

Matt smiled with honest pleasure.

The carving knife met some tough meat and its pitch rose to near-hysteria. Nick was obliged to raise his voice to answer Marina.

'Well, it's five star—though I'm not sure what that means— but it's a nice one overlooking the harbour. "Des Etrangers" it's called. It's French for "foreigners", funnily enough.'

'What d'you say?' The old man turned his face now towards his son.

'I said, It's French for—'

'Oh, we know all about you. Big'ead. *Five star.*'

'Dad!' Dave intervened, stayed the carving knife and turned round. The kitchen fell quiet, the only note was the clink of Matt's knife and fork; he'd started eating. He stopped, feeling eyes upon him, and slouched in pique; one foot kicked the leg of the table.

Marina served the old couple with full plates.

'Well . . .' Ken used the word to expand his disapproval. 'What's he want to be sloping off over there for? What's *good* about it over there? Spending money! Who wants to go abroad and be at the mercy of a bunch of strangers? Unless you're dodging something. All that showing off, walking about in posh clothes. You ask yourself why anybody would waste their time doing that. Pardon me,' he said to Astrid as she took her place next to Matt opposite him, 'but we always thought he was a nancy boy, me an' 'is mother.'

Matt and Emily looked at each other with naked glee.

'Boys didn't oughta care about fashion and clothes and coffee cups and using the right spoon and all that—eh, Matt?'

'Do you like fashion, Emily?' Astrid asked brightly.

Emily, with the premature breasts of the overweight child, was sitting in a tight top, her belly protruding. Her hair was cut into an orange helmet.

'No.'

'Are you into music?'

'A bit. Not much.'

'What do you like then?'

'She used to like pick 'n' mix,' piped up June. 'We used to give her Woolworth's vouchers for her birthday and Christmas and Easter; now it's closed, we're blowed if we know what to give her.'

Nick took his seat.

'There's a new taxi firm opened on London Road,' June said. 'They want four pound fifty to take you from Bulverhythe to Warrior Square! It's daylight robbery.'

'Eh, June.' Ken used his elbow on his wife. 'Old Shifty here, surprised he could tear himself away from his café society to come and get us today. . . . No thanks, dear, not 'ungry,' he said to Marina when she offered him gravy from the jug. He pushed the plate off its place mat, causing it to slop. He turned, drew in his chin and looked over his glasses at his elder son. 'Anyway, since you are a lawyer of some sort, you can give your old man some advice.'

'There's a bit more crackling left, if anyone wants it,' said Dave, rising.

'If I go by bus to the bingo, I have to change at Warrior Square. . . .'

'Will you give it a rest, June? Like a dripping tap, she is. Just if everyone could stop interrupting and listen a second, they might 'ear something.' Ken gave a tremendous sigh and the table fell quiet. 'Right. My will needs to be sorted. I want to leave everything I got to Dave, in trust for that boy there, young Matthew, to run the family business, but what I don't want is for her lot, June's family, to get their hands on a penny of it, see?'

June issued a gay laugh. She forked a piece of meat and put it into her mouth, then closed her knife and fork over the vegetables and roast potatoes. She sat chewing with her hands folded over the handbag on her lap.

'Now, you tell me how to go about it.' He leant back in his chair to squint at his elder son.

'What about Nick?' Astrid asked suddenly. She crossed her legs.

'Nick? Who is this *Nick* fella anyway? Thank you, young lady, but you're new to this family. You're not even in this family, matter of fact, so I'll ask you to keep your nose out.'

'She's called Astrid,' said Nick. 'I don't care about the money, let Dave have it. He's earned it. However, the fact is—because you are married—your estate will pass to June here. Even if you make a will leaving it to Dave, June could contest it under the Inheritance Act of 1975.'

'Could she?' Ken changed tack and recoiled from June now, and gave her a look down the length of his nose as if there were a viper in the nest. '*Could* she?'

'Oh-hoh!' June issued poultry noises. 'Innocent until proven guilty, please!'

Dave caught his brother's eyes across the table. 'I'm sorry, mate.'

'Do they ask you what you do for a living when you're abroad, the people you meet?' June addressed Nick, her head on one side. 'Do you get people bothering you for advice all the time?'

Nick finished his drink, wiped his mouth with the napkin and laid it gently on his plate, as if covering a dead body. 'Time to go.'

But Dave wouldn't have it. 'Oh no! Don't go, you've just got here, mate. I tell you what, if either of us had thought for a minute—back me up on this, love—if we'd thought he was going to come out with this load of shit . . .' He put two hands up to his bald pate, as if the ceiling were falling on him. 'I mean, Christ O'Reilly, this is really unbelievable, isn't it? First time we sit down in donkey's years and, I mean, you couldn't make it up, could you . . . ? I mean, Dad, you could have waited until pudding at least. Sorry, dessert, Marina, whatever, pudding, dessert, sweet, *I don't care*, Marina—it's not important, is it? I mean, the point is, he has to . . . I mean, like, Dad . . . Dad, why did you have to . . . ? I'll be sharing whatever I get with you anyway, Nick mate.'

'Absolutely not, Dave. You're a good man, and thanks, but no way. Like I say, you earned it.' Nick shook his head.

With his plate still untouched, Ken was devouring Matt with his eyes, grinding his teeth. The boy was picking crackling from a back tooth.

Dave was red-faced and upset. Nick was pale and apparently composed, but Astrid could feel his embarrassment. She felt badly to think that she'd pushed for this lunch; in truth she'd known it would expose him, but she'd not guessed how much. When he gave his elongated fake yawn, paired with a back stretch, she knew he was in real trouble.

'Right then—ready, Astrid?' He stood up. 'I came for your sake, Dave, but when it comes to Ken, well, it's a waste of time pretending.'

The children looked up.

'No. No! Nick . . . mate! Astrid, sweetheart! Sit down a minute!' Dave was oiling his head with his hands, working pig fat into his crown, bobbing in his seat. 'Oh, this is awful, I mean, this is just terrible. I mean, what about a simple sodding Sund'y lunch like other families have? Why can't we do that once in twenty years, eh?'

'I don't like playing games.'

'No, don't you do that, my old son, you speak plainly. . . .' said the old man, with a crafty smile.

'Ready, Astrid?'

'Yes.' She stood beside him now, hands crossed like a president's wife.

With careful diction, hitting the notes rather like a pianist, Nick said, 'Well, it was a really good lunch, Marina, and I'm sorry not to have done it justice.'

'Don't go,' said Emily, turning in her seat to face Astrid.

'You've both grown up so much, you two. Nice kids, Dave,' Nick said to his brother. He turned to Astrid with his hand out, indicating the door. She noticed the slight wagging tendency of his finger; it reminded her of Ken earlier. She mouthed a hasty 'bye' at Marina.

'Before you go,' Ken's chair scraped as he shoved it backwards, 'I'll need you to do something for me in your professional capacity. You won't refuse a customer, I hope. I shall pay you your usual rate. I don't ask no favours.' He put his hands on the table. 'I'll need you to do me a divorce, Gary.'

8

'He can fucking forget it,' Nick said, slamming the car into reverse while Astrid waved limply at the kids, who were standing outside in the cold to see them off. When Matt put his forearm around her neck from behind, Emily stuck her tongue out, making an expression of horror as if she were being poleaxed. Gravel flew.

'Who does he think he is? Henry the Eighth? He can just forget it.' Then, under his breath, 'Calling me Gary. Stupid old shit.'

She had to press her lips together to stop the smile.

'Gary,' she said with genteel effect, breathing life into it, making it sound fragrant. 'It could be worse,' she lied. 'Shane?'

'Thanks,' he said sourly. 'You sound really sincere.'

He'd gone pompous on her. When he was pompous, he had no sense of humour. Still, she allowed him that occasional transgression. Most men of his age were shabby and tight. They wore the same underpants days running until you caught them out. The same jacket did them twenty years. They spent their money only if they were with you—and only on eating and drinking—and they cut corners in all the wrong places, such as holidays and jewellery. They didn't seem to care what people thought, when that was all that mattered at all. But Nick had bought her a cocktail ring from Boucheron for Christmas. When she opened the gorgeous solemn box, she knew he loved her. She could see it right there.

It was best to be silent. She should sit and look amenable. But, a few miles further down the road, she broke her own embargo.

'Oh, Jesus Christ, Nick! For God's sake. I'm sorry about saying you should go. I don't blame you for not wanting to see him ever again. He's a horrible old man, isn't he? Look. You tried. And he just wanted to knock you back. Silly old sod. He's *jealous* of you. Obviously.'

But he didn't look comforted by any of that at all. In fact, he looked all the more rancourous. He looked like his old man. He was running through other lines of attack in his head, things he could have said to his father—rebuttals, matters of fact—and working through some cruel jibes.

'Marina was very nice,' Astrid said, sliding her fingertips in between his legs. 'She ought to try low carbs. Anyway. Perhaps we can have them over for lunch sometime, just your brother and his family. He's a nice guy, huh? Salt of the earth type.'

'Hmm.' He had the length of his finger along his top lip, his thumb in the crook of his cheek.

'Some lowlights would take years off her. . . .'

But he didn't answer and she sat there, prim, thinking about his accent changing in that kitchen. She tried squeezing his hand. 'I love you, darling.'

His eyes were hostile. 'Well then, next time listen to me! You had to push me into it, didn't you? The old man was right about that! You don't know anything about our family, so you should keep your nose out!'

'Nick! Don't turn on me, if you don't mind! Jesus Christ. Is it catching, or something, your father's nastiness?'

'Oh, wind it in, Astrid!'

They put it off, but an argument was brewing. She'd never known him to speak to her that way. She knew what she was going to say when she had the chance, in a fight, and in drink: 'It seems like you've got plenty of your father in you after all.' But she contented herself for the time being by fixing her gaze out of her side window, crossing her legs to point away from him, and saying under her breath, '*Gary.*'

And she found enough satisfaction in that to tide her over.

9

By five in the afternoon, Ken was asleep in the reclining armchair in his house, his head thrown back, his mouth open. He looked like he'd received two thousand volts. June was sitting on the sofa with her coat still on, her ankles and hands crossed, looking at the carriage clock on the mantelpiece. After a moment, she gave a loud cough. Still he did not stir. From under the sofa cushion she pulled out the Kays catalogue, and she sat there, moistening the pad of her thumb to turn the pages, occasionally folding over the corner of one and running her thumb along it to keep the place.

Over in Fairlight, at Longwinter Farmhouse, Matt was in his room at the computer screen, biting a fingernail, waiting for a download. He was thinking about the time they took his grandfather and June to visit his other grandmother, Lynn, in the nursing home. He could see his father with his hand on the roof of the car, the door open, his face sweaty and hopeful, asking Ken to change his mind and come in. Ken would not. Matt was sitting in the back with him and June. He remembered the smell of talc from June and, curiously, the smell of a hot-water bottle. He remembered the door slamming and the car shaking, and then he looked out of his window at the man with a melted ear. Like something out of the 'Thriller' video, the deformed old fellow had come to the car with his cronies—some limping, some hobbling—as soon as they parked up. The man with the melted ear stood mouthing something at them; next to him was another man with a goitre. Up on the balconies, the old girls were gawping.

'It gives me the willies,' his grandfather had said. 'Sod this.' He'd squeezed Matt's hand.

When the Yahoo page came up on the screen, Matt sprang forward in his chair. He put it in again, the word 'euthanasia'.

'For the benefit of that person,' he said aloud.

Emily was sitting in the toilet, looking out through the small side window and holding the bunched-up curtain against her nose. She was thinking about the girl called Laura who was her age and whether she was in some way a cousin and whether or not to put the Build-A-Bears into the attic when this girl came round. She was thinking how Astrid ran a spa. She'd go in there one day, and come out different—with long blond hair, in curls—and people would say, 'I totally didn't recognize you!'

Dave and Marina were sitting in the kitchen. Marina was on the small sofa and Dave was in the wing-backed chair opposite. He was sitting with his head down, his feet planted wide, looking at his hands. He had been like that for half an hour. Marina turned the pages of the magazine, all the while keeping an eye on him as she would a pot on simmer. When his shoulders rounded over, she got up and kissed his head.

'*Issa dreadfor terribor fing,*' he said, mimicking Ken. He looked up at her and cracked a grin.

For that was the way Ken had put it to Dave, over mugs of tea at Pelham Circle, with the old man sitting on the threadbare stairs of their latest development.

'*Issa dreadfor terribor fing.*'

'*What is?*'

'*To 'ave a son and not be close to 'im. You'd never do that, wouldya?*'

'*Matt's a good kid.*'

'*Yeah. He is, innie?*'

'*Do you want a biscuit?*'

'*Naargh. Gets under my plate. It's the worse fing. There ain't nuffing worse, if you think about it.*'

'*Pass them back then, if you don't want them.*'

'*Than losing your son, is what I'm saying.*'

'*No. I s'pose not.*'

'*Issa failure, innit?*'

'*Mm-hmm.*'

'*A cock-up.*'

'*Yup.*'

'*All right!*' He'd given him his peeved look. '*If you* don't *mind!*'

'*Eh?*'

'*Snarky. Rubbin' it in!*'

'*Sorry, Dad.*'

'*But what he done was wrong, wonnit? It was him what broke the family up.*'

'*He was only eighteen.*'

'*This long-life milk you put in 'ere? Leaves a funny taste, dunnit?*'

'You tried,' said Marina.

By five, things had changed. Matt was playing with a cricket ball in the garden; Dave was in the shed, finding the cricket bat; Marina was wiping the place mats; Emily was using a razor on one eyebrow.

June was in the hall of the bungalow behind Ken, describing developments in bus services in Hastings as detailed in the free paper and matching the company names to the new routes.

Ken was going as slowly as an iceberg through the hallway towards the front door. He parted his lips and ran his tongue across them. The words he wanted to say were moving ahead of him. The sunshine seemed to thicken behind the frosted patterned glass. When he got there, he found he had overtaken the words and lost them. He opened the door and felt the pain of the steel tread through his thin socks. The name plaque had fallen to the ground.

'He'll be 'ome by now,' he said. He stared out onto the forecourt at the place where the great black car had been just hours before. He put his hand on the light bristle of his chin and dragged on it.

He turned back into the fug of the hallway that smelt like cheese footballs and closed the door behind him. He picked up the phone and, squinting between numbers, going carefully, he dialled the number from the list on the wall.

When the phone was answered, his face changed.

'Oy! Big'ead! I'll tell you what you are! You're *nothing*! You're a stuck-up, jumped-up . . . *embarrassment*, that's what you are! Cambridge University? Fuck yourself! Advice? Don't make me laugh! Stuff it! You always was a big'ead, even as a kid. No. You and me, mate, we're finished! We're through! Not a penny! Not a single penny from me. I've got money you couldn't even dream of. You've no idea, have you, how much I've got. Gary? You there? Gary?'

He left the phone on the hall seat and went into the living room. He looked at June in bewilderment. 'I think he's hung up on me.'

'Is it making a funny noise?'

'Is what making a funny noise?'

'The phone. Is it making a noise, Kenneth?'

He went back to it and listened. 'It's going "doo-ort".'

'He's hung up on you then.'

He put it back to his ear and spoke. 'Can you hear me? Son?'

Then he slammed the phone back onto its wall cradle. It fell off and he slung it back harder. He stood and looked at it, ready as a boxer. It stayed. He faced her next with a snarl. 'What you got your coat on for? Eh? You going somewhere?'

'I'm not saying a word, Kenneth, *not* a word. I shan't get myself into trouble that way.'

'Oh, you! You think you're so clever! Don't cha? You're no use to anyone. More lonely livin' with ya than without ya,' he said, and he went back up the hallway, this time closing the door between the front room and the hall, and punched more numbers into the phone.

From her new position, crouching and bending by the side of the door where she was just looking for something round the back of the hostess trolley, June could hear him quite clearly.

'Put Matt on, will you, please?'

She touched her chest; it was not his fancy woman from the funeral parlour then.

10

'I don't care if he does die,' he said. 'I won't go to the funeral.'

When they got home from picking up Laura at the station that evening, he was critical about the supper Astrid made; he didn't like 'fruit with meat', he said, making a face at the lamb and apricot tagine. He sulked about the TV programme she put on, mocked the women on it so much she couldn't hear it. 'If they want to lose weight, why don't they just stop eating?'

He sat in the armchair rather than on the sofa with her. He seemed stuck on the same page of St Augustine's *Confessions*. He set it aside to moan that everything on the television was rubbish these days. Didn't she think?

'Hmm?' He pressed her.

She didn't answer.

'Over a hundred channels and nothing worth watching,' said

Laura, deadpan, 'and pop stars that can't play instruments.' Curled up on the smaller sofa, she popped in her earphones.

When Astrid turned the television off and picked up a book, he said that books these days were written by victims for victims. As if life were a pity contest, he said. Darwin would be turning in his grave! What was wrong with being brave? he asked her.

When she failed to rise to that bait, he complained about her mood spoiling the evening. So she went to the kitchen to have a good time cleaning the fridge. 'I've got my very own Ken now,' she said to herself as she doused and soaped the glass shelf in the sink.

He tried to elevate Laura by telling her how much he'd read as a child, how he'd been top of the class without fail—and never for a moment bored—and the girl raised one eyebrow and took her Nintendo DS off to the kitchen.

He was left alone in the front room.

'He reminds me of Granddad,' Laura said to Astrid, taking up a wet cloth and wiping over the evacuated jars on the counter.

'How do you mean?'

'Boring.'

'Oh.'

'It's like when you go for a walk with Granddad, he has to say stuff to spoil it, about history or nature or the sound of the river being like music or something. I never answer him. But he still does it. He says stuff like, Oh, to think the Anglo-Saxons washed their socks here, or whatever.'

The front-room door banged against the wall as he came out to them.

'Don't you have any classical music?' he asked, brandishing Astrid's iPod. He poured himself a glass of wine.

When Laura went up to her room, Astrid let him talk. They went to the conservatory so that he could sound off. She sat and listened with her hands clasped while he walked up and down, pointing at his reflection in the windows. First he expressed his moral outrage at having been 'hijacked'—he put it that way—over lunch, then he proceeded to console himself by taking the piss out of the old man. By way of conclusion, he announced that he was done with them, he was washing his hands of his family, for once and for all. It was final.

But he didn't get from her the reaction he wanted. She seemed distracted, to his mind. Oh yes, she joined in with him and echoed his sentiments and shook her head in all the right places, but she didn't seem to fully *get it*. He had to put things in *extreme* terms for her to even begin to *know* how he felt. He had to keep going over it. He needed something from her, but he didn't know what it was and neither did she, so he paced and gestured and fumed and she watched him.

'Poor you,' she said, at what was possibly the end of it. He checked her face for sarcasm, but there was that faraway blithe look on it that was so impenetrable. 'I'm glad I don't have this trouble with my parents,' she said.

She was thinking whether she oughtn't to empty the one bottle of Encona chili sauce into the other. There were two in the fridge. Or she could just throw one away; it was manky, it didn't look nice.

'That's a loaded comment!' he said, eagerly following her as she slipped back into the kitchen.

When the phone rang, he leapt at it; he snatched it from the cradle. She knelt to wipe out the bottom compartment of the fridge. He came over and kicked her bum with his socked foot and pointed to the phone in his hand. She took a deep breath.

'You daft old shit!' he shouted. 'You're nothing to me. Well, and you, you've not been a father to me! Normal? Normal? How would you know what was normal?'

Then he put the phone back.

'That was him,' he said, pushing his hair back with his hand. 'Ken.'

'Yes. I thought so.'

Words failed him. 'For fuck's sake! Astrid!'

'Shall we unplug it? Are we in for an evening of it?'

He sat down on a kitchen chair and looked suddenly defeated. He put his thumb to his mouth and chewed the side of the nail.

'You throwing that out?' He nodded at the bottle she was sliding into the bin's steel mouth.

'Yes.'

'Is it empty?'

'Yes.'

'Don't throw it away if there's some left.'

'Thank you, but I can manage the sauce bottles all by myself. What did he say?'

'Oh, I don't know. The usual.' He shrugged. 'Rubbish. I don't know. I didn't listen.'

Typical bloke, she thought. 'Poor old you,' she said.

He fell into a preoccupied stupor, thumbnail in mouth, eyes bulging, and—since she could get away with it—she popped into the bin the almost-empty bottle of brown sauce as well. She liked filling the bin. It was a pleasure akin to shopping. Perhaps even guiltier. She treated herself to a spot of non-recycling protocol by putting them in the household rubbish too. There were all sorts of condiments that could go.

He got himself a new drink. He made sure she heard him unscrewing the bottle. He was having whiskey, rather ostentatiously. He would want her to comment, or ask if he wanted ice with it, so that he could say, No, I'll have it neat. He knocked it back and made the proper noise, the sound a bus made before it moved off.

When they came back from the holiday, he told her, he'd change their phone number. He'd refuse to take calls from his brother; he'd break off with them all for good. He'd renounce them. And be done with it. His father was an arsehole and his brother, well, the truth of it was he was a loser. He'd called him a loser when the kid was only three years old and that's what he was: a loser.

'Who is?' said doe-eyed Laura, in her PJs in the doorway, pulling a mermaid's comb through her long wet hair.

'Nobody,' he said.

They had a laugh together upstairs, the girls, when Astrid took up the laundry and began sorting it in Laura's room.

'Fancy calling a three-year-old a loser!' Laura smirked, holding up some beads to the mirror.

'He's upset. Poor Nick.' Astrid patted the covers around her daughter's face to frame it and kissed her nose.

'Astrid!' he called upstairs. *'Astrid!'*

'Yes?' They clung to each other; they could feel each other's chest rise and fall, and they began to tremble with the wantonness of laughter.

'Astrid! Shall I call him back and tell him what I think of him

and that next time I see him, it will be in a box? No, it won't, though, because I won't even go to the funeral. Shall I tell him that?'

'If you want to, honey!' She stuck her nose in her daughter's hair.

'Mum.' Laura pulled away, and splayed her fingers to check the nails she'd painted that day. 'Mum. He's so lost his cool, it's like—freak *out*, man!'

'I know! But he can't help it.'

'It's like, *whoops!* There goes my charisma. I don't know how you can fancy him. Why don't you break up?' She knelt up. 'Hey. Then we could, like, move to London? So much cooler and we'd be nearer to my dad!'

On Monday, Nick was back at work. By Monday evening, he was saying that he was completely over it. On Tuesday, he had a few drinks and went through it again with her and made a call to the old man, telling him not to call him ever again, then he did the whiskey-and-bus-noise routine, and on Wednesday night, he came in miserable and just about jumped to grab the phone when it rang. His father must have slipped in something new, because Nick's voice wobbled, and he seemed to gulp: 'No, you did that! *You* did that!'

And when she asked him what he meant, he said he'd had enough of it all, he didn't want to talk about it. He got himself a whiskey, finishing the bottle into a tumbler, and put on the television. She stood open-mouthed, looking at him with his feet up on the coffee table. He had his shoes on.

'Nick! Shoes!'

'Leave me alone,' he said. 'Go and look after your daughter, or something.'

'Don't be so rude to me! It's not all about you, Nick! Not everything's about you!'

'Oh, fuck off, Astrid,' he said.

Quite a lot was said between them, up and down the stairs that evening, and finally he withdrew and hid under the covers while she sat downstairs with the whiskey ostentatious.

When he came in the next evening, they were curt but courteous; they had Laura there to keep them on the toes of their manners, and neither said anything about the night before.

'Would you like to eat now?'

'If you do.'

'Well, I'm not hungry—but if you are, we can.'

'Sure. Whatever you want.'

Pushing past the pussyfooting pair, Laura went with a heavy '*Excuse me*' to the bread bin. She made herself a sandwich and left the spread a mulch of crumb putty with the knife stuck in it, upright.

'I shouldn't be eating bread all the time. No wonder I'm borderline obese,' she said and went into the front room to watch television.

Astrid had imagined there would be an apology. She sat up in bed, with the covers at her chest, waiting patiently and in full make-up. He looked at her nightdress pointedly and then began to undress. She watched him hobble about the room in between the open suitcases, pulling each foot out of his trouser legs, bobbing about as if he were on the deck of a keening ship.

He removed his underpants without a care, showing her his arse fully; he draped them over the chair, then pulled back the covers and climbed in.

'What?' he asked, opening an eye to see her looking sideways at him.

'Nothing.' She turned out the light, pulled the covers up to her chin and wriggled down.

After a minute his hand felt for hers. In another minute, he was asleep.

11

‘I tell you what, Astrid,’ he says on the Saturday morning they’re off to the airport, swapping with her at the bathroom sink. ‘Listen to this. My mum used to say to me and Davie, I’m not kidding, I’ll flay you alive. . . .’ He cracks a smile over the side of his face free of shaving foam. ‘I’ll give you the hiding of your life. That was another one. Not your everyday humdrum beating but something to remember.’ She loves it when he shaves the little indented fur-row under his nose, the strip above the middle of his lips; what a funny face he makes then, he looks so proper. ‘Mind you, it was only talk.’

He wipes each side of his face, leaving blobs of shaving foam on his earlobes. (‘Oh, the way he holds himself, you can see he thinks himself a very fine gentleman,’ her mother said to her once, unkindly.)

‘Ken met his match with Pearl; they were both completely

bloody-minded.' The iced gem of foam on his Adam's apple falls onto his chest. He unwraps the towel from his waist. 'He was forty-odd when he married Mum, and he only did it because her dad died and she came into a bit of money. Sure of it.' He opens the glass door to the shower, the frame shaking in his wake. He turns on the tap. They stand there, dark and light, facing each other, the plain glass between them. Suddenly he's doused in water and his hair is flat to his temples.

'Mind you, they could both scream and shout. Christ! Even the dog was a nervous wreck. You've never seen a dog with diarrhoea like ours had.'

He sluices under each armpit with the soap. The glass screen is splattered with soapsuds. He puts shampoo onto his head as if he's cracking an egg onto it. His mouth bursts open into gasps, and his eyes screw tighter in the onslaught of the stream of water as he rubs and rubs his head. He looks so sweet, her one-man storm in a teacup. She puts two fingers to her lips and touches the glass screen and leaves him there.

Ten minutes later, he comes downstairs dressed as the country gent in his careful clothes, the check shirt and cords. 'Ready?'

She trims her grin, recalling how pleased he'd been to go to Laura's first sports day at school and been gutted to find himself opposite another father who'd been wearing identical clothes: coral trousers, Barbour and leather hat.

They're off to Gatwick, bound for Sicily. It will be good to have a break from this whole business with his father.

Just that very morning the phone rang at seven and it was Ken asking for the number of a fish and chip shop in the old town. 'Silly old fuck,' Nick said, hanging up. 'Why call us for that?'

'We're not bloody directory enquiries,' Astrid had griped from under her pillow.

According to Dave, Matt used the Internet to switch the old man's telecoms provider to one offering free calls evenings and weekends. Great, said Nick, good on him, *the little shit.*

The two larger cases are in the conservatory, waiting for Nick to put them in the car, and he stands looking at them, bracing himself. The dog, their brown and white springer spaniel, peers in at them, too dirty for admission, his face craven, ready for the jackpot of a welcome as much as for the disaster of dismissal. He cocks his head.

'Dirty old dog,' says Astrid. 'He knows he's off to kennels. Bugger off, Roy.'

They thought it funny to name him this, to call out: 'Roy, Roy . . .' But Laura doesn't think it's funny; she wishes the dog were called Biscuit. 'Whose idea was it anyway, Mum, to call him Roy?' she asked once on the way to school and Astrid knew, sliding her eyes and pausing before answering, that in such questions there was a subtle evisceration of Nick. 'Mine,' she lied.

'Yes, he knows we're going,' Nick says sadly, looking at Roy through the glass with a deeply sympathetic look.

They have time to lie down together and kiss before they go, don't they? she asks him, a hand on his arm. He taps his watch and sighs as if it's against his will. This is their shtick; he jokes that she badgers him for sex.

'I'd best get the other bags, love.' He plods upstairs dutifully and she follows him up, but he surprises her with an ambush at the bedroom door.

From the first night, he appointed their sides of the bed—he to the right, she to the left—and this is how he arranges them now, pulling her across him. They kiss on their bed.

'Handsome,' she tells him.

But he resists the tip of her tongue and jumps up. 'Enough of this lolling about, we've got a holiday to get on!' He gets up to zip the bags.

She lies there, her thoughts cramping at this small spurning. One thing leads to another: being girlfriend not wife; having no children of their own; her age; other women. This is always the terminus for this line of thinking, and on its benches sit beautiful women. Sometimes it seems to her that she lives in a flat world, like the bed they lie in. Jealousy to the east, doubt to the west, the past to the south, the future to the north—all pits to fall into.

'Come on then, we don't want to miss the plane,' he calls up the stairwell.

There are fifty women to every straight man these days. She has to be vigilant. Women are fighting—liberation's over and now it's civil war—and she's in the armaments industry: beauty. The other woman is rattling the handle of the bedroom door, a true competitor, just a dress size away. The sweet spot is the fear. Her fantasies thrive there; lust is a kind of terror.

When he takes Roy into the kennels, she checks her crow's feet in the mirror. You can never be the most beautiful woman, no matter how beautiful you are, she thinks. She hopes that this Sicilian destination will not present the problems of a Caribbean or, worse, a Brazilian resort. It has scarcely any beach, so it ought to be safe from sun-worshipping nymphs. She purposely chose a place that seemed a little middle-aged so that she'd compare well. When he gets in the car, she slaps the visor to and smiles guardedly. A true smile. A grin—God forbid, a guffaw—would show her age.

When they pass the exit signs on the motorway and he has difficulty reading them, he says he thinks he might need glasses.

'My eyesight's not what it used to be.'

She's pleased; every Delilah wants her Samson blind.

12

The phone went at just after six and Ken got himself out of bed with what he deemed discretion. June rose and fell several times in his wake, as if on a raft, and received a stray cuff as he flailed about. The carpet rose and fell, and the furniture whinnied and clanked, and the last noise to betray his clandestine exit was finally and explosively a trombone salvo from the bathroom. He had misplaced faith in the thickness of those walls.

Where he goes when the phone rings, she knows very well. He is at that woman's beck and call; she has only to snap her fingers. June knew it was her as soon as she clapped eyes on her. She met her at Pat's do. The vol-au-vent cases June got from Lidl, forty-eight of them, and filled them herself. That woman—Audrey—gorged herself on them. She must have had four or more. And Ken! He hung on to her every word, as if he were catching her crumbs. June asked people what they thought of the vol-au-vents and got some very kind words, but nothing from Ken. He was too busy ogling the greedy undertaker.

She has given up hope of much in the way of affection from Ken. She does feel lonely, but she's of the generation that understood very well, thank you, that no one likes a sourpuss, or a moaner, so you keep your troubles to yourself.

She has a nice son who is forty-six and lives in Wales in the countryside and runs a holiday camp for artists. He has an Australian wife. She has the school photographs of their twin children—Jeremy and Jemima—above the gas fire. Once in a blue moon they come to Hastings and stay in the caravan park.

The day before they come, Ken picks a row, so they have a miserable time of it with him griping and carping. And when they go, he's all good-natured—he has a certain spring in his step—and he has the cheek to ask her if she wants to say sorry to him for her behaviour of the last few days. Then he takes her out to The Italian Way and stands up at the counter, reminiscing about the days when the Dimarcos ran it and he and the Teddy Boys hung out there looking mean. As in tough, not tight, which is what he looks, standing back when the waiter brings the little plastic tray. Her purse snaps back and forth and provides the right money down to the last penny. It's never more than eight pounds. Seven pounds eighty as a rule for two minestrone soups with rolls. And then they're all done and back to normal again.

'I've been a fool for those eyes,' she says, lying there, hot and heavy of leg, rheumatism aching right through her, a bad taste in her mouth.

What a life. You never know how it's going to end up, but you don't imagine it will be like this. They ought to warn girls how it is, how it really is.

She gets up in time to see Ken, a stick figure in his black suit, up the far hill. She phones her son and gets his wife, Melinda.

'You never imagine your husband will get a thing for an embalmer—and an outsized one at that—that's one thing you don't imagine. Now, the thing is'—she coughs, 'Excuse me,' with nerves—'and I don't know whether you should tell my Andrew this or not—you know how sensitive he is. The thing is that Ken says he wants a divorce. It's because of her, Audrey Bury, Hastings' biggest funeral director. Ooh, it'll be for the money, I know that much. She's rich, that woman, rich. Rich from cheating widows. Rich from all the gold teeth.'

Then Melinda gives her a piece of her mind and afterwards June sits down, looking at the twins in their brown and gold cardboard frames and wondering if her daughter-in-law's fury didn't amount to some sort of abiding affection emanating from Wales and from the hearth of her own family.

She decides the best thing to do is to eat a pack of Bourbons right now, then starve herself in front of him until he notices. But she'd best prepare herself for the worst. At the small table in the kitchen she sets out the Basildon Bond pad with its ruled guidance page underneath the top sheet, and in her bird's-foot writing she picks out the following as a note to herself, to fold and keep as a moral stiffener: *Dear June*—that made her feel better in itself— *When you go away from Ken to Wales, please remember that he will not come after you because he's never done it before and it's not in his nature. When you leave Hastings, you leave Ken for good.*

She won't think about those eyes, though they're there between the loops of the 'o's. She folds the note and puts it in her bag. She makes a cup of tea and puts on the wireless. On comes Otis Redding with 'I've Been Loving You Too Long'. She sits and listens to the song the whole way through, unsandwiching the chocolate Bourbons, dipping the dry sides into the tea—Ken's way of eating them. Otis finishes things in a strangled sort of way, and when he's done, she switches off the radio and puts the empty biscuit packet into the bin.

In the beginning she'd gone off for hours and hours after rows with him, but he never came after her and, goodness knows, she dithered by the bus stop. She was a bus-stop dallier; she'd annoy the drivers with her umming and erring, her toe pointing in, pointing out. 'No, thank you, I'll wait for the next one.' And the bus would swerve off in an angry manoeuvre, rejected by a little old lady with a handbag. Oh, she dreamed of seeing her Ken come up the hill for her sake, to stop her boarding the bus! 'Dream on,' Ken would have said.

She takes a walk up to Lidl for a look-see later on that morning, going up the hill with her heart heavy, thinking about the very idea of leaving him, her last love, and she comes back down it again with placatory words on her mind, blinking at the sea. He can't help what he is, and she loves him! Oh, for those eyes! And the way he helps himself to a cream cracker and a bit of Red Leicester in the evenings, bouncing the little plate on his knee as they watch the news together. That's happiness enough, surely. And of course you have to bear in mind he's never had a mother.

This is the way her thoughts are going, and she's thinking of doing a posh dinner for him—she's got a ready-cooked roast chicken in her bag—when towards her comes a blue double-decker bus bound inland. She loves the smell of the back-draught as you board and the comfort of the seats, so nicely sprung. That bus could take you anywhere. It's marked up as going to Hawkhurst. From Hawkhurst you could get anywhere—London certainly, or Wales.

The bus driver is a woman. She has her head out of the side window and her hair is long and auburn, tresses and tresses of it flowing in the wind. It's truly something to behold. It is a sign.

'Just like Boadicea,' June says to herself, stopping and changing the bag to her other hand. 'Oh dear, oh dear.'

When she gets in the bungalow, she sits down in her coat in the kitchen and takes the letter out of her bag, unfolds it and reads it through once more.

'Hawkhurst,' she says. She pushes up her glasses on one side of her face to wipe the corner of her eye. 'That's where I'm bound.'

13

The rental car crosses the bridge from Syracuse to the isle of Ortygia; a baked Alaska of sandstone, melting into a turquoise sea. The outpost of successive civilizations before and since Christ, it has survived sieges and earthquakes and invaders: Greeks, Romans, Vandals, Goths, Arabs, Normans, Jews and the Sicilian aristocracy, each disinheriting each other by dismantling their churches. Where grand palm trees lean over the ruins of a Greek temple, they hesitate in their hire car at a roundabout until they are squeezed and harangued forward by a collective will and expelled like a cork out of a bottle through a narrow street of tall buildings into a courtyard.

Astrid spots the hotel's small sign fixed to the wall. They park alongside green bins reeking of dead fish.

They are graciously received in the marble of the hotel's reception, upgraded to a room with a sea view, and the young bellboy goes behind the little tin car, beckoning Nick with his hands to a parking space on the promenade.

He's never happier than when he's reversing into a parking space, she thinks, watching Nick in the car. You could drive into a space like that straight—but no, a man has to reverse into it. She stands there grinning as, from a saunter, he breaks into a little run.

'What?'

'Nothing.'

The bellboy shows them how to use the card to access the room and power it. The air-conditioning hums. Nick flutters before him with the apology of a mime artist, to show that he has no change to give him.

She goes to the shutters and braces the handle on the double doors. The hum of the air-conditioning stops. She tests it again. She shows him how to do it and he does it too and they look at each other.

'Bloody clever,' he says and does it again.

She stands on the balcony in the afternoon heat, squinting at the sea, then looks to her right across some seven other similar balconies. Above her and below her, the double-doored balconies are in symmetry. It reminds her of the advert for Chanel perfume in which rouged sirens step out onto balconies such as these and holler elegant abuse.

'They shout out *égoïste* in that advert,' she says to him, 'those women on their balconies. So French. It would never have worked in England. Can you imagine it? Thirty English women yelling out of their council flats at a bloke.'

'*Oy, shit'ead!*'

She laughs. 'God, Nick, you sound just like Ken.'

He's standing outside the bathroom, dabbing his sweating face with a hand towel. He pulls the underarms of each side of his shirt to his nose and makes a quizzical face. 'Oh shit, you *are* your father,' she says.

''Ark at 'er, going on like a drippin' tap. . . .'

She goes to hang up their fine things, cardigans over the shoulders of dresses, his shirts folded and stacked. She leaves their underwear in the bag and closes it—you never let a cleaner glimpse your smalls.

Then she locates the mini-bar underneath the television and whips it open. She twists off the top of a small bottle of red wine and takes a glug and hands it to him where he sits on the bed, feet planted wide, happy to watch her.

'I love mini-bars.'

'Twice the price.'

'Twice the fun. Always tastes better.'

'You daft cow,' he says, still in his father's voice, taking the bottle from her and having some too.

'It does, though, doesn't it?'

They finish it off, wipe their lips and jettison the bottle in the bin.

Stepping down the grand chequered stairwell of Hotel des Etrangers et Miramare, she hears the slovenly sound of rubber hitting tile and, with effort, by splaying her toes, keeps the new flip-flops stuck to the soles of her feet and proceeds more discreetly. This is Sicily! She has in her shoulder bag a photocopied map of the town and she withdraws it in the lobby and strides into the sunshine. Nick dallies, looking at prints on the walls, detaining her with his exclamations. She wants to 'be here', to see and be seen. She has an al fresco martini in mind, or a Campari and soda down by the water, among the stylish.

The receptionist gives her an encouraging look, as if to say, Go on—the water's lovely! The bellboy arrives at the electric doors and with a swoop bids her join the outdoors. '*Prego*,' he says.

'*Prego!*' She knows that one.

'Have a good day,' he adds rather too quaintly.

'Yes, all right, thank you very much,' she says briskly. He's seeing Judi Dench, not Kate Moss. He thinks she's past it. She feels for her sunglasses and lowers them like a visor. It spoils her mood. The flip-flops look cheap. She smells of airplane.

Finally, Nick comes loping after her. He wants food; a late lunch or an early dinner. But she wanted to dress for dinner! They turn up the hill, away from the beach, his hand firm on hers, shushing her, enjoining her to come with him his way, and she complains and tries to wriggle her hand out of his. They head across the scorched piazza and dip into a shadowed side street and, with his hand still firmly clasping hers, he indicates to a loafing kerbside restaurateur that they'd be interested in a table. The man extinguishes his cigarette and smoothes down his apron.

'Please!' he says, demonstrating the way in.

'It's such a nice day,' she laments. 'It's so nice to be away from home, to be in the sunshine, and to be near a beach.'

'Let's have some fun. We're on holiday,' he says, towing her in his wake.

'I know,' she says testily, 'but why does it have to be your holiday?'

He turns to shield her from the other diners, who are looking their way. His eyes are warm and cajoling. 'Look, silly billy, let's eat and have a nice bottle of wine and get this thing off to a good start. Shall we? It'll be romantic!'

It's agreeably fetid in the tiny room of five tables. The owner has an easy smile, broad hands, and a grey ponytail. His sidekick looks like a backward yokel from a Pagnol film; he has buck teeth and darts about with extravagant confusion. The owner is decisive; shortly after they have hesitantly pronounced the names of a few dishes, he whisks away their menus with an approving flourish. They have ordered plates to share. Baby octopus, deep fried, followed by spaghetti Siracusana and mixed salads, a bottle of water and a bottle of wine. The wine and water are served immediately.

He says to her, as they shake out their paper napkins, 'We'll have to start viewing some places when we get back, sweetie.'

'Oh,' she says. Since the lunch at his brother's, he's mentioned once or twice their moving. He complained that he was sick of the quaintness of their home with its beams. Yet they fell in love with it when they saw it just a year back. It reminded him of Gamekeeper's Cottage, he said, the home he left at eighteen. Not fit for human habitation, he joked. He'd like something with underfloor heating. Maybe in East Kent for a change. She had decided to follow her mother's example in man management and neither cross him nor reveal her hand, immediately. Rebuttals, refusals and difficult things—confessions—were introduced into conversation in company. Her mother did it over a hand of cards, Astrid intends to do it over stuffed mini-peppers.

They clink glasses and drink.

'Dreadful about Sam and Andy splitting up,' she says, moving to the mollifying subject of other couples' problems. 'No doubt she'll come to see you soon at work.'

'Yes, I know. I'd thought of that. I'm not sure I could act for her, though. Really. It's not that I'd be against him; I'm for the court, really. . . .'

Her eyes wander about the room. She strokes her forearms. *He has chosen that they should eat, he is choosing where they should live. He has chosen the wine.*

'. . . there is an unspoken obligation within my instructions—well, I won't go into it, it's rather complicated—so although it wouldn't be like I was really acting against him, however . . .'

'But it would. Wouldn't it?' she says. 'And once he got a letter, one of those pompous ones—'

'They're precise, not pompous. You use the word too freely, for things you don't understand generally, I've noticed.'

'Well, put me in my place, why don't you!' she laughs hollowly. 'Whatever you think, a letter from a solicitor is a pisser for most people. Still, if people didn't fight and hate, you wouldn't have a living.'

He looks at her empty glass and purses his lips.

'I'm lucky. I get to see the best in people,' she says, reaching for the bottle.

'You see what people want you to see, Astrid. I provide a rather deeper service. Sometimes people want to divorce, you know. Well, of course you know. They want it more than anything. So as not to live a lie, as the cliché goes.'

'Oh no, you're wrong, sometimes I see the real person. I saw you, didn't I? I saw who you were. You said I did, anyway. Or did I see who you wanted me to see? Maybe I'm only just beginning to see the real you.' She knocks back her wine. Her eyes look sloppy.

'Maybe.'

'Maybe.'

He can't wait to try the food, he tells her. He'd been reading about it on the way there in the airline magazine. They fall silent. He points out a framed vintage print for Lavazza coffee. They have the same one at home.

'Reproduction,' she says coldly.

On shifting ground, her mind works sideways. 'That stupid ad. That Chanel thing. It reminded me,' she says, 'how I used to want to be beautiful. A star. You know. Someone who flings open doors. With red lipstick.'

'All girls do. Laura does, I'm sure.'

'No, she doesn't. She's into pet rescue.'

'Is she?'

Her wrist is loose and the wineglass sways dangerously free. 'I don't know, the women when we crossed the piazza, they were just so amazing looking and here's me well past my best. In flip-flops. Do you know, I can put a day on it. I lost my looks on one day last November. I did. Really. I woke up, looked in the mirror and said to myself, Well, that's that then. Gone. It's true. I have to accept it. I have crow's feet.'

'Only when you smile.'

'Oh, thanks a lot. Well, that's one way of making sure I *don't* smile anymore.'

He refills her glass briskly.

'You know, it gets me down; the business of beauty. Bev was doing a pedicure last week and this woman's toenail just fell off when she was painting it and she ended up holding it. That was funny. It's good when it's funny. But it's not funny enough. They ask you what you know about cosmetic surgery and stuff, our clients, and they all want to change themselves and lately I keep thinking—is this healthy? I mean, do I go with it and form some sort of partnership with a surgeon to do Botox and fillers, or do I ignore it? I mean, I can of course completely understand it.' She sighs flamboyantly. ' "You're beautiful", was what you said to me in that restaurant, you know, over lunch the first time we went out. That feels like years ago now.'

A plate of baby octopus in pale yellow batter is placed between them; it is piping hot. Nick picks up the half-lemon and looks at her.

'Want lemon on it?'

'Whatever you want.'

With his fork he begins to pick poker-faced through the strange shapes and selects the longer limbed of them.

'Try it, it's incredible,' he says and offers her a forkful, tentacles waggling.

She shakes her head.

'Nice man,' the owner says as he empties the last of the bottle into their glasses and nods at Nick. 'Your husband?'

'My partner.'

'Another bottle?'

'Yes, please,' says Nick.

'I hate that word,' she says. 'Don't you? *Partner*. As if we're Starsky and Hutch.'

They eat the rest of the octopus in silence, averting their eyes from each other.

'Want this last bit?'

'No, you have it.'

'No, it's for you.'

'No. Thank you.'

When it comes, the spaghetti is as thick as soba noodles, cooked al dente and coated in crushed garlic, anchovies and breadcrumbs. It is a woolly and pungent dish. He keeps his head down. The food is bloody marvellous. He intends to shovel in as much as he can.

'Why is it that women are only as good as they look, do you think, Nick?'

His mouth is full. He points to it. He has already tried to explain to Astrid that he finds a woman's face interesting with age. He likes to see life in a face—not as in liveliness, but the life that has happened. When he looks at her, he feels like he has a vantage point in which he has before him both the girl and the woman; he can see how she was and how she will be. While she was off shopping for an anti-wrinkle cream in duty free, he sat at the bar and glimpsed through the glass wall the condemned coming into arrivals up the escalator; a long line of girls with hair in ponytails to the side, glum, treading down the backs of their Uggs, their faces pretty but blank.

'You must get sick of me asking you how I look! We're only going next door, you say. Won't you be cold? Who's going to be there anyway? That's what you say, and there I am sleeveless in November, kitten heels in dog's mess, bulging out of my hipsters. I mean, I wore hot pants to the pub at Christmas. What possessed me? I'm forty! I looked at my skinny jeans on the radiator last week and they looked huge. There was nothing skinny about them. I'm deluding myself, aren't I?'

He blows out, takes a drink. The fat rises in a frothy belch. He blows out a second time sideways.

'Speaking of which, I tell you what, Nick, I did laugh a bit to myself at your brother's house. When you dropped your posh speaking voice! *All right, geezer . . .*'

He takes a sip of wine. 'You've drunk too much,' he says to her.

This is the same accusation he levelled at her Wednesday night when she came upstairs to renew their argument. It seems now that the argument is still there, left out on a table like a board game abandoned mid-contest just waiting for the players to resume their seats.

'You've run so far from him, Nick, but you are him. Ever since that lunch, I don't know, but it's like he's possessed you.'

'Well, you, you're like your mother, Astrid.'

She's shocked. They've shared jokes about Linda hitherto. There's much to smile at. Astrid's mother had long ruled out carnations and gypsophila from her flower arrangements. She gurned at Venetian blinds and built-in garages. She cringed at cladding. She reviled water features and gave short shrift to wallpapers, patterned carpets and pastels too. She ruled in favour of muted neutrals, and claimed she always had, and she could argue avocado was aqua. She lived in terror of someone breaking in and messing up her cushions. Poor Malcolm, they said. Good old Malcolm, they said. When he met her parents, her father, who'd been a manager of a printing company, made her cringe by saying to Nick, the solicitor, 'We are only humble folk.' And since then Nick had taken the mickey out of this, repeating it in a yokel voice and pulling his forelock. 'He didn't mean it that way,' she'd said to him. 'He meant it as a joke. Isn't it a quote from a book or something?' Her father was always talking in quotations, to boost himself. This one had failed him with ghastly irony. Nick harped on about it: *'We's only 'umble folk, zerrr...'* She loved her father. Her father wrote stories for women's magazines in his spare time; romances. He put her mother first. He still brought her flowers.

'You're obsessed with appearances. Just like Linda. Really. It's so shallow. You talk about *my* business but what about yours, love?'

There's a touch of Ken in the use of the word 'love' and it's this that undoes her.

'At least my father's not obnoxious and common! I'm beginning to see a different side of you, and it's not funny. It's not funny at all.'

Other diners are looking at them.

'I have no interest in pursuing this conversation,' he says. He tosses his napkin onto the plate of food he's been enjoying so much and gets up and goes outside to pace up and down the alley and fume and, in his head, call her stupid and vain and anything else he wants.

14

He met her in Rye two years before. After a shabby one-night stand fuelled by silly drinks in a silly bar, he fled to a place he remembered as being thoroughly proper, if not positively fuddy-duddy, for redress. Rye was not unlike Ortygia; both were island citadels.

He stops at the newsagent's now and consults a guidebook in English. This is the right thing to do. He will use erudition to bolster himself, to prove himself to both of them. This is who he is. He checks his watch. Five thirty. He will give it ten minutes before he goes back in. He flicks through the book and looks sideways, left and right, and then up and around. It is certainly more Catholic than Rye, Ortygia. He can see what they meant in the guidebook about its baroque excesses, a place where wrought-iron balconies bulged, critters on cantilevers cowered, architraves leapt with nymphs on the hoof, balusters dripped foliage and bas-reliefs trembled, with ancient scores being settled in fretwork.

Nice, he thinks, if a trifle over the top. Rye is far more demure.

On Piazza Archimede, he takes a seat and orders a coffee granita. Over the fountain soft-breasted Artemis is posed in eternal
provocation with a bow slung across her and arrows behind in her
sheath. Something about her forthright expression reminds him
of Astrid.

Rye was not burgeoning with immortals in marble. Rye was
where mortals panicked, and strove to catch their breath. Rye was
rather like a Walnut Whip whose cobbled streets mounted steeply
in tiers to a conical form. 'For our time is a very shadow that pas-
seth away' was the motto on the church that crowned the summit.

The isle of Ortygia is quite flat, it makes a good stage. A police-
man remonstrates theatrically with a lone moped driver. He has
stopped the traffic on the piazza, and now Nick sees why. Twelve
medieval drummers come round the fountain with long cloaks
and leather boots, making mincing steps, followed by a procession
of maidens each holding petrol-station posies.

He'd gone to Rye that time to embrace getting older. He persuaded himself he was more game pies and log fires than he was
strobe lights and hand-shandies. He knew Rye as a boy. For a
number of years his mother had a stall in Rye's Thursday market. He used to sit under it on school holidays, reading books, or
else he'd wander its streets, treading the ankle-turning pebble-set
hills, and browsing bookshops with an aloof adult manner ready
for any challenge, with twenty-five pence in his pocket. The book,
the mere fact of it, distanced him as much as the seclusion of the
under-stall. He was glad enough to remove himself from the
squalor of the cattle market, with its pens and poo, giving in to
poor offers on chipped bric-a-brac.

'Would you take twenty pence for it, darling?'

Dave was motivated sufficiently by the prospect of a bag of chips in payment to run around getting Pearl and the other stallholders their teas.

And of course he'd share them with Nick. Sometimes they would sit with their chips and wooden forks and watch the man with the Kevin Keegan haircut lift the side of the lorry, to display shelves of packaged goods. He'd begin with an item at a time, usually electrical, occasionally cosmetic, proclaim its many merits, then start dropping the price wildly. The boys would nudge each other when they spotted the stooge and, sure enough, a woman would pipe up from the crowd, 'How much? Blimey, that's cheap!' Then, in a loud aside, as if confidentially, 'I bought a telly off him last month and it was top quality.' Waving a crisp note in the air, 'They're up Argos for twice that price! Over here, mate! I'll 'ave one, darling!'

They enjoyed those shows, and he'd have the rest of Dave's chips after he finished his own. 'You can 'ave 'em, I've 'ad enough.'

Good old Dave. It wasn't for the bookshops, or the fuddy-duddies, that he was drawn back to Rye that weekend, he reflected, watching the medieval crowd toss their flags on high, it was something to do with the taste of weak vinegary sweet ketchup. He could conjure its taste even now. It was certainly not Heinz. Watered down, it ran along the chips and dripped out of the bag rather than congeal. To his mind's eye comes now the vision of Dave with his mouth round and open, not daring to close it, in a quandary as to what to do, because the chips were so hot. ''Ot, innit!'

He went back to Rye because he missed them. And he found Astrid.

On the street that ran above the marketplace, parallel with the train tracks, there stood a renovated warehouse, dubbed 'Rye Spa'. He was stopped in his tracks by the herbal fragrance from its open doors. It reeked of purification and he weakened. He wanted cold alabaster hands on him, water over his head, shorter, cleaner hair.

Astrid appeared to him as light: smooth, shining and fair. She came towards him from the desk and said she'd take him herself. She was dressed all in black with a pale blond bob and red lips. For a person to look like that, their home too had to be immaculate, their handbag had to be neat, their toenails trim, their relationships kind and tolerant. He asked her out to lunch.

From the first heady days of car-park kisses to the hand-in-hand walks with the dog two years later, through talking—talking in wine and talking in bed—they learnt how to work in unison. She put him first, even above Laura, and they'd had little cause for quarrel thus far.

Given the *Tom and Jerry* model of a marriage he'd witnessed growing up, it was perhaps no surprise that before Astrid he chose the weakest of potential enemies: girls who were at a disadvantage to him—dimmer, younger, less educated, poorer, speaking a foreign language. Sure, for the most part they connived in his superiority. He knew that they played dumb, but that suspicion was generally the last thing to be aroused.

At first, his relationship with Astrid seemed to offer elements of the old; she'd only stayed in school to sixteen, and she was feminine, almost submissive, in her mannerisms, but she owned the spa, a profitable business, and she was his age. In bed with her or talking to her, he felt two things he'd never felt before: exposed and grateful.

There were all sorts of things about love he didn't know before her: the emergency of wanting to be honest which, it seemed to him, was what real love did to you; the fear of loss; and the risk of becoming ordinary.

In the early months, when they set up home together, he came up with a working model for the smooth running of the domestic machine: *A man wants to be good and a woman wants to be beautiful.* But that was only valid in the courtly phase. After that, there was sustaining the relationship. That needed a rule too, and he had that down: *Do not call the other person a piece of shit. Don't see through them.*

Paying for private school for Laura gave him a paternal role in her life and helped found the family. He likes to drive her in to school, turning up *Girls Aloud* on the radio, and imagining himself the fond papa. It was all like playing Mummies and Daddies. Nobody minded when he was mistaken for Laura's father, except for Laura. 'Because I have a daddy already, you see,' she'd warned him. There's a little bit of Margaret Thatcher in that girl, he'd thought, swallowing his pride.

He loved them with practical acts: he made the fire, carried the shopping, cooked a breakfast or took Laura to the pictures when Astrid was tired. That was the life he wanted. He had his fire and game pie.

What he didn't want was arguments. He had enough of it at work. His clients all said the same thing: 'We want this to be amicable.' He could punch the air every time he heard it. He didn't. Instead, he said: 'We want that too,' and added, for the sake of candour, 'but it never seems to go that way.' It never did.

The 'D' words were best avoided; you can't avoid death once

you're born and you can't avoid divorce once you're married, that was his drinking brag.

Every day he looked down from his office onto the shopping street and saw people struggling to get home; good people, and yet if he got any of them into the chair in his office they'd sit as they all did, shaking and tongue-tied, using pseudo 'legal terminology' and going on about fair play, but it was stunning how quickly a short course of shock therapy by correspondence could unravel in any one of them a murderous hatred.

Their home was a haven from it all, until just before Christmas. They've had to unplug the phone some evenings. Astrid says she doesn't understand it, and he doesn't either. But she goes further. She says she can't understand why he rises to it, why he starts shouting and swearing back. 'That's another evening spoilt,' she'll say. Like it's his fault! He doesn't like the way she looks at him nowadays, with her hands on her hips; she stands before him face to face, mannish. She looks him in the eye. Like Artemis, he thinks sourly, leaving some change on the table and heading back towards the newspaper shop. He can't reconcile this Astrid with the girl he met in Rye, whose eyes drank him in, whose smile was pure praise.

'It's so childish the way you and your father go on and on at each other,' she said.

But he knew from his work that this type of thing, this raging, this ranting, this haranguing, this hating, was in fact quite common between grown-ups. It was just that he never thought he'd be susceptible to it himself.

15

'Gary Goodyew!' Her smile knocks him back.

Nick's standing between magazine racks. He's opening and closing his mouth, running his hand through his hair. He's been lucky, too bloody lucky. In going back to Kent he's not met one of his old girlfriends and now, here in Sicily, it has to happen. Ah shit, he thinks, this is the last thing I need.

'Morwen.'

He gets a shove; a man pushes past him to the counter. 'You look good,' he says, using the muscles honed by half a lifetime's insincerity even though he means it.

'You look just the same!' The teeth have been set straight, he sees, but, as if her mouth hasn't had the news, her lips stay parted after she speaks.

He has a flashback of them on the floor in Toby Farrow's sitting room. He kept his coat on. Why? Was it cold?

'I can't believe it!' When his dreaming brain is seeking a guilty feeling, it goes straight to the image of her—and there she is, centre stage, on a surreal scene, toothily dismayed, something like the ghost of Christmas fucked up. He can see her when she came into school after the announcement was made, when she was received in the quad, duffle-coat hood up, with all the fuss she'd never had before, the pats on the back and the girls bending down to peer into her face, keen to see what tragedy looked like. 'I'm an orphan now,' she said to him, when they walked to school. She had hairy knees, he recalls.

'Twenty-three years it is, Gary!'

He lets himself be jostled with her out onto the street. 'On holiday?'

'Yes.'

'Good. Good.'

'You?'

'Yes. Husband? Kids?'

'No, I'm afraid not. I was married, Gary, but we got divorced.'

'Never mind.'

'Are you divorced then, Gary?'

'No. No, no, not me. It's my business. I'm a solicitor. Family law.'

'You always was a clever boy!' She stops to marvel at him, standing in the sunshine, just beatific, hands on hips. He never did know whether she was innocent or a touch slow. 'It's amazing the way our minds play tricks. I mean, I don't see a line on you or nothing, Gary; you're just the same.'

'Oh no! Jesus. Let me help you there'—he points to his forehead—'hair gone there'—and to his waist—'and an extra couple of pounds there, I expect.'

'What about there then?' she says, poking his chest. 'Your heart, Gary. Anyone claimed that?'

'Oh, that's all in order, just about! The occasional run, you know, to keep in shape.'

'You sound so upper class, Gary!'

He is speechless.

'Fancy meeting you again, and here! I don't know! It's like a dream come true.'

'Yes.' He rolls on the balls of his feet.

Her eyes glisten as her smile spreads.

'Well,' he goes on, his mouth running ahead, 'come and have a drink with us, if you'd like to. My girlfriend's at a table in a little restaurant just down here. Come along, if you'd like. It's a bit crowded, but I expect they can find us another chair. Or we could have a drink later on, or another day. . . .'

'All right then, I'll come along for a quick one! Why not? We're on holiday, aren't we, Gary?'

Morwen, who was so under-prepared for adulthood, has aged well; she still looks girlish. They'd called her 'Kipper Chest' at school. No one asked her out. She wasn't asked to dance at the disco. She wasn't picked for any team or party. Even puberty left her out. She was the girl who hung around with the asthmatics, eczematics and gender uncertains who ate their lunches in the lab, afraid to brave the open spaces. And when everyone else was affecting world-weariness, she was utterly ingenuous. She came from the state system and was thrilled to be at grammar. She kept her socks pulled up. But, though he kept it a clandestine arrangement, they used to walk to and from school together every day for four years, only meeting up well out of sight of the school's bounds. Then, at seventeen, she lost her parents; they were killed in a car crash on the A21.

He indicates the door of the restaurant to her, and lets her pass before him, but cranes his neck round her to left and right. Parting the bamboo blind, he is ready to see Astrid's smile like a flick knife, transforming woe to a bright greeting. But the table is empty and the owner is standing there with a pained expression on his face.

'Sir, your wife, she has gone away.'

'Oh, great,' he says with relief, 'good, thanks, that's fine. All right at the same table?'

All the forty years of his life push him towards the seat he sat in, opposite the woman he loves, to sit now opposite the woman that on balance he'd probably least like to have seen again, give or take one or two others. He alternates grin with grimace, clutches the menu, cranes his neck for the waiter, and she sits there just plain happy, fanning herself, moving her head in wonderment.

When he put an arm around her in the church porch that day, after the announcement, she closed her eyes and opened her mouth. He'd *had* to kiss her. Then she said, 'Are we going out now?'

The owner comes and changes the tablecloth, with the sniffy air of room service changing sheets.

'Won't she mind, though, about you being here with me, your girlfriend?'

'No, not at all. Why should she? Hmm?'

Nick orders a bottle of the same wine and she draws closer to the table in jolts, holding the chair.

'You look even more handsome actually, Gary.'

'Oh no!' He slumps. He puts his head in his hands. 'Morwen.

You'd lost your parents and by Christ I let you down. I am so sorry. You see, well, I just couldn't . . . at *that* age . . .' He feels for the most hygienic lie. 'Get my head round your loss.'

'Gary, I *understand.* Don't feel bad about it. Death, you see, it's tricky. No one's comfortable with it, are they? Tell me now, do you still bum-suck a cigarette?'

He has never bum-sucked a cigarette, and he doesn't smoke nowadays except in emergencies.

'I'm afraid so!' He affects a wry look. Would she like to eat something? He drums his fingertips on the table.

'To be honest with you, Gary, I've stuffed myself with cake this morning. Have you tried the cannoli?'

'No, is it good?' He glances at the door as the strings jangle in the wake of someone leaving. Most of the tables are now empty.

'Holy cannoli!' she says with a little musical laugh and shows her teeth. 'They're little sort of flute things and they fill them with this sort of patisserie cream.' She makes a circle with her fingers and thumb and pokes it through a few times with the forefinger of her other hand. He gives her a damp smile; it's an unfortunate gesture. 'Mmm,' she licks her lips, 'they're so delicious. You don't know whether to suck the cream out of them first or just bite right into them. I suppose you remember my little weakness, Gary?'

'No.'

'Chocolate fridge cake? Hello?' She waives the owner's offer of tasting the wine, 'No, you go ahead and pour it, love,' and when he turns the rim and lifts the bottle, she says, 'A bit more,' and then she raises her glass. 'To old friends.'

'So. What do you do now, Morwen?'

'Well, I have my own bookshop! And we do jacket potatoes and things too.'

'Nice.'

'Yes. It's lovely. Seriously, you should come and visit! You'd love it. All those books!' She sips on her wine, likes it and gulps at it. 'I was never as clever as you lot, of course, but one thing I do have, Gary, is a good memory.'

He can see her now, sitting on that hillock waiting for him when she was all centre parting and solicitation: 'I wish I could get the hang of this maths. I wish I had someone clever to show me how to do it. . . . Cor, aren't you clever, Gary? You do it just like that, don't you, and it takes me *hours*. . . .'

She was his starter girlfriend. Nobody knew.

'I remember you was my first kiss.' She makes a face, grins sheepishly. 'And the rest!'

'Ah.' He winces. 'That.'

Then all the intrigue and bravura drop clean off her face and the naked sadness brings to mind how Laura looks on a Sunday evening, when they pick her up from her dad.

'I let you down,' he says. He offers her his napkin. She takes it from him and touches the tip of her nose. 'About your parents.'

'I have a very nice little cottage of my own in Peterborough,' she rallies. 'I've done all right. Not by your standards. Oh, Gary. You were such a lovely boy! When we used to play Monopoly, you used to let me win, you did. You was a really good person, once—you know, before you got popular. Before the world got hold of you. Can we go outside and smoke a cigarette, Gary? That all right?'

He trots after her. They stand just round from the restaurant in a side alley, below its windows. He lights a cigarette for her and one for himself. She clasps her thin arms as she exhales.

'I don't really smoke anymore,' he says.

'Classic! You got me smoking and now you've quit and I can't give it up! I only done it to impress you! That says it all! I did try and contact you at Cambridge, to be honest. They couldn't find you. Oh, Gary, you was my first love.'

He pulls her to him and hugs her and pats her back. Inside the restaurateur draws a breath as he reaches over the plates of anti-pasti and draws the blind on them.

When they go back inside, there is an atmosphere, Nick finds. The owner has put on the television and stands with his back to them, arms folded, to watch a dubbed American soap.

The slippery little sidekick sidles over to their table.

'We close now,' he says, but he uses his hands in a placatory way to indicate they should stay sitting. 'No, no, Signor, you please stay here and it is no trouble but we do not need more people. Like you.'

'*We do not need more people like you,*' Nick repeats in amusement for what he supposes to be a bad translation.

She laughs. 'Oh, Gary! You are funny!' She's sitting there, with her chin resting on a hand, beguiled. 'Gary,' she muses, heavy with nostalgia.

'I have to tell you,' he says with comedic confidentiality, glancing left and right, 'when I left school I dropped "Gary", and since then I've used my middle name. Most people know me as Nick.'

'Nick?' she says, stricken. She sits up and her hands fall away from the table. She looks askance, across the room.

'What? It's just a name.'

'Then why change it?'

'Because it's a bloody awful name.'

'So's Morwen.'

'Well, yes,' he concedes.

'So, you just don't like "the sound" of it, your given name, Gary.'

'No.'

'Now I don't know whether to call you Gary or Nick.'

'It's really not important! It hardly matters, a name after all, what's a name? I could be Ricardo or Bernardo or—'

'Yeah, but you wouldn't have changed it to Lee or Barry or something, would you? I mean, all the time I was looking for Gary Goodyew. . . .'

He yawns exaggeratedly, leans back in his chair. 'Look, it's hardly as if one's Christian name reveals some sort of hidden truth, is it?'

She holds his eyes with her own. 'Do you know what, Gary . . .'

He raises an eyebrow.

'You make this journey alone, whatever your name is. Some people can't take that and all they can do is pretend it's not true. Me, I used to listen to the rain on the windowpanes at night, and I got to love the feeling of being alone after Mum and Dad died. I sort of trained myself to it. That's the truth of things, you see. We are alone. I know it and other people are pretending. So change your name, change your game, whatever you want, I don't care, pretend if you want to, but surely a clever boy like you knows when he's pretending.' She drains the glass. 'Do me a favour.'

'You think I'm shallow.'

'You are what you are. Or maybe you're not. Perhaps you're

just a face you borrowed or a voice you heard. Perhaps you got yourself off TV or out of a book. Perhaps you're someone you saw on a train. I don't know. That trench coat!'

'We all wore trench coats!'

'We was supposed to meet on Big Side the day I left, and you never came. You never even said goodbye, Gary. I overheard that Sebastian Double-Barrelled-Cockface saying to you one time, in the common room, "Find someone your own class, man." Now, what does that mean?'

He puts a hand in the air.

'What does that say about you?'

He asks the sidekick for the bill.

'You were a snob, that's what it says. The sort of bloke who'd sell his own parents for membership of the right club.'

It occurs to him this is not what most people mean when they talk about meeting up with old friends and getting to know each other again. He wants to run to Astrid and smell her good hair.

16

On the way to St Leonards you pass through Silverhill, a cross-roads of discount carpet stores and blacked-out pubs resembling any South London intersection, and it's there on the brow of the hill: the sea. The ground drops away from beneath you and, shaped by the buildings either side of London Road, it's like a glass raised for a toast.

Ken steps off the kerb to cross London Road to Norman Road. He's on his way to see Audrey at Bury and Bury Funeral Directors. It's like a sanctuary; when Ken goes through the doors, he's back in the past where everyone was courteous and decent and hard done by and hopeful.

It breaks his heart that that world's gone. He's so lonely in this one. June is a modern woman and no good, he's decided. The nearest he gets to feeling right again is in Audrey's funeral parlour. What a woman she is! Women like her used to live on every street, in every village—they'd help with the birthing and the lay-ing out—a strong pair of hands. Old Mother Perry came to their house when his mother died, and stayed on and taught Pat how to cook and look after them. Women weren't all for themselves in those days. Dave told him how Pearl said to him, last time he saw her, be it long or be it short, she was devoting her life to growing vegetables. Send her my regards, will ya? he'd said. But whether she got them or not, he didn't know. There was no word back. Well, *his* life, be it long or be it short, he was going to spend in the company of good persons. Like what his Pat was. Persons what thought more about people than they did their china animals and buying things and gambling and spending money. Kind sorts. Not persons always trying to have one over on you. Persons he could trust, who cared about him. A good woman was what he was after now, most urgently.

He told Pat, Don't you worry, sweetheart, don't you worry about nothing, the angels will be handing you right into the Lord's arms themselves, girl. She didn't want to do it, she was against it, you could see that, but he'd left the window open like Audrey said to and there was the singing of the birds as the sun came up. Daft little sods, he'd thought, singing their little hearts out as if every day were the Creation. And he sat with her there, holding her hand, and he was holding it tight when she took her last breath.

'That there is the only woman who's ever loved me proper,' he'd said to Audrey when she came in.

In the middle of the road, on a traffic island, he takes a buf-feting from the wind as he faces the sea. He stands there, hopeful of something from it. But since Pat never said anything to him about the sea, since she only gave it a cold shoulder, nothing helpful comes to mind.

She relied on people, did Pat, on the goodness of people, and she gave some credit to flowers and dogs but, though they lived by it all his life, she never praised the sea. She didn't like cats neither. She was seven years older than him, his sister, and she was like a mother to him and she took real joy from doing the things he wanted to do. She was only twelve when their mum died, and she was eighteen when their dad joined up.

From time to time, on a fair day during the war, the two of them sat up on the shingle of the beach, with her calling out after him, even though he was yards from the waves, 'Careful you don't catch it,' or, 'Watch you don't get a soaking,' and he ran at it, made a small hullabaloo, and then ate his sandwiches next to her, keeping an eye on the demon tide she dreaded, scrutinizing it between his toes, heard its rushing and hushing in between their chatter. They'd stay until Pat was 'proper browned off' with the seagulls. 'Gerroff out of it,' she'd cry with a ghastly shudder as they swooped in on the scraps, and he'd chase them away for her. At the end of the picnic, tidying away, exchanging admonitions one to the other in apprehension of mess, they shook out the crumbs from the blanket and shut the tin tight, the two of them pressing it down together.

Those were the happiest days of his life.

So now, when he looks at the sea, he is appalled that it's still there and just the same—a pale snoring ogre. It appears smooth and inscrutable, vast as any notion of God, but it's troubled and, like a disturbed mind, it turns its problem over and over. With its undercurrent on the prowl, it's ready to take each of us by the ankles and lay us out.

Roger's on reception when he steps through the door. His face falls. Roger is the driver and coffin-maker. He's a loafer and slow with it, Ken thinks.

He has Roger call Audrey for him. He takes a chair and waits. Roger hands him the phone, blushing.

The man's always blushing—more or less a simpleton, he is—and Audrey would do much better to have a pair of hands with a bit of something up top an' all.

17

It would be the prettiest seaside village in the south-east, if it weren't for the parvenu that stole its name. The Old Town of Hastings nestles in a horseshoe of grassy hills, hidden from the new town that has risen beside it, beyond the West Hill. The Old Town is a haven of Tudor cottages, with stained-glass surprises, horsemen's lanes and leafy bowers. Windows are thrown open to views onto the pebble beach, where fishing boats lie amid the black creosoted fishermen's huts, erect as sentry boxes. Smugglers once staggered ashore here, ankle-high in stones, to slake long-salted thirsts. The morris men still come forth in May, with their blackened faces, and the beardy men dance in front of the pub on the seafront, knocking sticks, lifting their knees and sounding the springtime hoorah. There is a pretty greengrocer's, a delicatessen, numerous fish and chip shops and a host of bohemian tattoo parlours and vintage boutiques.

Audrey Bury lives in Armada Cottage on All Saints Road, a row
of medieval hovels, upper floors bellying out over lower floors,
with doorways mottoed to the memory of sometime seafarers. It's
the prettiest street of all, beloved of film crews. They look quaint,
those places, but you can't live in them. The doors are four foot
high. You have to stoop. The floor's not level. Audrey's mahog-
any standing mirror on wheels rolls downhill. She keeps hauling
it back where she wants it, but it just trundles off again under its
own steam, towards the window.

Funny, her parents thought she was up her own arse for moving to the Old Town. In a way, she is; right up it and doubled back
on herself. Her back aches all the time. The only time it doesn't
ache is when she's lying down in her bedroom, but even then she's
like an ogre with her nose against the window. They could only
get the smallest of beds up the stairs in segments. It's her crucifix.
There's just about enough space for a peck on the cheek.

A large woman, she chose this winsome confinement because
the area is better than anything else Hastings has to offer; its small
homely businesses are run by former Londoners, feminine men
and manly women whose deft hands can convert humdrum into
boho and who like a drink. You're friends with them in minutes.
Audrey shares with them the knowingness of a forty-something
woman; all husky appetite and brawny forearm.

Come the odd day off, she's outside rather than in. She dith-
ers along the pedestrian thoroughfare of George Street. There's
the smell of weed in the air and rancid fat. The food is a very
pale imitation of modern fare; they call them paninis when they're
squashed rolls, and the orange cheese runs like paint. The pubs are
dingy. Gormless men congregate there with their shaven heads, a

knife in one of their socks, faces pitted like oranges. Outside any pub there's your standard loser, pulling on the choke chains of four or five bull mastiffs, feeding his dog friends chips from the bin while, in return, they pee over his shoes. Old men with long beards and novelty captains' hats sit on benches, shaking to the tune of Parkinson's. The gulls stir the sky, each call and cry a hackle-raising warning.

She sits down outside a bar with a large glass of red. This feels festive at least. Her mobile rings and it's Roger, her right-hand man and the only other full-time member of staff, and he tells her Ken Goodyew's in, just sitting, and she says that's fine, tell him she'll be in shortly. She drinks up. She looks at the trestle table next to her. The young people have either dyed white hair or dyed black hair. Assembled, they look like a chess set. They are discussing the benefits of being a hermaphrodite. She leaves her glass drained, squeezes past the young people and goes to get the car.

He's a nice old boy, Ken Goodyew. He's a bit of vintage chic himself in his smart clothes and shiny shoes; looks like he left the hanger in his coat. Since his sister died, he's been in every other day. She let him sit and keep the old lady company before the funeral; then, after she was buried, he just kept coming in. At first it was on the pretext of this or that to do with the headstone, but within a week or so he made her a proposal.

'My boy Dave's running the business and I can't sit twiddling me thumbs. Got to have something to do. It's a nice family sort of place 'ere, innit? I like to be useful.'

She was short-staffed and so she agreed he could help out, casually. Not that there was anything casual about Ken. He was born to the business with his dress sense.

'Don't want nothing for it,' he says, but she gives him a tenner here and there. He's been with her to a nursing home and the hospital to pick up the deceased. Far from being squeamish, he's practical and interested in every aspect of the work. He praises the way they refer to the deceased as if they were still living: Mrs Edmondson, Mr Dixon and so on. 'I appreciate the way you do that, Audrey,' he says. He likes the way they dress smart and have clean hands. He likes their quiet voices and good manners.

'I say, Audrey,' he said one afternoon, sitting in reception having a cuppa, 'when I come in 'ere, I feel myself.'

Roger had given her an old-fashioned look and she'd had to stop herself smiling.

In his spare time, Ken likes to pore through the funeral plan. ''Ere, I say, Audrey, it's like a menu, innit? It's like ordering off a menu. Bet you don't get many of your punters come in and book up this way, do ya?'

'I wish we did. It would make it much easier, Ken.'

'Cremated or buried? Audrey? What would you 'ave?'

'Well, it's according to your religious views, Ken. Do you believe in the Resurrection?'

'Oh, I dunno about that one, Audrey,' he whistles, 'dunno about that one. . . .'

'Well, it's like with a holiday; there are options. It's how you want to travel. Whether you want to go club class *somewhere* or whether you'd prefer to go economy *nowhere*.'

'I don't believe in 'olidays,' was all he said.

Later on he said, a-quiver with the giggles, 'I say, Audrey, I've got time to think it through, ain't it? I'm not kicking it tomorrow, am I? Eh? Eh?'

'I've never had anything like it,' she'd mused. 'A groupie.'

'He's sweet on you,' said Roger. Ken had been in every day for three weeks by then. 'It's that or he's a necrophiliac.'

He had a schoolboy's sense of humour, Roger. He got a clout one afternoon from Audrey for typing up an old joke on the coffin plaque for Joyce Haynes, who died a spinster. *'This one returned unopened.'*

'Blimey,' said Ken, 'that ain't right.' And he cast Roger heavily critical looks.

'There's nothing wrong with a touch of levity, Ken,' she said to him. 'I like to confound people's expectations of a funeral director.' Her parents never used to say what they did for a living. If you told people what you did when they had a hand in your bag of Revels, they'd whip it out quick as a flash, drop the chocs. They'd never take a cup of tea from you. Other times they'd ask you about the handles and whether you half-inched them.

'Have you worked with anyone we'd know?' a woman gushed at a house-warming party.

'I don't know. Do you know a lot of dead people?'

'Oh. I thought you said you were a film director!'

Ken preferred his own jokes. ''Ere, Audrey, tell you what, you've got an advance booking from Ken Goodyew. Oy, the living are queuing up for your services! I don't mind if you want to use it in your publicity. Get a nice picture of me. 'Ere, Audrey, listen—"Wanted dead or alive". Eh? Eh? Get it? How about that for a caption? Tell you what, I'll let you buy me dinner in return for using my mugshot. 'Ere, Audrey, you ever taken out an old geezer like me before?'

'I have, Ken, but he's been in a shroud.'

Her mother warned her not to let on about what she did for a living until she'd seen a chap a few times. Other girls were getting warned not to sleep with a man on the first date, but she was told to crack on with it. They'd been few and far between, though, and here she was forty-odd, with a clothing rack of black, a fridge full of Müllerlights, and an eighty-year-old for a suitor. It was a rum do.

She drives at a dignified speed down through the Old Town, but makes quite an impact on the traffic. In front, cars pull in, pull over; across from her, they slow down, their drivers look away; and behind her, cars slow and lengthen the distance between them. At the traffic lights, an elderly man stops, assumes a military bearing and removes his cap.

When the lights change, for the hell of it, Audrey floors it along the seafront like something out of *The Dukes of Hazzard*. She hits fifty as she passes the pier. She cuts quite a figure in a speeding hearse.

18

❦

A boat trip, lunch and a visit to the catacombs came and went the following day and Nick treated it all with mute disinterest. He was supercilious when he did speak, either lofty or cryptic.

In front of the Duomo on that Monday evening, couples stroll hand in hand across the great white marble piazza, back and forth, before settling on one of the five similar restaurants with tables for two.

Nick and Astrid watch them with pointed absorption. Each of them affects a gaunt melancholy. They reach for their glasses of wine as soon as they are served. They take dutiful sips. They have ordered a pizza to share, though they have each admitted that neither is hungry.

On the cathedral steps, a tall man with hair pulled back behind his ears holds out his hand for a woman in a strappy dress. She has the poise of a dancer. As he pulls her into him, he uses his mobile phone to take a picture of the pair of them, in front of what was once the temple of Athena. A man in a wheelchair is parked at a table next to them. His friend hoists him up. The disabled man slumps. The friend does it again. The man slumps again and his glasses on a string fall off and hang about his chin.

Astrid misses the spa. The clients she got in there were the sort of women she liked: malleable, the behind-your-back type. Fortunately, she never had to deal with any of the Annie Lennox sort: opinionated and messianic. She enjoyed conversation in the half-hour slots during which she applied the colour. She could give vent to anything she needed to, shorten a few long faces and, after a day of it, leave feeling generally very satisfied and ready for a bit of male. She missed the company of women. Especially now, when they'd had a falling-out and she had no one to speak to.

Of course she didn't discuss the entire ins and outs of their business! She hadn't time for the whole kit and caboodle with the apprentices doing the rest of the foils when she moved on to the next client. No, she edited the story down to what he said (that was bad) and what she did (that was good). She reasoned, as ever, that if she was telling perfect strangers the ins and outs of their lives, she ought to tell her mother. So, from time to time, they met for lunch. 'I've never liked any of the men in your life, Astrid,' her mother said to her once. 'Well, I love him,' Astrid had replied as they worked side by side, fork by fork, through the cheesecake, coming to a truce at the crust.

'I don't come on holiday to get drunk as a rule,' Nick says when she proposes another bottle of wine.

'Oh, wicked!'

'I've never liked that expression used that way.'

They sit in silence. The friend hoists the man in the wheel-chair once more.

As the white façades retreat into the night, she implores him, 'Nick? Where are you?'

He doesn't seem to hear; he makes no answer. She pays the bill to spite him and to relish, in that curiously feminine way, griev-ance added to grievance.

When they go to bed, he launches himself onto his right side, facing the wall. In the morning, when there is a light between the shutters, he wakes and goes into the bathroom. Windowless, it is dark in there. He stumbles about; he's desperate for a pee. He reaches left and right for a light pull. He tries the light switch on the outside wall. He flicks it on and off, on and off, on and off. Nothing.

'The fucking lights are broken,' he says out loud.

He goes to open the shutters. He goes back across the floor to the bathroom. The bathroom is still impenetrably dark. Shit, he'll have to call downstairs and ask whether it's normal to have a power cut here.

'Put the key card in the slot in the wall,' says Astrid.

'Which slot?'

'The one right in front of you which says, in English and Ital-ian and French, put your card in here to turn on bathroom lights. That one,' she says facetiously.

'Thank you!'

When she hears the lights ping and flutter and warble into action, she rolls over onto her stomach. 'Some holiday this is.'

She can hear him shaving, showering, drying himself—the usual routine, but at speed—and her heart beats faster as she wonders why he is getting up at this hour, and then he's got his clothes on in what seems like seconds.

'I'll see you up at breakfast, I assume,' he says dourly before he leaves.

With the wardrobe shaking in the door's wake, she sits up and looks in the mirror at her tired face in the morning light.

Up at the rooftop restaurant, where breakfast is served, on a buffet table laid with pristine white linen, there is a crushed almond granita circulating in a drinks machine and a bottle of prosecco in a silver bucket hinting at honeymooners. Some fat-bottomed tourists in khaki shorts are bending and exclaiming over the custard-topped pastries.

Outside on the terrace, the morning is spread out over the harbour, and there is a pink and violet tinge to the birdless sky. Nick is sitting at a table for two, gazing across to the modern port with its industrial area and docks. There is a noise coming from it which sounds like a giant vacuum cleaner.

But he is in Kent in 1987, in a field, sitting, waiting for her to come as he'd promised he would. The damp cold at his ankles, the sun on his crown and a faint smell of sheep shit. The ghastly delay between one crow calling another. The rumble of the road.

Astrid sits down opposite him.

'Are we to carry on with this argument all holiday, Nick?'

'No, I don't suppose so.' He looks nobly pained.

From her seat, she can see the tops of the buildings, square and domed, baroque and rococo, everything adorned and embellished, everything poised for a perfect day; a ruffle on a sleeve, the flick of a lock of hair, the lifting of a baton.

'Let's have a nice day today,' she says. 'Let's be friends again. It's a lovely hot day for the time of year.'

He offers her a wan smile.

Making do with that, she turns to admire the far plains on the other side of the harbour. When she finishes her coffee, she catches him looking at her forlornly.

They go down to the bit of beach closest to the hotel. The hem of sand that gives onto the harbour is fringed with stones, cigarette butts and twigs from the pine trees behind. Sparkling in it are the soft gems of washed glass in all sorts of colours. Three or four old men sit in their trunks on towels on a wall; walnut-skinned, they waggle their toes, their hair silver as if the sun had taken a blowtorch to it. Three older women, large and dark, stand in bikinis and sun hats, making scornful noises, with their hands on their hips, knee-high in the water. A young black man is washing his arms. The seawater on his back is like marbles.

'Have you seen this here?' Nick says out of the side of his mouth, to Astrid. Beside him a young couple lie kissing.

She shrugs.

After only a few minutes of sitting there, at the end of Nick's hotel towel are two terrier-like holes, the wet sand churned like toffee where his heels have dug. He is looking at the couple again, she sees. What's wrong with him? She takes a look. The young couple are using each other's bodies like furniture, with casual intimacy. The boy has the girl's lower tummy as his headrest, lying at a right angle to her; he is smoking a cigarette while she talks.

Nick gets up. Shaking his towel with disregard for the irritation he causes, he rolls it briskly and stows it under his arm. 'Going back to the room,' he says. It takes him a couple of goes to get up the wall. He makes his way up round the Fountain of Arethusa, leaving Astrid behind, open-mouthed, her paperback in her hands.

She looks at the couple again, lying alongside each other, facing one other, touching fingertips to fingertips, soft as fruit in a bowl. She leans back on her hands and closes her eyes to feel the sun and thinks of him, of Nick, her last love. Your body is like a garden—I know its quarters, the brush at your upper chest, the soft moss on your lower back.

When she opens her eyes, the tears in them smart like sea-water; still she smiles as hard as she can.

19

When he came in, just after five, he found her reading in the room, and she looked up to see his scowl—a deep furrow in his brow gone maroon in the sun.

'I came here to spend a week with you, not on my own,' he said.

The irony made her gag. 'Why don't you just fuck off, Nick?'

He sat down on the bed. He picked up her book and looked at it, then put it down.

'I must tell you . . .' he addressed her as if she were a client, 'on Saturday, I met an old school friend here, a girl—well, a woman now, but I knew her when we were young.' He cleared his throat. 'I took her virginity. She was very vulnerable, because her parents had died, and I let her down pretty badly, as it happens. I ran into her when I left the restaurant. I brought her to meet you but you were gone. Anyway, all I'm saying is the conversation was uncomfortable, to say the least. I can see now that I could be accused of being rather callow.' He looked at her. 'Do you know what I mean?'

'Yes,' she said through gritted teeth. 'I know what fucking callow means. I wish you'd stop using your words like you get a triple-letter score every time.'

'This girl, this woman, she set me straight about the kind of person I am, unfortunately, and it's hit me quite hard.'

'How do you mean? What on earth are you on about? What does she know about you? You were just a teenager when she knew you.'

'I don't have a mother and father. Not because they died, but because I cut them out of my life. People hate me. This man burst into my office last week and called me an arsehole. He said it was thanks to me he'd had a heart attack!'

She made a face. 'I had this woman once who said I'd ruined her sex life with a bob. People just want someone to blame.'

'He said to me, If I ever see you crossing the road, I'll run you down.'

'Oh, I don't suppose he will, Nick.'

'He came up the stairs, shouting, Where's that cunt—'

'I bet a few heads popped up then.'

'Astrid!'

'Well, quit your job then! Do something nice, fuck you.'

'That girl, Morwen—'

'Moorhen?'

'Morwen.'

'What kind of a name is Morwen when it's at home?'

'Welsh.'

'Welsh! You slept with someone Welsh?'

'She's not Welsh.'

'But you did sleep with her?'

'Twenty years ago! I told you! Look, she was in love with me. She said I was her first love. She said she's been trying to find me ever since. ... .'

'Stupid cow.'

'But she couldn't find Gary Goodyew of course, because he doesn't exist anymore. She went really nuts when I said I'd changed my name. She flew off the handle. She went on about how I'd been untrue to myself and just about everyone else. And she's not far wrong.'

'Well, you haven't been untrue to me, have you?'

He stood looking out across the harbour, his back to her. He didn't answer.

After a while, he turned round, his eyes small, and said, 'She's down there, on the beach.'

Astrid pushed past him and leant over the balustrade, holding it tight, and saw a single woman, on a towel on the beach in a navy-blue swimming costume, meditative pose, legs crossed.

'That the one?'

He nodded.

'Is she waiting for you, or something?'

'I don't know. Maybe. I mean, in a sense she was always waiting for me.'

He hung his head and sat on the little tin chair on the balcony, looking out to sea. He didn't hear the door close.

When he looked across to the beach, he saw Astrid, taking the steps down past the fountain two at a time. She hopped off the wall onto the sand. Morwen looked up as Astrid approached.

There must have been something of Artemis in her expression, for Morwen stood up. They faced each other, hands on hips, then first Astrid, then Morwen, looked towards the balcony at him.

He did not think a wave would be appropriate.

There was some conversation. Morwen folded her arms across her chest and put a leg out to one side. Mistake. Astrid slapped her. He could see it was hard because Morwen reeled. A man stood up, but didn't move further. Astrid clambered onto the wall and went back up the stairs.

He retreated quickly from the balcony, closed the double doors and stood in the dim room, feeling his cheeks burning. He heard the swagger of the elevator, then the ping of its bell, followed by the sound of her flip-flops slapping the marble floor, coming closer and closer. When the door opened, he saw a wild woman, nothing like the girl he'd met in the spa.

'She said the wrong thing,' she panted. 'I asked her how she felt qualified to ruin my holiday with her half-arsed opinions, and she asked me what my problem was and—well, as you'd say, I've never liked that expression used that way.'

She went to the mini-bar and helped herself to a can of beer. She was shaking.

'I can't believe you just did that,' he said.

'I'm tired of being good,' she said, and then she drank.

20

It's a hell of a threshold to cross.

'Come on then, Ken.' She uses her thumb like she's hitching a lift. 'You wanted to see an embalming, you said.'

Ken baulks at the double doors. He gets a grip and follows her through. The mortuary is a large open space with a triple-doored fridge to the rear and three rolling tables, all of which are occupied. The incumbents are each covered by a sheet. On the wall is a chart with names, weights and dimensions written in marker pen. There is a kitchen-like installment of wall and floor cupboards, and a counter with a steel sink and a flush sluice.

He stands just inside the doors, rubbing his hands together. 'Parky in here, innit?'

'You wouldn't want it hot, Ken,' says Audrey, uncovering the body closest to him to reveal a corpse in a paper gown, to all appearances a wax dummy with sparse hair. The old girl's face is aghast, mouth open and eyes open. Her limbs are withered like twisted cabbage stalks; her yellow feet have curled toenails and the toes overlap. The luggage-like label with her name on it is poked between two toes for safekeeping.

'She looks like she fell in the fat fryer, don't she?' he says hoarsely. 'She looks like she was bracing herself for something? She's like . . . *it's coming, it's coming* . . . you know? Why do they want her embalmed then?'

'The sister's in hospital. Otherwise I wouldn't do it. What they're after is a pre-deceased appearance, but—' She pulls a plastic apron out of a dispenser. 'Well, it's like so many things. It's all about keeping up the illusion. For the living.'

She takes plastic gloves from a drawer and puts them on, blowing into each to make a balloon hand.

'My older son's gone off to Italy on his holidays, Audrey.'

'Has he? Lucky man.'

He looks at the dead woman and his jowls sag. 'We didn't have much of it in my day, that's all.'

'Well, there you go then,' she says amiably.

On the counter is her open briefcase; it contains a rolled velvet bag, its ribbon loose, a large container of Elnett hairspray and a large grubby make-up bag branded Boots No7. She gives a five-litre Hozelock spray a pump once or twice.

He looks at the woman's name tag: Barbara Bailey. She has sandy-coloured curls, permed at the front of her head, slightly unkempt and stringy now; the rest of her hair is short and pressed flat, like a lawn trodden down. Audrey passes her gloved hands through the front of the woman's hair, tenderly. 'All right, love,' she says. 'Here we go.'

'With my Pat, see, I'm glad the way it went.'

'Oh yes, that was a good one.'

'This lady resembles her, Audrey, don't she?'

'She does a little bit.'

'Just didn't know how it was going to get me,' he says quietly. 'She's gone, though, ain't she, Audrey? This here Barbara. You can see it's just the shell of the person, ain't it? There ain't nobody there. It's like a suit of clothes, innit? She looks like she was a nice lady, don't she? Neat and tidy. Her hair was always done nice, Pat's was. Thursdays was wash and set. Must do my 'ead, she liked to say. And she did her baking the same day. Did her cleaning on a Friday morning. She was very regular in her ways. Just dragging the duster about, she'd say, but she'd do it proper. . . . My shirts always smelt good.'

'You were very fond of her.'

'Cor, I should say. She weren' 'alf good to me.'

Audrey goes over to a small CD player and presses play. She waits for the first notes of the piano to knell. She takes away the paper hospital gown to reveal a green inflated stomach ripe with putrefaction. She puts the gown across the woman's private parts for modesty. The ribcage is high and almost apart from the stomach, like a large chicken carcass. She goes to the taps and runs warm water into a plastic basin in the sink. She puts in a squirt of liquid soap and takes a large bath sponge and squeezes it, then she begins to wash the body, starting with one arm, going to the other, and from top to bottom she wipes down each limb and then the torso, going gently over her neck and breasts and giving the lightest of touches to her stomach.

He wants to make a break for the door, but instead he stands teetering.

Audrey squeezes the sponge out between each limb and before she does the face. There are wispy stray hairs about the chin and upper brow, and the cheeks are sunken, the eyes open and yellow and grey. She dabs at the poultry neck. The head is so far back that she props it with a small pillow. Audrey takes the bowl down to her feet next, unhooks the label with her name on it, and washes the feet, over and under and, with a small smile forming on her lips, goes between the toes as and where she can.

Ken puts his fist over his mouth.

Next, from the velvet roll, Audrey withdraws the aneurism hook, the separator and scissors. On the right-hand side of the lady's chest, above the bone, she cuts the skin and separates the tissues to find the carotid artery that is like an elastic band. In behind it she slips the separator and, using thread, ties off the artery either side. She pumps the handle on the Hozelock spray another time. Bending over Mrs Bailey, she says, 'All right, dear, here we go.'

'All right, dear?' Ken seconds her, gawking at the dead woman with all the false cheer of a game-show host. 'Jesus Bleeding Christ!' he says when Audrey makes a nick in the artery and inserts the end of the tubing from the Hozelock into the woman's neck. 'Bloody Nora! You're sure she's dead, a'n't ya, love?'

Audrey gives two or three hefty pumps, then she picks up a bottle of hand lotion and squeezes an amount onto her hands and rubs Mrs Bailey's hands in turn.

'There we go,' Audrey says, turning them over to see them becoming pinker. 'That's good,' she says, 'we're on our way.'

''Cause you want to be sure, don't you, love? I mean, you'd want to 'ave done all the necessary just to be doubly sure, wouldn't ya?'

From the sink she picks up the trocar, a three-sided hollow steel instrument, triply bladed, and approaching the gurney, she jabs it with confidence into the stomach just above the belly button.

'You'd want to be sure of it, wouldn't you!' he cries in a high voice.

Audrey turns on the hydroaspirator that whirrs and hums and draws the excrescence into a bell jar. A sickly flatulent smell is released. 'Cancer,' she says. She thrusts the knitting-needle–long trocar about here and there inside the woman, vacuuming her stomach. Checking backwards over his shoulder, he sees the waste is running into the big jar container. She places a hand over Mrs Bailey's ribcage and feels about as she aims higher. 'Sorry,' she whispers as she feels the ribcage collapsing, bones being fractured and the vital organs being punched each in turn, last of all the heart. She puts her forehead into her upper arm, onto the checks of her cotton shirt, and wipes it there. She looks down at the container once more and watches the blood hitting the sides of the jar like scarlet fireworks, leaping and making patterns.

'You all right, Ken?'

Ken is swaying like a carnival inflatable on a rope. 'I'm all right, dear. You carry on.'

The left side of the woman's face has become lifelike. Audrey reverses the direction of the tubing into the carotid artery, now towards the head, and keeps an eye on the right side of the face, even as she continues to vacuum about inside the ribcage. 'That's looking better, Barbara.'

She turns off the motor and empties the waste into the sluice.

'We're all done, Ken. You still with me, are you?' she says, snipping the thread at the neck.

'I'm just feeling the blood return myself,' he says. 'Bit rough, ain't it?'

Audrey takes a small four-pronged comb from the briefcase and tends to the lady's hair, teasing out the permed curls as best she can. She picks up the photograph that has been lent for reference. She hands it to Ken. In the snap, Barbara Bailey is in her fifties in front of a Christmas tree. She is wearing an Austrian-style skirt and jacket, and smiling with the glee of a child, holding a tiny sherry glass with two hands. She has redeye. He turns it round and sees, in the genteel cursive script of her generation, the inscription 'Christmas 1994'.

'I'm gonna have to part ways with my June, Audrey.'

'Oh dear. That's a lot to bear for both of you.' She cleans the inside of Mrs Bailey's mouth with a small piece of sponge and, using tongs, puts a long wad of cotton wool down her throat, then she packs her nose too. 'You know, you can't blame your son for wanting a holiday, Ken. It's all most of us think about, really: escape.'

'In all my life I never done what you do, Audrey. I never done nothing 'ard, like this. Nothing for others, you know. I tell you, Audrey, you do a marvellous job, you really do. I couldn't do it, myself.'

'Thank you, Ken.' She takes the needle and thread and stitches Mrs Bailey's mouth together, going behind the lips into the gums and up through the septum of her nose. Once it's trussed shut, she presses it into a softer look with her fingers. She pulls Barbara's eyelids over the plastic eyecaps. 'You die alone, but if you pass through kind hands, well, that's something.'

She applies a beige cream foundation to Barbara's face, putting a dollop on each cheek and her nose and brow and rubbing it in, particularly around the nostrils, then rubs lipsalve forth along her cracked lips, puckering her own as she does.

'There you go, Barbara. Remember me when I come into your kingdom. A dab hand with the make-up brush.'

'You done her proud, love,' he says. But a corpse can never resemble a woman with a sherry glass by the Christmas tree. He looks at the photo again. Barbara Bailey is showing teeth in the photo, and there's something about the narrow hunch of her shoulders in the shot; it's as if she's guarding the moment with her life.

Ken looks at Audrey and wishes for her all the things she deserves and a good man to love her. He wishes it as hard as he can.

One eye comes open. The hands fall away from the sheet suddenly. They hang either side of the table, swinging. Ken clutches his chest and steps backwards.

'It's not the first time that's happened,' says Audrey hastily, giving him a reassuring smile, putting the eyecap back in its place and folding the woman's hands across her chest.

21

On their last night they sat on the most populous promenade, in need of other people without having spoken of it, and drank wine and ate pasta, crammed in between tables of couples, elbows tight to their sides. This was where the hoi polloi came for their suppers, the citizens of Syracuse and suburbs. This suited them so well they soon fell into their old happy way of denigrating the people around them.

'I can't stand goatees.'

'No. They're either effeminate or pretentious.'

'Or fat men use them to make a chin where there isn't one. Sometimes you have someone more or less bald and they have one, and you sort of want to turn them the other way round.'

He'd felt that the past was like a raised fist, ready to strike. But now he felt better. He had someone who believed in him so much, she'd fight for him.

'Oh, Jesus. He's wearing one fingerless leather glove, Nick! Don't look! Can you see it? Oh shit, it's got studs on the knuckles too.'

'That's Italian men for you—not afraid of looking gay!' As their coffees were settled before them, he said, 'I might have been clever at school, but I was a complete duffer when it came to—'

'Matters of the heart?'

'Yes. I mean, I wasn't a *complete* prick. I felt sorry for both of them, you know, Ken and Pearl, not being happy. I was eighteen.'

In the swimming baths, his father, half-submerged, looking with hatred at their mother as she came down the metal stairs into the pool, and Nick saw her the way the old man saw her. His mother at the back door, handkerchief in hand, and Nick saw his father through her eyes.

'I was more of a prig than a prick. You see, I'd decided to have a career in law, because I wanted to deal in truth. It seems laughable, I know. Anyway, Dad was away for a couple of months. He was just "away". But a friend of mine saw him on a train with a woman. Her husband had left her a pub in Eastbourne, apparently, and he couldn't resist it. Anyway, I decided I'd tell Mum, but that I'd do it when we were all there so it would all be above board. I think I thought we'd have it out in the open and somehow, them being the grown-ups, they'd make sense of it. Well, Ken went berserk. I'll never trust you again, he said to me. He packed a bag and went to leave, and I think he asked her if it was what she wanted. And I remember all she said was, I suppose you'd better. And Dave, he went with him. I never expected that either. He said, We can't just throw him out, he'll be all alone! And there we were, she and I, Mum and me, in just the space of a few hours, together in that house, half a family. The woman wouldn't take him in, so they ended up in the caravan park.'

'I don't know why he didn't go back, Ken.'

'He couldn't. There was no way back.'

He could remember a shepherd's pie on the side ready for the oven. She gave it to the dog after Ken and Dave left. She put the Pyrex on the floor. He could remember the noise of it on the tiles and hitting the skirting boards with the dog's nose pushing it round and round and her watching, mesmerized.

He drank his coffee down. 'And hey, so much for a mother's love,' he said, his voice tinged with the bitterness of the dregs. If he went to kiss his mother, she turned away from him. She hated him, that was plain. All right then, he said. In the summer, after his exams, he left home.

He called Dave from Cambridge during that first Michaelmas term. Dave and his father were sharing digs in Hastings then. He thought he might come down.

'Best not, mate,' said Dave. 'Dad's still hopping mad.'

There was only the communal hall phone in college. He called his mother a few times but had little in the way of a conversation, and gave it up. He spent Christmas in his room at Cambridge. He wasn't supposed to be there, but nobody caught him. He'd left a back window open and climbed in on Christmas Eve. In the Lent term, the phone rang a couple of times and the girl who lived closest to it would shriek up the stairs, 'Is there a Gary here?' There was no reply. And after another call or two, she said starchily, 'This is Downing College, Cambridge. We have no "Gary" here.'

And that was it. Apart from the occasional call from Dave, no contact. He didn't ask anyone to his graduation. He moved to London to do his law conversion course. A year or two later, there was Dave's wedding. A village-hall affair, with heavy smokers in shiny suits, elbows out, jogging along to Level 42 songs, balloons in clusters of three, not much in the way of speeches, and a scuffle or two when the bar closed. His mother didn't go to the party. His father made a song and dance about not speaking to him there. He was with June.

On a Christmas Day in his twenties, after a few drinks, he called his old man to say he'd got a place in a firm, and his father told him he'd like to knock his 'bleeding block' off. You're nothing to me now, he said. Apparently, his mother felt the same way, for he heard nothing from her.

He had never imagined they'd turn on him as they had each other.

'You're lucky your parents are so normal,' he said to her.

Her parents functioned as a couple; his didn't. Ken and Pearl went straight to a scrap, were nimble with name-calling, quick to up the ante and reckless with ultimatums. When it came to his father's chauvinism, his mother was his equal sparring partner; she hated men. If Astrid's dad, Malcolm, would not exactly say sorry, he would take out the bins, mow the lawn, run a bath for her, make a cuppa. If her mum, Linda, would not exactly say sorry, she would at least call out that the programme was starting.

Ken and Pearl would finish the milk to mock the other's tea, cook separate meals, sleep apart, begin the day in grudging silence and end it with a shrug or a curse. He'd go, or she'd go, for one night or two. The entire village would know about it. Time passed, wheels of the mind turning, turning, grinding meat into mince. And yet he could recall too some wonderful times, when they laughed with each other, and he and Dave egged them on, when they spoke in funny voices, like a comedy double act, their voices shrill and wild, and they seemed to reprise some old-time vaudeville act with him calling her 'Mother' and her calling him 'Father'. And just occasionally there was something flirtatious to it and their dad would whisper something to her and all they'd hear was the sibilance of it—though maybe a whole word would slip out here and there—and then their mother would come over sly, then grab him and order him to kiss her. These were thrilling glimpses of the promise of adulthood for those two small boys.

'It's hard to know what love is,' he said, 'it takes some working out.' He took her hand and kissed it. 'She's really something, though, my mother,' he said.

'That's the first time you've said anything like that.'

'You should meet her.'

She laughed. 'Hang on, I'm just getting over Ken.'

'I miss her,' he said miserably.

He thought he saw Pearl in Tenterden, a couple of months back, coming down the high street, swaying with the weight of the bags she was carrying. It was hard to tell if it was her. She was wearing men's clothes and her hair was salt and pepper. She stopped, grimaced, put down her bags, looked up at the church tower and unzipped her jacket as if she were having a hot flush. She resembled, he thought, her father.

Before they left Ortygia and the Hotel des Etrangers et

Miramare, he and Astrid made quiet fierce love. They arrived in exhilaration at the same place at the same time, together, then fell apart, gradually extricating themselves bit by bit, swapping limbs, trading a leg for an arm, and sighing.

They slept holding hands.

22

⁓

'Try and cheer him up a bit. You know,' says Audrey, explaining to Roger that Ken will be going with him to fetch the body. 'It's his idea of a day out.'

But Roger is not prone to small talk; he's economical with everything, and not just the truth, and when he does issue a statement, it's accurate. Otherwise he's rarely perturbed, trusting the limits to original thought and deed.

Ken sits beside him, winding himself right up in his rival's presence, resenting the man's very breathing.

'Don't say much, do ya?'

Roger passes him his bag of Glacier Mints.

'Who're we picking up then, up the hospital?'

'Dead woman.' Roger pops a sweet into his own mouth, arms locked, an impassive expression on his face. Only his drooping eyes change shape and become round, when the minty sensation tingles in his mouth.

The corridors of the hospital are sallow. Roger has a piece of paper to present to the reception desk. Ken stands back, waving people between himself and Roger with unappointed officiousness, his face as deliberately expressionless as a guardsman's. He likes wearing the black suit. He's got black socks and black gloves. He offered to buy his own hat, but Audrey dissuaded him. 'When the time comes, Ken, we'll see you right with a hat.'

Roger's wearing a dark navy sweatsuit. He is leaning on the counter, waiting for the woman's direction, moving a sweet around his mouth.

Ken rolls his eyes. 'Blow me, you'd think we'd come here to use the facilities.'

Roger swivels as if hinged to the counter at the elbow. 'Won't be long,' he says. Between Roger's knees is the folded gurney and body bag.

Ken looks him in the eye. 'You weren't in the army, were you?'

'No.'

'I didn't think so.'

They head to the female geriatric ward, with Ken's soles like a snare drum on the floors. A man in a green top directs them to the far bed, with the curtains drawn around it.

Their arrival creates a stir through the ward of crippled-up womenfolk, as if they were film stars. As best they can, the women hoist themselves and there are catcalls. It makes Ken jumpy, but nothing impedes the slow, plodding, donkey-like way of Roger going about his work. Ken catches sight of an old girl with half of one leg amputated and bandaged, lying there three-quarters akimbo with her nightie awry.

'All right, darling,' she rasps.

'All right,' he replies evenly, eyes front.

Roger's disappeared and Ken's like the understudy, trying to get through the curtains but failing to find the parting. The curtain rings clatter and the material flaps, and the old girls are all sitting up, passing comment and laughing.

'Don't worry, sweetheart! No rush! She ain't goin' nowhere!'

'Nicely turned out, innie, Wendy? For an old boy!'

He points a finger at the one-legged troublemaker to warn her, which sets them off, from laughter to racking coughs and back again.

When he makes it through the curtain, he shrugs his collar off his neck and shakes his hands away from his cuffs. 'Right now, let's see about this,' he says, standing well back.

Roger has the gurney unfolded, the wheels locked, and is placing the body bag onto it, smoothing it out.

'Mothers' meeting out there,' says Ken.

The body on the ward bed has been more or less tossed into blankets, vaguely concealed, like chicken in a basket. Roger peels back one of the plastic-backed paper blankets to take a look.

'Come on then,' he says, and he and Ken go to lift her. Roger takes the shoulders and Ken the feet. Ken holds his breath and averts his eyes. The woman's long curled toenails drag across the front of his jacket and a toe gets caught momentarily inside his lapel. He checks Roger's face. In the great calm expressionless shape are two sad eyes that look like those of the boy left out of the team. The sag of his shoulders, the resigned way of his, tell the story of a man disappointed. They lower the wrapped body onto the gurney and Roger arranges it in the body bag. The lady's face has a shocked expression, mouth and eyes wide open.

'You done a good job there, mate,' says Ken, catching his breath. Roger zips the bag. 'I'll let you do the honours,' he says, finding the side of the curtain, 'while I keep the animals at bay.'

Roger gives him a shy smile and dips his eyes as they wheel the body past the women. But they're otherwise occupied now. On the TV, a woman has won something and the woman with the half-leg is saying, 'Oh my God, I can't believe it,' and she means it. Whatever it is, it's fantastic. She's delighted; she looks around to find any face she can, to share this good luck a bit, like offering her grapes. She points at the TV.

'Yeah, good, innit?' says Ken. 'Cheerio then, ladies. Get well.'

'That you, Kenneth?' pipes up a voice from the last bed on the right as they begin to wheel the body out of the ward.

'Jesus Flaming Christ.'

It's Pearl. Two sons, dogs and cats, five houses and money problems; they were married for just under twenty years and he hasn't seen her for more than twenty since.

'All right?' is all he says, and he stands there, hands at the end of her bed, one corner of his upper lip twitching.

Pearl turns to address the black woman in the bed next to hers. 'Oh yeah, smashing! D'you hear him? Here I am in a hospital bed, laid up, and that's what he says to me. *All right?*'

The other woman laughs as if she's been poked; it's a short-lived response. She's wearing headphones; her eyes remain on the suspended TV screen.

Roger has lumbered on, solo, pulling the gurney.

'I'll be with you in a tick, Roger,' Ken calls after him, stuffing his hands in his pockets and looking at his ex-wife. There was always something Victorian about Pearl: useful and harsh, sly and sentimental. She was a good-looking girl and she didn't stand for any flannel. And flannel was what he gave her. It became just so much easier not to go home and get an earful. 'Unkind!' He used to upbraid her, 'Unkind!' 'But not untrue!' was her retort. What he objected to was that she wasn't any kind of Pat. She wasn't doting, or patient, or quiet, or careful, or willing to go second, or last, or without.

Pearl rises, and Ken shrinks. Her elbows push into the pillows, and his hands delve in his trouser pockets. She rolls her eyes to the ceiling and they come back white for a moment until she fixes on him her uncompromising eyes, dark as sloes.

'See Jill there,' she says. He looks at the woman with the half-leg. Her mouth is moving to Judy Finnigan's on the TV as if she's the ventriloquist. 'One leg. Lost her tits. You'd look at her and think she was unlucky, wouldn't you?'

She'd replaced her sex appeal bit by bit with a caustic sort of humour. Very quickly, she was headmistress of the school of hard knocks.

'That Jill, she's bald more or less. She snores at night something shocking. So loud it wakes us all up. She lies over there, her nightie up to her armpits—it's a sight for sore eyes, I can tell you. She gave her kid away. Half-caste he is. Gave him up for adoption and he comes in with his wife and kids to see her now! Can you believe that? They come in and call her Nan and sit with her and they laugh and chatter like you wouldn't believe.'

He gives a reed-thin laugh, makes a glancing acknowledgement of Jill, nodding at her as she's looking their way. She offers them a childish wave, folding her fingers a couple of times.

'You take a good look at her, Ken. Do you know what? I'd trade places with that woman. She's got a sodding sight more than me. So you can stuff your "all right" and sod off back wherever you came from.' She shuts her eyes.

Falteringly, he approaches the visitor's chair at the head of the bed and he stoops to whisper. 'Sorry for your troubles, Pearl. Anything I can get you while I'm here?'

Her chest rises and falls.

'No.'

He hovers. 'What about them chocolate bars you used to like? I could nip down to the café and get you a Bounty bar.'

She opens her eyes. 'I'm diabetic; you might as well bring me arsenic.'

'You look well.' He smiles. 'Considering.'

One eye separates from the pack. It was her party trick, her lazy eye; she could do it at will. And there was the way she bit the tops of beer bottles, and the arm that never set after she broke it at the elbow and she could flick it this way and that. Those were just some of her tricks. She could recite famous poems; she could recite lines and lines of them, word perfect.

'You used to be able to do the splits, din'cha, Pearl?'

'What are you doing here anyway, Ken?'

'Voluntary work. Doing my bit, a'n' I?' He looks round for support.

She laughs as if he's made a crude joke. 'Save it for someone

who believes you. You wouldn't do nothing 'less there was something in it for you. Pull the other one. So, what are you doing?
Nicking the rings off the fingers of corpses?'

'That's right!' her neighbour bursts out, nodding and grinning,
eyes on the screen.

Ken gives the woman a sour look. 'Loud, i'n' she? That's an
unkind thing to say, Pearl. And it *ain't* true, as it happens.'

'I know you, Ken.'

'Mmm-hmm!' comes the resounding note of her neighbour's
approval of what's happening on the TV.

Ken flinches aggrievedly, and turns his back on the neighbour
to block her. 'You sin the boys at all, Pearl?'

'David come in to see me. You sin 'em?'

'Not a lot. Went to Dave's place not long back.'

'Oh, did you now. With *June.*'

'You sin Gary at all?'

'Nicholas, you mean.' She turns her face away from him, and
it's then he remembers her fully. He knows the slackness about
the mouth and the way the eyes slide.

'Naargh,' he lies. That's a habit formed early on, when he was a
kid; you didn't tell the truth so as not to make a person feel worse.
You hid your luck, whatever it was. And it wasn't just about spar-
ing the other person's feelings of course; it was also a case of not
wanting to have to share whatever you had.

'I thought you had,' she says. She could always smell a lie.

He sits down on the chair. 'Not a word.'

'Miserable little shit.'

''Ere, Pearl,' his voice quavers, delight stirring, 'that's our son we're calling a miserable shit! 'Ere, remember when we got him that set of drums for his birthday and he said to us, *That it?* Cor dear! Miserable! Always talked posh, dinnie? Thought he was better than us. Used to give us that funny look, dinnie, even as a baby? You used to say, Look at 'im, Ken; 'e's givin' us that look! Like he'd smelt something bad, wannit?'

'With Dave you'd get a thank you, but not with Gary.'

'We used to call 'im misery guts. We used to say to him, Can't you look on the bright side a bit?'

She eyes him cynically.

'Christ, you look old.'

'I am old, a'n' I?'

'Hoo-hoo!' chortles the neighbour.

'Turned out like you, Gary did. No regard for anyone but himself.'

He says nothing, but moves his teeth in his mouth.

'Christ, it nearly killed me giving birth to them boys. But I tell you, it killed me again and again cleaning up after you lot, making your dinners to be treated like dirt. . . . Never a thank you, and if I was ill—God forbid—you'd moan about it being women's business. Minute you had spare time, off you went the three of you, off on a jaunt without me. When I mopped the floors, I used to cry into the bleeding bucket and think to myself, Well, that's a way to do it without making a mess, and I used to say to myself, if my mind wandered, Now, don't give over to dreams and fancies, Pearl, don't go dreaming. . . . But, Ken, just something! Some sort of a thank you. You never once got me flowers. You never did nothing for me. Not one of you ever said you loved me. And then that Mrs Morris, she said to me, They only treat you like it because you let 'em. And she was right. What a stupid cow I was. Still, I got what I asked for. Didn't I? Look at me now.'

'Don't upset yourself, Pearl,' he says. He feels for her hand on the sheets. She lets him hold it but looks away.

' "Mother" you used to call me. *Mother!* Oh, look at Mother in a temper. *'Ooo's* upset Mother now . . . ? Oy, Mother, where's my shirt? Mother! Dogsbody, more like.'

He squeezes her hand, hopeful for a change of subject. 'What's the matter with you anyway, Pearl? Why're you in here?'

'Broke my leg on the back path.'

'I always said we should get some nice big modern paving slabs out there.'

'That's right, chuck away them bricks that's been there hundreds of years. That's you all over. Make a parking lot out of the garden. Cover the flowers in cement. No, thank you.'

'You got your own way in the end, though.'

'Yes, I did. My own way.' She throws his hand aside. 'Well, here we are now, Ken. You're an old man and I'm an old woman. Neither of us thought it would work out like this, did we? Still, you've got some daft cow to do your washing, I expect. You and the boys, you'll all have found someone else to pick up after you.' Her eyes, he sees, are wet. 'I never thought it would end like this.'

'It ain't the end, Pearl.'

'Ha.'

He takes a handkerchief from his pocket, white with black trim, and hands it to her. 'Here. Here you go, Pearl. You can hang on to that, if you want.'

She lets it lie in her hand. 'Thanks.'

'I'm sorry, Pearl.'

She doesn't reply; her fingers twitch at the handkerchief.

He stands up. 'See you then.'

She is staring into the mid-distance, head on one side. 'Shall I come see you again?'

She doesn't answer.

After a while, seeing the black woman looking at him, he goes off round the end of the bed and is about to turn the corner of the ward when she calls out. 'Ken?'

'Yes?'

He turns.

'If you see Gary, tell him he can call me. If he wants.'

'All right, Pearl. I will. Cheerio then, Pearl.'

And all the way down the corridor towards the main entrance he says to himself, I'll do that for her, I'll do that for Pearl.

And when he rejoins Roger at the van, and sees the big fellow leaning against it, sucking a sweet and looking up at the sky, he says to him, 'That was my old missus, that was.'

He stands opposite Roger, with his hands in his pockets. He sniffs a couple of times, clears his throat, rises on the balls of his feet. 'Fancy them women in there carrying on that way!'

Roger moves the sweet to his other cheek.

'Cor, she can't half give a man a tongue-lashing, my Pearl. And all them women—ears flapping! You should have 'eard it, mate.'

Roger pops the door locks with the key.

'I tell you what, mate, I never bin so insulted in all my life.'

'You need to get out more then,' says Roger implacably.

And all the way along the Ridge and down through to Silver-hill, Ken's wheezing and exclaiming, 'You could say that, Rodge,

you could say that,' and he starts up one of his own jokes in retali-
ation, ''Ere, what about that woman in there, old Peg the Leg?
Reminds me of the one—how does it go? Listen to this . . . 'ave
you heard the one about the lady with half-a-knicker? That's the
punchline, innit? How does it go? That one.'

23

Poor old Pearl. Ken is sitting in reception with his hands together between his knees. He is remembering when he met Pearl, in 1960. Things are coming back to him he'd not thought of since: the smell of the creamery, Jepson's, as you went through the door, sweet and suffocating in a way, and the steam rising while the old girl poured from one pot into something like eight cuppas; and the slops going down the steel griddle, the dumbwaiter going up, shouts of warning, a wet cloth going round an ashtray and onto the next, the ashtray spinning, making wet rings on the table; and her sitting there in a tight frock with her sister's cardie on her shoulders, one button done up, trying to talk big, finishing every sentence 'I'm sure'.

Audrey's at the computer doing a name plaque. She gets Roger to check the details for her against the sheet of paper in her ring binder. Roger slips a pocketful of wrappers from his sweatpants into the wastepaper basket, sideways. He stops at the little printer tucked away on the rolling shelf behind the reception, gives it a little chuck under the chin as it obediently engraves the plastic faux-brass plaque. Then he disappears through the double doors into the great beyond, the mortuary.

Audrey squints at the computer screen and taps it.

'We had John Hickmott's family in today, Ken. They said they had a reading but no music chosen, then the young lad pipes up, What about "Smoke Gets in Your Eyes"? He loved that one. Dear God, I said, don't you think it's a bit inappropriate? Mind you, if I had a penny for all the times it's "All Things Bright and Beautiful".' She shakes her head. 'That John Hickmott, now he had a good death, like your Pat. His last words, according to his wife, were: "I feel like shit." He went off to make them a cup of tea and she found him ten minutes later, sitting at the kitchen table, dead, and the kettle boiled. Lovely way to go, that.'

' "All Things Bright and Beautiful",' he repeats grimly, shaking his head. 'That's no good. You want to get it right. You only die once. Some are more rousing than others. "At the Name of Jesus" or "Onward, Christian Soldiers"; they're stirring. But what you're after is something on the way it goes—a man's life, you know—how quick it goes.'

'I could murder a cuppa, couldn't you?' Audrey says. 'Where's that Andy? He's supposed to be on teas today. It's gone eleven. I said to him, to Andy, You were friends with John Hickmott; why don't you say something at the crem? They haven't got a vicar of their own. He loves it, does our Andy. He's what you call a lay preacher. Loves it. This one time, Ken, he was warming up for the service and he came down the stairs here, just above where we're sitting, reading from his booklet, and he reads ever so slowly, a word with every footstep, and he's saying very solemnly, "For ... the ... Lord ... himself ... shall ... descend ... from ... heaven ... with ... the ... voice ... of ... the ... archangel ... and with ... the ... trumpet ... of ... God ... and with a shout ..." when all of a sudden Roger, *Roger* of *all* people, bursts out, *If you like a lot of chocolate on your biscuit join our club!*' She leans forward on her elbows and whispers, 'I think it gives him the willies—the death thing—and sometimes he just sort of breaks loose.'

Ken cocks his head. 'Thinking about it, Audrey, make sure you've got on my plan that I don't want no embalming, ta. Put that down, will ya? Be just like them lot to have me done. I'll have Psalm 90 read out, though, if you could put that. "You bring our years to an end, as if it were a tale that is told." That's a good one, that is.' He stands painfully, putting a hand to his lower waist and grimacing. 'Just going for a jimmy, if you don't mind.'

'You help yourself, Ken.'

Passing by, he touches her shoulder. He can feel the thick bra strap through her blouse.

Poor old Pearl, he thinks to himself as he staggers into the toilet. He wrenches the door closed behind him as he squeezes into the confined space. In a moment of panic, in the dark, he loses his footing and scrabbles with his hands for the light. And as he does, he says to himself, Dear God, don't let my boys turn out like me.

When the light comes on, he looks into the mirror at the face which surprises him daily; only the eyes give back any of his idea of himself.

He doesn't stand to pee anymore; he undoes his trousers, lets them slide and lowers himself down to sit and enjoy come what may. Dribs and drabs. Ah, for the days of pissing a bottle over like knocking down a skittle with a bowling ball. He is sitting there like Max Wall, shoulders back, chest out, gripping his lapels and straining. He lets one fly and it's more than air. Never mind. He likes a wooden toilet seat.

We must have a water closet indoors, Pat said, and she saved up and got them one. It was sandwiches for dinner, toast for breakfast and cake for tea. A bit of ham from time to time, Shippam's paste and the occasional boiled egg. The only downside to it all was the constipation.

When he was seeing Pearl, he used to go home with a quarter of liver pâté for Pat. He didn't dare tell her he was seeing someone. You're not leaving me, are you? she said when he told her they were getting married. He was thirty-eight then. You want children, I expect. I never had none. I couldn't, could I? Had to look after you, didn't I? She had a knack for making you feel bad. Women did. She used to say, So long as *you're* happy, in that way of hers.

He looks left and right, to the side, on the floor, and over to the vanity stand. No bleeding paper! He sighs.

'You all right in there, Ken?' comes Audrey's voice.

He leans forward to seek the roll.

'Yes, yes,' he says. All he needs is her forcing the door to find him arse in the air, scavenging. With his trousers around his knees, he leans towards the slatted door of the long cupboard to the right of the sink unit and yanks it open by the brass knob. It's shelved and inside, side by side, are dark brown plastic containers, row upon row of them stickered with names. Christ All Sodding Mighty! There are dead people in the lav.

'Did you say something, Ken?'

There are also a couple of toilet rolls, mercifully. He unwinds, bandages his hand, wipes his behind in a sawing motion. He looks. He jettisons. He starts unwinding and bandaging again, staring gloomily ahead; there are Jeans and Joans and Grahams in there. He closes the door with his foot and sits there, shaking his head, saying to himself, Dead people in jam jars! And then he thinks to himself, Christ, that'll be me, Ken Goodyew. And out of nowhere comes another trickle of wee. The miserable little sound says it all.

He emerges sideways, like he's hiding something. One shoulder is higher than the other. He clears his throat to get her attention.

'I shall have meself a burial, Audrey, if you could write that down an' all.'

She offers him a finger of her KitKat. 'Any reason, Ken?'

'I'm a Christian. I believe in the Resurrection, don' I?'

'That's cool, Ken. That's cool. Fair enough.' She looks at him contemplatively.

'Just going to have a sit-down in the family room, being as no one's in there. I feel a bit outta sorts. It takes it out of you, dunnit?'

'You go ahead, sweetheart. Help yourself.'

Like a dog on wheels being pulled in fits and starts, he goes mechanically along the corridor past the two chapels of rest. He peeps into the maroon of one of them. It's a narrow room, just big enough for a coffin lengthways and a person at each side with one or two more at the foot. It's carpeted in dark red and the point of focus, behind the head of the coffin, is a stained-glass window with a brass crucifix on its ledge and, on a lower shelf, the alternative option, a white porcelain dove.

'I'll have the cross,' he says wearily. 'Stuff the dove.'

The family room beyond is rustic with leather sofas and a fireplace. He drops himself onto the sofa, nodding along the items on the far ledge under the two frosted windows: the dried flowers, the box of tissues, the Bible. Yes, this is where they will sit when Audrey says to them, in her matter-of-fact sort of way, 'It's all been arranged and paid for by your father.' He couldn't even trust you not to cock that up.

He wipes his eyes with his cuffs, one by one. It feels as if there's the weight of a hand on either of his shoulders, pressing down on him. He starts, and his neck jars trying to see who's there, behind him.

It's his old dad in his string vest, braces down, with a tea towel around his neck, as he used to look when he shaved at the kitchen sink.

'Cor dear, scared the living daylights out of me. What you doin' behind me like that?'

I always was, son. I always was right behind you.

24

That evening Nick opens a bottle and makes a fire, and sits drinking the red wine and stirring the fire. His eyes cross and his vision blurs. In the blaze he sees them again, his mother and father in the garden at midnight, down on the front path, between the rose trellises. He and Dave are kneeling up on his bed at the window, and he's holding the curtains shut, not letting Davie look. 'It sounds like someone's murdering someone, don' it?' Davie said, thrilled and horrified and proud.

Their dad said that he didn't like coming home to find another bloke in the house. But she didn't care at all. Her hair was cut serviceably short and mannish. Her forearms were strong and scarified from the thorns and brambles of the garden, with the thinnest knotted threads of a vermilion hue. And, indeed, this was her only jewellery now. She wore a woolly hat in winter and summer, pulled down low on her brow, which, combined with her perpetual frown, gave her the look of a day-release patient, and she wore shapeless sweatshirts and men's cords, clogs in the summer and lace-up working-man's boots in the winter. Nick squirmed to see her feet up of an evening, with her hairy legs and thick socks crackling on the dry skin of her feet as she rubbed them together.

The boys didn't understand. She didn't come to meet them from school. She didn't make their lunches. She didn't come to school plays or sports days, and they didn't ask her—because, if she came, she wouldn't be wearing a dress or do the right things. She'd embarrass them. She seemed to find it funny when Nick took her to task: 'You're not like other mothers.'

She mimicked him. 'Because I'm not like other mothers . . .' she'd say over and over again in mock-posh elocution, apparently very pleased. He couldn't for the life of him see why she was not ashamed of the indictment. He had meant to bring her to heel, for all of their sakes.

She crooned and broke her heart over the animals. Formally, there was a menagerie of rather overindulged animals: chickens, cats, a disturbed mongrel, cross German shepherd and Dober-man, and a wilful and highly strung male goat. Informally, this extended to itinerant toads, rabbits, pheasants, foxes, even voles, shrews and field mice. Yet she was harsh with the boys. She made them do their own washing by hand in the sink. Nick paid Davie to do his on occasion, and then welshed on the deal. They were to cook their own teas when they came home from school and it was Nick who fried the half-moon Findus Pancakes and Davie who boiled the kettle for Pot Noodles, with much equivocation about the precise location of the 'fill to' level.

Whenever the old man came in, they traded insults in the kitchen. He took an aspirin or two from the boiler cupboard, slammed other doors for good measure, then tiptoed up to the bedroom to change his clothes and go out again. But Pearl spoke tenderly when she came upon the pair of them standing upstairs at the bathroom window, watching his van go down the dirt track. 'Come away from the window, my lambs,' she said.

She took to the garden. She had her realm; the woman in the woods. The brick house was three-quarters surrounded by woodland, and to the front its view gave onto steep fields which rose up to hide it, and it stood in its own magical fiefdom like something Hansel and Gretel might have stumbled upon. It had been built on a great estate, to house the gamekeeper, and the sheds when they moved in were full of traps and snares and baskets left behind. It was typically Victorian, with its triple-hipped roof, three windows up, two down and a middle front door. A craftsman had given the windows brows of alternating yellow and red brick. A brick path went up from its front door to the gate, and across the front of the gate there ran a small stream—thus the house's ingress resembled a moat, and it was across this that he and David went to school of a morning. He went the virtuous path to the grammar and David went off at an aside to the comprehensive, and both of them set out in the mornings to the twentieth century, leaving the nineteenth behind them.

Their mother would scarcely accommodate modern facilities in the house. The shower was a miserable wee down your back, and she wouldn't have central heating. There was just a single wood-burning stove. The boys slept in their clothes. The house was cold even in summer, so they spent a great deal of time outdoors, he and Davie making camps in the woods and sneaking off without being made to help her in the garden.

When she first dug the vegetable garden, she pulled out of the black earth bottles with marbles in their necks, earthenware jars and broken china, and she urged the boys to come and dig for treasure with her—and that was a thrilling afternoon, to be filthy with their mother, flinging about them plump worms, grasping and tearing at roots, in a state of wanton greed to unearth, perhaps, something whole.

'A teapot, a teapot! Without a spout!'

And how complicit they were then, thick as thieves the three of them, with their arms plunging into the past.

'It's something you plunder,' she said, about the past, about the dirt.

She was either dull or dazzling. Bad news, bills and matters relating to Ken, were related with a loose mouth, often chewing something, with her lazy eye off looking elsewhere. Surprises, first fruits from the garden and the goings-on of the critters were delivered with eyes that could make yours glisten too, so pleased they were.

This wilful woman, whose delights were cheap or free, this woman who pulled things from the ground that no one else wanted, this was the mother who gave him life. But there was another mother, the one who wanted to put him back where she'd got him from and bury with him the father she said he was like.

She hasn't called him in years.

'When you think of the smell of your homeland,' his ex-girlfriend Natasha asked him once, sentimental for the Ukraine one Christmas, 'what does it smell like? For me it smells like our black round bread, warm from the oven.'

'Dirt,' he'd said. 'The soil.'

When they were in their teens and their mother had nursed back to life the antique roses, established her cottage-garden wilderness of hollyhocks and foxgloves, and had infant fruit trees still on their leading reins, the gamekeeper's granddaughter came to gaze at it all from over the fields. She was more than ninety years old. Standing up, sniffing the intruder, short-haired and fierce, their mother must have seemed formidable, and she'd have called after the dog in such a way that the reproach fell on the trespasser rather than the dog. But she'd softened as she strode forth, seeing at last the tiny lost eyes under the grey perm.

First Davie, then Nick, came home that afternoon to find the old lady in the dining-room side of the front room. The one concession their mother had made to 'change' was to take down the wall between the two downstairs rooms, on account of the terrible cold in the dining room, but there was still a distinct chill to that side. The old lady explained that it was in that room that the gamekeeper's youngest daughter died of TB, when she was only twelve years old. She showed them how the other children lined up outside and waved goodbye to her through the window.

The house was full of ghosts. If you listened at night, you could hear them, moving about the house.

'It's bigger than us, the past,' their mother told them. Certainly it was bigger than Ken and Pearl. It was a jealous house; it loved her and kept her. The rest were mere lodgers. They left.

Property was Ken's thing in the late eighties, and he kept costs

down by living in the properties as he renovated them after they
separated, and by having Dave do the work with him. Every
dwelling place was a 'digs', developed, then sold or let. He had
no home until he begrudgingly bought 'Perchance' when he was
seventy.

The door to the gamekeeper's cottage had been closed to all
of them for twenty years. The path across the fields had gone,
according to Dave. The long grass had reclaimed it, the stile had
been knocked down, the orchard of fruit trees now fully obscured
the house. It was concealed. The gate at the end of the track was
padlocked. There was no mailbox, no house name. It was as if
the drawbridge had been pulled up. As Nick had said to Astrid in
Sicily, there wasn't a way home.

25

On her weekend off, in lieu of a laugh, since she's over forty and more than seventeen stone, Audrey chooses a numbing. These are strange times, she considered that Saturday morning, on her way to The Fat Ox in Icklesfield. It was muggy and fly-ridden in the winter, and in the summer there was hail. It was a time of turmoil. Maybe it did portend some greater crisis coming: first the recession, next the pandemic.

Since she gave the business a marketing overhaul and made it more sympathetic to modern 'tastes', they'd become the funeral directors of choice in the area. She and Roger were full time, round the clock, and they had on the books another eight working in shifts.

She consulted with them all when it came to the new slogan.

'*The dead—it's a living.*' This was Roger's suggestion. The others agreed it was fair. No one could think of anything else.

So, she decided to go with her own idea: '*When the worst thing happens, we will be there.*' It was on all the stationery and on the front window in appealing soft italics.

'All right,' Roger had said warily. 'If you think so.'

'What?'

'Nothing.'

'No, go on, what?'

'It's a bit soft.'

'Soft?'

'American.'

'In a good way, though?'

'No.'

'What—you think it's dodging the subject?'

'There could be plenty of other worse things and we won't be there.' Roger was reliably cautious.

'I think the clue is in the subtitle: funeral directors. I don't think we'll be getting called out when the teenage daughter's up the duff or the cellar's flooded.'

'Sounds like we'll clean up the mess, or get rid of the evidence.'

'When the worst thing happens, *we will* be there,' she said, trying it with a new emphasis, like a woman in a changing room giving a skirt a bit of flounce.

'It's like being the Grim Reaper.'

'No. Not at all.' She'd laughed, but she'd felt a bit annoyed with him. 'Bugger me, Roger, you're like the Reaper yourself sometimes. It's like pushing water uphill, getting you to show a bit of enthusiasm.'

He took it badly. He stood there for a moment with his mouth open—just as if the worst thing had happened—and then he dashed off. She'd never seen Roger dash.

He kept himself busy in the coffin room and they didn't exchange more than a few words for several days. He was quiet, even for Roger, and there was no eye contact whatsoever. If she came up, he was sitting there doing the crossword; the question was a particularly complicated one that required him to press his forehead upon the newspaper.

So, they stuck to business. She gave directions, and he went. There was no chat, nothing in the way of their usual laughs. The body appeared in the mortuary, she attended to it, he gave her a hand to get it in the fridge, to put the waste bins into the street, and then he went off to plane coffins or polish the hearse. And he left on time. It was then she realized that his normal routine was to hang about with her, having a coffee, having a chat and, on the odd occasion they went to the pub, she'd have a glass of wine, and he'd have a juice.

He went to AA meetings. She'd seen him waiting outside, grinning shyly while the big boys and girls smoked, waiting to go in. He only grinned when he was terribly afraid, she knew.

He was heavy and lonely. So what? Who wasn't?

She was on the board for the National Association of Funeral Directors and went occasionally to speak at conventions. When she did, she left Roger in charge. She kept it to a minimum. He was so pithy when it came to phone conversation that the caller was treated to something only just short of silence.

'Hello, hello?' the long pauses caused the caller to say.

Eventually they'd get this much: 'Name? . . . No, of the deceased . . . Thank you.'

It seemed to put him too much on the spot, the phone ringing. He went red. He dithered and let it ring too many times, hoping she'd take it if she was there. Interpersonal skills were not among his talents. Lugging bodies, lugging coffins, lugging spare wheels: these were his talents. And turning up. Not to mention the placid demeanour that supplied his response to even the good things in life—such as when he won a tenner on the lottery, or she treated them to a fish and chip lunch—as much as the worst things, such as his wife leaving him.

The customers liked him. He was a shoulder to cry on—and they did, and he just stood there, immobile, but with a touch of spare pride in his cheeks. There was something consoling in his stoic presence.

Before this little upset between them, she'd gone away to Birmingham for a few days to speak at a convention on pandemics, and his pleasure at having her back seemed to be more than was warranted by being relieved of phone duties. He went to meet her at the station and joked and larked about as he took her case from her, swinging it about as if it were light as a feather. He was like something out of a musical, she'd thought, gay as a lad.

'Pandemics are becoming your special subject,' he'd ventured.

'So it seems!'

'There's one coming then, is there?' he'd chuckled.

She'd done a double take. Roger had become an extrovert in her absence.

'Sure as eggs is eggs, Roger. We've got a contingency plan that will be the gold standard of the south-east.'

'It's me, isn't it?' he'd laughed.

She'd confirmed it.

'Righto,' was all he said, but he whistled all the way up the steps from Warrior Square.

When the hospital called day and night, as they had last year with the MRSA crisis, it was Roger who unfailingly went. There were so many of them in there from the funeral companies, he said, that they were obliged to tip the stretcher up and hold it vertical in order to pass each other in the corridors.

'When this here pandemonium comes,' he'd quipped as they turned into Norman Road, 'I'll be nose to nose with the corpses in corridors.'

If any town succumbed to a pandemic, it would be this one. It was an already weakened population on the brink of collapse. Nearly everyone in Hastings was a full-time alcoholic. She wondered what it was in him that kept Roger off the bottle now. It wasn't the pay, it wasn't responsibility to a family, it wasn't a sense of Christian duty, but he just showed up—every time he was needed—without much to say but with ready hands.

They talked about how things were going: people dying fatter, younger, done in with drugs and booze, suicides, old people neglected, with no families to call on, funerals unattended. How it was unusual to pick someone up from their home. It wore you down; you had to speak about it, but you couldn't go bandying it about. Drink helped in her case. She'd have a few glasses back home, on her own more often than not. Unlike Roger.

And unlike Roger she had been brought up to it, the job. She was fourteen years old when she first went with her mum and dad to pick up a body. An old girl, it was, and her nightdress kept coming up as they put her on the stretcher. Her old dad kept shouting out, 'That's your job, Audrey, to keep her bleeding nightie down!' To give her some respect.

She couldn't go much more than five miles away on her days off, so here she was at The Fat Ox, under a set of dirty great pylons in a little village where no one knew her and she could sit and get properly drunk, far too drunk to drive, and have a room for the night for thirty quid. She'd sit outside from lunchtime onwards with the pylons buzzing and humming and doing God knows what to her head, and sometimes she'd pass out at a picnic table after ham, egg and chips. Sometimes she'd go inside and have a big dinner, and she'd sit there straight-backed like a bloke, fists on the table, looking like a long-distance lorry driver, assuming masculinity to avoid interest. She'd drink to the end of the bottle and then she'd go up the back stairs to the bed where the pillows smelt of head sweat—and that was good, because that was how a man smelt—and she'd sleep until breakfast time.

The only thing she wanted, really wanted, was to be kissed and loved and told 'You're a good person' by someone she could believe.

In the morning light she lay on that bed with an arm out, palm open. She couldn't imagine how Roger did it—what kept him at the job, and sober too. It was heroic. It didn't make sense. There was no logic to it.

26

~

The crematorium attendants have a little side room from which they control the music and lights and she, Roger and Ken, all suited and booted, have a quick chat with another funeral director in there about the good weather being a surprise that April.

Andy, the lay preacher of burnished hair and baby face, is inside the chapel—their zealous sergeant major, who can speak without embarrassment about the fire in his heart for the Lord. When he is not paging away the funeral procession, he rides the East Sussex hills on his tractor. He could be a corporate man, so clean and regular-looking is he, were it not for the radiance of his smile. He has spoken well of the deceased, on few notes, then gone on to push the envelope of faith and presented the mourners with an opportunity to meet Jesus Christ. Most pass. They'd rather not meet Him or his Old Man a minute sooner than they have to.

The Hickmott family, amounting to six people, have shuffled in to sit side by side on the same bench and bear with bowed heads the admonition of death. The services run every half-hour to the same format. From the side room they can hear that it's only Andy who's actually singing along to 'All Things Bright and Beautiful'.

'People don't sing these days,' says the attendant, a tall bald man with clouds of hair above each ear. 'You never hear them singing, do you?'

There is a unison of disapproval.

'It's the committal now,' Audrey says, and on the monitor they see the curtains coming round the coffin.

'That it?' says Ken, aghast. 'That the lot?'

They can hear Andy saying, 'I am the resurrection,' as the doors open and the farmer comes towards them, eyes electric.

The family follows his lead and assembles in the courtyard next to the racking for the flowers, and each of them takes a turn to squint at the messages on the bouquets. The widow traces the writing on the cards with her fingertips and her daughter says at each one, 'That's nice.'

'Where's Audrey?' Ken whispers to Roger, startling when he realizes she's not there.

'Off with the Two Ronnies,' Roger whispers out of the side of his mouth.

Ken gives him a sharp look. 'Pull yourself together, fella,' he says.

Casually, Roger ambles off, hands in his pockets. He goes down past the Book of Remembrance Chapel into what looks for all the world like a school canteen, with great big waste containers on wheels outside, and he glances up to see the big steel chimney smoking.

Audrey pops down there from time to time to see the chaps who load the furnaces; they're so often forgotten. At Christmas she tips them. They are both called Ron.

When Roger comes in, he finds the three of them standing in front of four crematories—ovens, steel and glass fronted, with little steel trays underneath their doors. The shorter Ron brings forth a steel bucket for inspection, and Audrey pokes her head in to see the charred metal hip-bone replacements. He shakes it as if he wants a contribution. 'Raised a thousand pounds for the hospice recycling these last year.'

'Good for you, Ronnie. How's the missus?' Audrey asks him.

'Don't ask,' says the other Ron, coming forward and wiping his forearms. 'She give me this 'ere cookbook for my birthday and she said, I haven't wrapped it because you only tear the paper off.'

The other Ron shakes his head.

'When did it all start? I thought. When did it all start going wrong . . . ?'

An electronic alarm bell sounds. One of the Rons opens the hatch and pulls John Hickmott in his £299 veneered chipboard coffin onto a trolley and the two Rons wheel him across to oven number four, still talking to Audrey in a friendly way. When they open the oven, there's a big raging orange heat and they load John Hickmott's coffin into it and close the door, and fix it to, turning the big iron handle.

'All she does is watch the telly. Why would anyone spend their time doing that?'

'Do you like watching the telly, Roger?' The taller Ron addresses Roger, knitting his brow and folding his arms.

Roger lifts his shoulders briefly. He glances warily at the oven door.

'Want to see where we are with the hospice bucket, Roger?'

'No.'

'Man of few words, 'im. Innie, Audrey?' The Ronnies grin.

'He is.'

'Solid, he looks.'

'That's right.'

Under such attention, Roger is visibly awkward, ready to be brave, ready to be amused, ready to be whatever he's called, ready for praise, ready for abuse, and all of these considerations show themselves in a slight parting of his lips.

'Come on then, sweet'eart,' she says to him. 'Best get back.'

Ron sticks the bucket back on the shelf to the side. 'Ta-da then, you two. Nice to see you. 'Ere, Audrey, you're the only one of the funeral directors who does come and see us, you know.'

'We're the untouchables, us two,' says the other Ronnie with a grin, leaning against the wall above the computer.

On the concrete concourse, behind the fencing, with the clouds passing over the sun, in the new grey chill, she stops for a moment. It has come to her. There is no logical reason to do this work. She turns round and faces Roger.

'Why don't you do what you really want to do, Roger?'

She sees in the shadows of his eyes the vestiges of other shamings. She holds his head and kisses him on the mouth.

27

They go with the family to the pub on the Ridge, The Harrow, where the son orders sherries and bags of nuts, and raises his glass to the ten or so of them at the bar. Andy steps in with his orange juice aloft. 'To John Hickmott!' The family give him grateful looks.

'May he rest in peace,' adds Ken, swallowing his thimble of sherry back as though it's a whiskey that burns. 'Your health.'

Roger and Audrey exchange looks.

Andy takes this opportunity to continue where he left off in the crem about how when Jesus broke the bread with the men on their way to Emmaus, he was really breaking Himself and how in that moment they knew Him and it was when they knew Him that he disappeared. He has the mourners in the palm of his hand, hemmed in as they are between bar and bar stools. There's a lot to the passage but he hopes one point will fall hard and true.

'Jesus comes to us in our hour of need in many guises to comfort us. We may not recognize Him. He may come as a friend or a stranger.'

He inhales the yolk-like line of orange juice from the bottom of his glass, swallows, licks his lips and smiles down at the short-legged Hickmott family. Furtively, the family exchange appalled looks.

Ken's cheeks glow after the third sherry and he says to Audrey, 'Nice in 'ere. Nice, innit?' He looks about himself and sniffs with satisfaction.

There are brass horseplates and dusty bunches of hops about the place, and a horror of a carpet with a geometric pattern worn into being less of a visual nuisance than it once was. Taxi cards are stapled to the beams. These cards bring to mind June, so he accepts another sherry when it's offered, and repeats himself.

'Nice to get out. Your health.' He raises his glass again. ''Ere, Audrey, how do you fancy being wined and dined tonight? I'll take you to The Italian Way, if you like. Buy you a meal out.'

Audrey flashes a look at Roger. He's standing there as if the music's stopped, clasping his shandy tight to his chest, eyes high and distant, looking sufficiently embarrassed for all three of them.

Driving back, with Ken in the passenger seat of the hearse, leaning in towards her, she is reminded of a holiday she took to Mexico as a young girl, and how, late at night, after dancing at a bar on a beach until the early hours and losing sight of her mates, she'd taken a taxi back to the hostel and it had seemed to her that the driver was going the long way, or the wrong way, with his eyes betwixt her pedal pushers. So she took him through the details of the embalming process. He'd dropped her off smartish.

'Penny for 'em,' says Ken.

'I was just wondering, Ken, whether you've finished your research, so to speak?'

'How do you mean? *Ree-search*?'

'Into the matter of death?'

'Well, you see, the big question's still not answered.' He clears his throat, eyes on the road (the back of a truck looms with its finger-written plea in the dust of the rear window: 'Wash me, you tosser'), and goes on, 'Careful, love!' He feels a nervous tic break out under his right eye. 'See, I had a mate whose last words were "I'm not pegging out yet". So, what I'm wondering is, how do you know you're going and what does it feel like and what 'appens?'

'Oh, don't ask me.'

'Well, who else can I ask? I ask June and she just starts laughing. Nobody will tell ya straight.'

'Because they don't know for sure.'

'Yes but *you* know, don't you?'

'I haven't passed on yet, Ken!'

'I know, I know,' he says. 'I know that, Audrey, but of anyone *you* must have an idea.'

'I wouldn't like to say.'

'Well, let me put it like this. I take it you believe in Jesus Christ, and what I'm asking is, is it Him that comes for you, direct like, or does He send someone else, like someone from your family, and does He take their body, does He look like them when He comes so as not to scare you, or does He stand behind them, or what? Because this fellow I knew, we was in the Territorial Army together, he said to me when he had a heart attack that he'd seen Jesus sitting on a tree stump, just sitting there, and he said to me, Don't you worry, Ken, about dying; it's beautiful. I don't know what he meant, but he was very certain of it. See, will He be there or will it be a disciple, or something? Will I know who it is? Which one, I mean.'

'Well, I don't know, Ken, like I said. As it happens, I'm not conventionally religious.'

She slams on the brakes as the car in front stops unexpectedly at an amber light. Ken slams his right foot down harder. They come up right behind the car in front, nose to tail with not an inch between them.

'Cor dear. I say. Puts it into perspective, don't it? Whew.' He loosens his tie. 'Not conventionally religious? How's that then?'

She keeps her face on the windscreen, her eyes blank.

'You're not one of them atheist lot, are you?'

'No. I believe in Him all right. . . .'

Ken nods and looks past her out of her side window, then looks again. He claps a hand on the side of his neck. Standing in the bus shelter is his June. Transparent rain hat on, tied under her chin, she's got a suitcase on wheels with her that he's never seen before. Coat's all done up, but not as buttoned up as her face. Lips are tight, eyes narrowed, and she's waiting for a bus.

'I believe He's a bit of a creep, to be honest, Ken. Sending floods, and pandemics and all that. If He can make a paradise, why make us put up with this? Because we're bad? Where's the sense? He made us and He made the world. Either unmake us or put things right. Right?'

Ken looks back over his shoulder and watches the figure of June grow smaller. Soon a bus swoops down on her and she's first in the queue—he knows that, but he can't see anymore as they go round the corner towards the next lights. He nods and nods as they move forwards through Silverhill.

Two elderly nuns cross in front of them, all toothy chat and grins, each with a carrier bag, cross-swinging.

Audrey's passion grows. 'Look, this God of ours in the Bible, either He's not the big "I am" or there's been a right royal fuck-up. 'Scuse my French. Look at the weather! So many people die miserable and broken and alone. When you see what people's dreams are reduced to . . .'

He nods. June's left him. She's gone and left him! That ain't no shopping trip, unless she's gone and bought the suitcase in Lidl on special. She bought some waders in there once. What the bleeding hell for? he asked her. They was four ninety-nine. We could go into the sea with them on. What the bleeding hell for? She probably paid a small fortune for that case.

'I don't get into talking about it often, Ken. It's very personal, isn't it? Religion.'

'Oh yes.' He gives her an avuncular smile.

They always have a fish supper on a Friday.

She's lost her marbles, daft cow. Going off with a suitcase on a Friday evening.

'When you see what we see every day, you count your blessings. It's not like it's one thing in particular which makes me think this God fellow's no wiser than you or me; it's the day-to-day suffering. How little people have, how little they want, how little they give. Like I said, if that's God's image, then I'm not interested. No. Look at us!' She gestured to the next batch of shoppers at the crossing, zipped up and browbeaten, giving the green man wary looks. 'Grubbing about for a quid here and there, and then we die.'

Christ Almighty! The carrier bag under the mattress with the forty grand in it! Christ! He's got to get home, get in that bedroom and get it!

'Lights have changed, dear,' he says to her, grinding his teeth. 'Go on, you'll get through the next one if you step on it. Take the outside lane,' he says to her hoarsely. He's clutching his chest, head slammed back against the headrest, mouth open, spittle stretched like a spider's web.

She glances at him. 'See, that's why it's not good to talk about it,' she says. 'Now I've gone and upset you.'

28

Spring came suddenly mid-April; a sudden florescence of the hedgerow was followed by a hurrah of blossom on the apple and cherry trees. On Nick's drive to work through villages and fields, up hill and down dale, he revelled in the renewal and the signs of an enduring way of life: a blackbird on a white weatherboard roof, handwritten signs for fresh eggs, the new lambs and old windmills. These persuaded him that all would be well, notwithstanding the bad budget, the corrupt parliament and news of a pandemic.

One would have thought that staying together was a matter of survival, but it wasn't so at all. If people had homes with good central heating, they ought to count themselves lucky, he'd joked with her the night before, in the draughty old kitchen where even in April the fan heater was on full blast. He stood by it, scalding one trouser leg. The dog dipped its nose to it too, blow-drying its

russet locks, casting upward glances. With property prices slump-
ing, tempers were fraught. That week Nick had a man disinstruct
him. When Nick pointed out to him that his wife could claim
some of his business, and certainly sell some of its assets, he went
berserk. The divorce petitions—whose grounds always ranged
from the mild-mannered 'We had different tastes' or 'He did not
share my interest in gardening' to the crude 'Our sexual relations were non-existent' and vulgar 'He was mean with money'
or 'She's a drunk'—went from one to two clauses to upwards of
eight or more. This was a sign of the times.

'Your father called again.' This was the substance of many
of Kitty Ho's intercom calls up to Nick's office since she'd been
instructed to take messages only from Ken Goodyew. But this
morning when she buzzed up, she said, 'Your father's here.'

When he came down, the old man was standing in reception,
giving the framed prints and striped wallpaper a cold shoulder,
standing to attention, ready for a fight where there wasn't one to
be had.

'Don't tell me, you've come about a divorce.'

Seeing Nick appear in the far doorway, Kitty Ho on the front
desk bit her lip and hung her head. She had her bag on her lap
and was going through the make-up purse, making a noise like
a hamster on a wheel. When the phone rang, she mumbled into
her mouthpiece, 'Alcock, Maycock and *Goodyew* . . .' as if it were
a catechism, and sat up with fresh lip gloss.

Nick showed him through the sprung door. They went up two
flights of stairs. In the corner of each stairwell, back against each
of his partners' offices in turn, he waited for the old man to haul

himself up using the banister rail, then he led him into his own
and closed the door.

On the top floor, in his attic office with its blistered sash windows and low ceilings, there were strings of dust suspended like
molecular models, drifting, only occasionally disturbed by human
tantrums. The far wall was lined with boxed files and legal tomes
bound in magenta or black and gold, and in the spaces between
there was random fluff. The only sign the cleaner left was a dis-
coloured stripe across the carpet from the swipe that went against
the grain. He used tissues to freshen his desk and computer screen
and wondered if Ben Maycock and Stuart Alcock did the same. It
was not something he'd asked on one of their weekly pints—the
'Monday moan' up at the pub on the way out of town.

He'd driven in, full of optimism, although his cheer had begun
to fade along the high street on seeing another two shops closed,
the colonnades dropping a tooth from their smile here and there.
And now, to cap it all, in his office, as if the last wind of winter
had blown him in, was the old man.

Ken had a great raindrop on the tip of his nose.

Perched on the side of the desk, elevated, Nick reached for
the box of Mansize and chucked it towards his father, who sat in
the clients' chair below him.

'Go on,' he said. 'Help yourself. Everyone else does. What's she
done? Got shell in your egg?'

His father blew into the tissue and poked it into each nostril in
turn. "Ooo?"

'June.' Nick accepted the returned tissue and threw it in the
bin under his desk.

Ken shrugged and looked broadly peeved as he took in the room. 'She's half-inched the money, 'a'n' she? Gone and run off with the lot.'

'Really? A lot, was it?'

'For'y thousand or more.'

'Christ.'

'It was under the mattress. Can't trust the banks, Kenneth, she said. Can't trust 'er, more like! Thieving Welsh! Conniving and cheating. You can't trust no man Jack of 'em.'

Nick put fingertips to brow and donned the pained expression that he wore so often, sitting there. 'So. Have you *spoken* to her?' And in the word 'spoken' was all the consensus of his age, chock full of condescension.

'Course I have. I've called her all the names under the sun!'

'Have you *discussed* things? I mean, have you asked her what her intentions are?'

'Wake up! She's run off with for'y grand in 'undred-paand notes! I thought you was trained in this sort of thing! I want the money back, dunn' I?'

'Well, I'm afraid I don't think the law can help you.'

'Oh, I know that all right. When was we the sort of people that went to the law? Christ Almighty, my poor sister nearly messed 'erself when I told her you was a lawyer. Naargh, we're going to go and get it back from her—you, me and Davie. The three of us.' He brightened. ''Ere, remember this one? "Taffy was a Welsh-man, Taffy was a thief." You know that one, don't you? Laugh! We used to sing that one, didn't we? You and I, when we went round the building site. And it used to make that arsehole—what was his name, Owen Bendover or something?—it used to make him go red in the face, dinnit? Welsh twit. There's a lot of truth in them old rhymes. That Owen, he drove home on the dumper one night and we never saw him again. Down the bleeding motorway to Wales on it, I shouldn't wonder.'

Nick hid a smile by dipping his head. He did remember the man. He adjusted his cufflinks. 'To be honest, I doubt you'll have much success getting it back that way either. She'll just say no.'

'I'll give her a good crack round the side of the 'ead that'll shape her up quick.'

'Don't be ridiculous.'

'She ain't a big woman.'

'We're not going to Wales to give her a hiding. You'll have to start divorce proceedings and include that sum of money in your statements. I doubt you'll get it back. You might even end up giving her more.'

'More?' he cried out. 'More? See, that's what I mean about this lot in government these days. In my day, someone stole something they got banged up, now they get a sodding golden handshake! I want it back. I earned it!'

'I've heard this a thousand times before from people sitting right where you're sitting. June is your wife, not some stranger. You shared a life together.' He sat in his chair. 'Let me do you a favour. Take some advice: forget about it. Forget about the money. Do you love her or not?'

'Love her?' Ken snorted. 'I could wring her neck for what she's done.'

'I'll tell you what I ought to tell my clients. You, as a bloke, you're shafted. Just accept it. But let me tell you something else.' Warming to his theme, he could hear Kitty Ho coming upstairs with the coffees clinking on the tray. When she wedged the door open, the girls in the next office could hear him. 'I had a client in here today, a woman. She has breast cancer and her husband is divorcing her. She instructed me to agree to his terms, whatever they are. She wasn't interested in the money. She said, Let him have it—I don't want to waste whatever life I have fighting him for money.'

'No, ta,' said Ken, adjusting his lapels and flinching away from Kitty Ho when she held out the cup to him.

'Do you see my point? You're not a young man yourself. You are seventy-nine. In a way, you're in the same boat as that woman.'

'I'm eighty. November the twenty-fifth. Same day every year. Anyway. He drives like a flaming maniac, your brother. We'll be under a bleeding lorry if he does the driving. On and off the brakes, he is, all the time, jumpin' on 'em. I say to him, Don't you use the gears?'

Kitty Ho slipped out of the room.

Nick stood up and walked to the window. 'You didn't hear a word I said, did you? Do you know, I have to ask myself if anyone does? They get in that chair, they have a quick blub and they don't listen to a word I say. They just want their money.'

'Well, that's what you're there for! That's your job!'

'Yes, that's right.' He went dejectedly, hands in trouser pockets, back to his chair. 'That's right.'

Ken banged the table with his hands. 'And he don't listen to a person talkin', Dave don't! He nods and that, but he ain't really with ya. Sometimes I don't know if he's the full shilling.'

'Don't you ever think that to put up with you—'

'I'll pay your petrol money!'

Nick laughed. He looked at Ken; he shook his head, and his smile spread to his eyes.

'What? What you laughing for? What's got into you? You daft git. Give over. It ain't funny. Pack it in. Blimey, I hope you don't treat all your customers this way. You ought to take it more serious. It might be funny to you. . . .'

Nick shook his head and laughed and laughed. And in the next office the two women exchanged looks over their partition, and the older one with the spiky gelled hair said to the younger one with the pageboy haircut, 'You don't hear that sound much round here.'

'Do you know what?' said Nick, pointing his pen at his father, 'I'm going to do it. I'm going to drive you to Wales. Because *you*, right, *you* will never learn. You're too old, you're no good to anyone, you're selfish and you won't change.'

'Thank you,' said the old man, relaxing at long last.

29

In the morning sunlight, Nick drove past the picture-book castle at Bodiam, then took the humpback bridge his mother used to floor the car to fly over, and crossed the steam-railway track with the sound of their boyish cheering still ringing in his ears. On through Cripps Corner and Sedlescombe the car followed the lanes, dipped and ducked, roller-coastering up and down the rise and falls of the Kent and East Sussex border, plunging into shadow from light. On rainy days these roads ran like rivers; they were valleys cut into the land, prayed over by chestnut trees. Their steep banks were root-clad and their rich soil fed the springtime show of primroses. He left the countryside behind at the archway of the Ridge where a sign salutes one's arrival in Hastings, the birthplace of television.

From that point it was all downhill, in staggering semis, until the sea washed in and washed out again. He drove along a grim line of disused retirement homes, bungalows and pylons towards Rye, to pick up Dave in Fairlight first.

His brother was ready for his day out, standing outside the door with a carrier bag in one hand. He was dressed like a teenager, wearing a hoody and sweatpants, and was all giddy anxiety, wheezing and sniffing. Once in the passenger seat, he talked ninety to the dozen, going between Marina's foreboding and the old man's bull-headed determination to recoup his money, which caused him excitable disbelief.

Dave worked a dissent the way a sheepdog worked a flock. He was saying of both June and Ken, 'Course you can see it from her point of view,' or, 'You can't blame him, right?' And before they'd even got to Bulverhythe, Nick had noticed how his brother finished every sentence with 'right?' or 'eh?' in his ruthless pursuit of consensus.

The old man, immaculate in a black suit, took the front seat after Dave hopped out and got in the back.

'All right, Dad?'

'All right. Let's get going.'

Ken sat stiff-legged, a hand staking each knee, while from behind, Dave subjected him to a gentle ribbing about being dressed for a funeral. Ken merely sat there, his forehead glittering in the sunlight.

They were at Clacket Lane services when, too late for Nick to make the exit with grace, Ken shouted out, waved and pointed and ordered him to pull over. Nick threw the wheel to the left, with his right-hand tyres just scraping the grass verge. His father clung to the side of his seat with one veined hand and to the door handle with the other. They pulled to a stop in the car park and

Dave fell back into his seat. Ken moaned about nearly piddling himself before he got to the loo, then got out of the car with one, two, three efforts and went hopping off towards the side of the services. Dave jumped out too and Nick sat there, running his finger along his top lip. The old git! It beggared belief.

After a while, Dave came back with another carrier bag, stopped, smacked his head with his palm and said through Nick's open window, 'Blimey, mate, do you want something?' He proposed a coffee and a doughnut, or a bacon sandwich or a Big Mac, and, having been turned down on these, went rifling through his bag to offer in the alternative a Yorkie and a Lucozade.

With Ken back in the front seat, they hit the motorway again and Nick heard the noise of a ring pull. He looked in the mirror to see his brother sipping on a Carlsberg. He checked the clock on the dash. It was five past twelve.

His brother's eyes were wide and blue and innocent.

'What?'

'You all right there, Dave, are you?'

'Yeah. Great. Thanks.'

'Having a nice day out, are you?'

'Yeah. Anyone want a crisp, Dad?'

Ken shook his head. 'Get under my plate.'

'Nick?'

'No, thanks.'

'Suit yourselves.'

They fell silent again for some twenty miles or more. Nick enjoyed driving and usually found it meditative. The peace was interrupted now and again by a slurp or belch, the smell of which named and shamed the culprit as either bacon or beer and obliged Nick and his father to lower the windows from time to time.

Astrid had received the news of this trip to Wales coolly, and the dog had looked with insight and pain from one to the other as they discussed it, his brown eyes straining to see into them.

'You're going to *Wales* then,' she said. 'I suppose you'll look up your old girlfriend.'

When he told her Morwen didn't live in Wales, and that he'd no interest in seeing her anyway, she softened and gave him his cheese and biscuits in front of the TV.

Unable to bear silence, Dave, with his head wedged between their seats, held forth. 'And Matt, right, I'm playing that Xbox game with him, right, last night, and I'm, like, driving the quad but I can't get the hang of it and I keep crashing it and so the little sod, right, he wallops me round the head every time I get it wrong with the butt of his gun. In the game, right, not in real life, but in the game. But your handset vibrates, you know. Just slaps me in the head. I mean, I got the giggles, right, didn't I? I was cacking myself laughing and Marina comes in to see and I'm, like, the kid's duffing up his dad for his driving and old Matt's got the giggles as well and then I'm in such a state, right, that I just total the quad and we fall out, the pair of us. He's this huge green soldier and I'm in bleeding pink, of course, and he takes his gun and puts a bullet into my head, right behind the ear, ever so neatly, and that's me done, dispatched to the great beyond.' He raised his can to his lips. 'I tell you what, mate, I was crying tears.'

Ken's jaw was clenched, Nick saw.

'I suppose your, um, your Laura gets you playing them games, does she, Nick?' Dave finished the can and scrunched it in his hand. Ken flinched.

'Not really, no.'

'You should give them a go, mate. I mean, even though us lot, our age, we're total spazzers compared to the kids. You all right, Dad?' he asked, raising his voice.

Ken covered his ear. 'I'm not Mutt 'n' Jeff.'

'Sorry.'

'You reek of beer.'

Dave opened another can.

'What's wrong with you, David?'

'It's just the one or two, Dad. For the journey.'

'Bleeding good thing you ain't driving, innit?'

Dave was sandwiched between their two seats, a hand on each of their headrests, almost panting with enthusiasm. 'It must be more than twenty years since we was all in a car together.' Ken ground his teeth. Nick peeped under the visor to see the motorway sign. Dave looked like he was in a rugby scrum, with his face squashed on either side by the seats. 'Do you remember, Dad, how we knew you was home of an evening because we heard the horn on your car? *Beeeeeeeep* it would go, round about midnight like that, and you'd driven into the back of the garage, pissed. And your head fell on the wheel and me and Mum one time, right, we had to go and pull you out the driver's side. Do you remember that, Nick?'

'What a load of cobblers. You're talking out your be'ind,' said Ken, feeling for his lapels. 'I never done drink-driving.'

'You lost your licence, Dad,' said Nick. 'For a year. You got that Irish navvy chap to drive you.'

'I was stitched up for that by old Shit-for-Brains—what was his name?—the publican at The White Hart. He was matey with the copper, wer'n' 'e.'

'Mum was wild.'

The old boy took off his glasses and wiped them on his jacket. 'Coo dear, boys, she could scare the livin' daylights out of you, couldn't she? Coo dear. What a gel. Never seen nothing fiercer in a housecoat in me life. They was all scared of her down on the site. Here's your fucking sandwiches, she used to say when she came down. Choke on 'em for all I care, sod ya. Coo dear, the blokes used to laugh and she'd turn on them. What you effing laughing at, monkey face? she used to say. Nothing, Pearl! She'd turn them to jelly. Women didn't eff and blind in them days.'

'She made you sleep in the garage once, didn't she, Dad?'

'That was when I brought that polecat home from the pub and set it off round the house and it bit 'er. She was always trying to get me out in that garage, but I could worm my way round her all right, back in them days. I used to say to her, Don't do it, Pearl, my darling, be a sweetheart now. . . .'

'You used to sing her that song, Dad. The one about the dear silver that shines in her hair.' Dave's nose was at his father's sleeve.

' "Mother Machree",' said Nick.

Then Ken started singing it in the same way he used to, with a pleading warbling voice, full of penitence.

> *I love the dear silver that shines in your hair,*
> *And the brow that's all furrowed and wrinkled*
>   *with care.*

I kiss the dear fingers, so toilworn for me,
　Oh, God bless you and keep you, Mother
　　Machree.

In the driving mirror, Nick could see Dave's face soft with long-ing, his eyes gleaming, his face smooth and wrinkle-free, and he remembered the boy on his birthday—first down at the table, not so worried about the presents, just ready to be important. And he remembered him dressing up like Action Man and marching up and down the front room while his father slapped his leg to keep time, and he remembered him standing to attention during the Queen's speech, so his father could approve—anything to gain points. He remembered too how he'd reappear after a falling-out, his eyelashes in spikes. And when Nick ribbed him, on and on, accusing him of having cried, he'd deny it.

'She used to say, I ain't got no grey hair—didn't she, Dad? I used to cringe at her calling the blokes who worked in the ga-rage dirty filthy bastards and all that. But, get this right, they ask after her even now. How's old Pearl? they ask me. She's wicked, your mum, they say. Funny, because we was so embarrassed by her as kids! Weren't we? Do you remember, you brought some girl home, Nick, and Mum was laying into the dog? Just scream-ing at the poor sod, calling it a bleedin' little bastard, and it had only chewed up a slipper, or something, but she could go off on one, couldn't she? She'd just sort of go mental, and then the next minute she was all right again and calling you duckie.'

Drop me off here, Nick used to say to her, well before the

school gates. Isn't that your mother? they said from the side of the stage, before the play started. Oh God, I told her not to come.

And now it comes back to him. She did call him after Cambridge. She called him when he was taking articles in London. I'm working, he said. I can't talk here, now—as if he were developing some sort of life-saving medicine. She may have called when he was at Cambridge too. He can't remember.

But he does remember how Dave had to fight for her love, because he, Nick, was the golden boy, the one who got a scholarship to private school, who went to grammar school, the one she talked to her friends about in sustained bafflement, and it was Nick who got the boiled egg and soldiers while Dave hunted around for a bit of bread to toast. And it hurt him to look in the driving mirror at his brother, nigh on forty, still trying so hard to find his place and to look too at his father, glowing with the talk of their mother.

She was missing. They were there but she was missing.

'She'd 'arp on a bit but she used to let me kiss her,' said Ken. 'She 'ad them cheeks like peaches. She was a good woman, no matter all her hard talk. She was what you call lenient underneath it all. A heart of gold. And loyal! She could call you all the names under the sun but she wouldn't stand for it from no one else.' He put a hand to his chin and rubbed it, his eyes narrowing as if seeing the past through a keyhole. 'It was only that she was disappointed, see, and it crushed her some'ow.'

Nick saw that Dave's buoyancy, an extravagance, was slipping away from him and the years were coming back and claiming his face. His eyes started to dart, to run for cover. 'Yeah but, Dad, you was good friends, weren't you? I mean, you used to laugh. I remember the time of the Jubilee, when you dressed up. . . .'

Their father turned his head to look out of his window and Nick could see the muscles in his cheeks working.

'She's not dead. We're talking about her as if she were dead,' said Nick.

His father was silent. Dave sat back in his seat and Nick simply gazed at the road. They had another two hundred miles to go to recover something his father didn't need from a woman he didn't love. They were making the wrong journey, but they were doing it together.

After a few minutes, Ken piped up with sudden sprightliness, 'Here we go! That Irish bloke what did the driving! Kevin! He said to me one time it was Irish for your 'eart, Machree was. That's what it come from, the Irish!'

'Your heart?'

'Mother my heart,' said Dave.

And nothing more was said until they were just about to pass the next services, when the old man threw his left hand in the air like he was hailing a cab, and after he caused the car to swerve off the road once more, he fell to bemoaning his driver again and hobbled off with thunderstruck face and a curse on those who held the doors open for him.

30

They slipped through the knot of one little town after another, going great guns on a bridge, skirting a pedestrian precinct, then, rebuked by a WHSmith or a Clinton Cards, going tail between legs back to a roundabout and sometimes exiting the town on the road they came in on. Dave was doing the map reading and, although he tried to bring a party approach to it, after more than six hours in the car they were beyond jollity.

'Oh, happy days,' he said, rejoining them in the car with another four-pack at a small Wild West petrol station which sold, it seemed, rope, playing cards and Harp lager.

They stopped at a pub to ask directions, and were told to turn round and go five miles back down the road by which they had come until they found an unmarked dirt track.

'Could be left, could be right. Not sure.'

A man with a pen at a newspaper looked up, thoughtful. 'What the fuck's a "croque-monsieur"?' he asked.

It was dark, and in the full interior illumination of the car, their father wasn't getting any more gracious. Far from it, his concentration was focused on man's second-best prize: revenge.

Dave larked about as they got in the car. 'Did you hear his accent?'

'Welsh,' said his father darkly. 'Say no more.'

'It's like—what's the name of it? That movie when everyone looks up at them when they come in. What's it called, that film . . . ?'

Nick shook his head. 'That hasn't narrowed it down for me much, mate, I'm afraid.'

Dave was pickled, lolling about in the back. He started dripping on about how Nick's problem was he'd always been 'sarcastic'. Nick was apprehensive, as he switched his lights between bright and dim and squinted for the unmarked road, that things were going to go badly when they got to June's son's house.

'Do you think there'll be any argy-bargy?' Dave asked his father.

'He's a nancy boy, that Andrew,' his father said in the dark apropos of June's son. But given he'd said it about him too, it didn't give Nick much comfort.

'He must hate your guts.'

'Why? Why would he?' asked the old man, querulous with indignation. It seemed that the power of insight he'd shown on the M42 had dissipated on the border of England and Wales.

'He's gonna try and lamp him one,' Dave muttered. 'He's gonna take Dad on, but don't worry, Dad, we're right behind you, mate.'

'You wanna be in front of me, not behind me! God give me strength. I'm nearly eighty years old! You're half-cut and him, he's liable to try to give 'em some of his so-called advice.'

'What's the plan then, chaps?' said Dave, sitting forward, hanging on to their headrests.

'I don't know,' said Nick. 'Have we got a plan?'

'Naargh,' Ken said, looking thoroughly disgusted. 'We go in, ask her for the money and we leave. Then we'll find a room for the night in one of them Happy Eaters.'

Dave laughed.

''Ark at 'im.' Ken nudged Nick. 'Bag o' nerves. Boozed up. No good to anyone. He'd have been court-martialled.'

'So, we're not bringing June back with us then, Dad?' Nick asked.

His father grunted.

Nick put the lights on bright. To their right were two pine trees, just as the barman had said. He turned the car into the unmarked driveway which ran alongside a field to the left and a forest to the right. They could hear the hooting of an owl when Nick wound down his window to squint at a name on a board. 'Here we are then. Nut Hall, it is. Like taking coals to Newcastle.'

'Well . . .' said his father, expansively pejorative. He put on his trilby.

The drive ended in a turning circle. Nick pulled up in front of the stone cottage. The wheels crunched on the gravel, making the noise of bubble wrap being popped. A dog started barking.

'Right,' said Nick. 'It will all be quite civilized, I'm sure. No need for you two to get all up in arms. Just stay cool. Let me do the talking.'

But he hadn't reckoned on Melinda.

31

Good evening. Sorry to disturb you at this ungodly hour, but I bring you one bitter old man, one drunk on a day trip and a solicitor to relieve you of forty thousand quid. This was what was going through his mind as they approached the only source of light, two stripes of it escaping round a curtain behind a long glass pane.

'No door handle!' said Dave, swaying, gassy with lager fizz.

'It's called a window,' said Nick, standing back on the gravel.

'A French window,' Dave said in his defence. He trod next along a flower bed, the wrong side of a box hedge, and found another door. 'Bell don't work.'

But Nick was already at the arched door with the wrought-iron knocker, tapping.

When the door opened, there escaped the smell of curry and onions, and in the fumes and light appeared a great stocky woman in socks, shorts and a bandanna and T-shirt.

'Isss Rambo,' Dave whispered to him.

Her face and hands were daubed with what appeared to be dry clay. She folded her arms over her breasts. She stood there, feet planted wide, and with a roll-up in the side of her mouth she said, 'Yih?'

'Hi,' said Nick, fawningly. 'Hi, I . . .' and he was about to make a great rhetorical circumnavigation of the matter of money featuring enquiries after their health and the children's and coming to that of June's, but he was forestalled. Melinda saw Ken, standing back in the half-shadow behind Nick, his eyes bright with aggression.

'Oh, it's you. *Kin*,' said Melinda, unimpressed. She took a drag and let the smoke out the same way it came in, through a crack in the side of her mouth. 'She won't go back to you, you know.'

'Steady . . .' said Dave, behind his father like a boxing trainer, on the balls of his feet. 'Steady.'

'June!' his father bellowed. *'June! You in there?'*

Melinda raised an eyebrow. Her cheeks were flushed, her eyes bold. 'I told her you'd only married her for her money.'

'June? It's me! Ken!'

'I think she might have got that one, Dad,' said Dave, stuffing the tips of his fingers in his hoody pouch. He bent slightly at the waist. 'All right, Melinda.'

'All right, Dave.' Melinda was leaning against the door, leisurely. 'She can't hear you, *Kin*.'

'Course she can 'ear me. *June! It's me! Ken!*'

Melinda's smile loosened her mouth's grip on the damp roll-up and its light died. Her pupils were large and, with her hair tied back and her brows and hair all of a uniform pale red, she was a very open-looking woman.

'You got a nerve, haven't you?' she said to Ken, with amusement rather than contempt. 'And you must be the older son,' she added, looking at Nick, a note of scorn in her voice. 'Well, well, well. It looks like a *real* family.'

Her lines were working out well for her, Nick thought bitterly, recognizing in himself the humble desire to be liked above all else.

'Melinda,' he tried, 'I think we might do well to all sit down together and have some sort of discussion, maybe hear June's point of view?'

'*June! Will you get your bleeding fat arse out 'ere!*' Ken cupped his mouth.

'He was never what you call a great motivator,' said Dave, rubbing his hands. 'Witches out 'ere, love; do you mind if we come in?'

'Why not?' said Melinda, closing her finger and thumb on her roll-up and slipping it into the pocket of her cut-off jeans. 'I reckon I can handle you three all right. Come on then.'

Ken made a doorway lunge at her—he seemed to have a thing for threshold confessions, Nick noted. 'Listen, we don't want no trouble, we ain't come for that. I've always had respect for you and Andrew and been generous with you, a'n' I? You can't fault me for that. Is he home? Andrew?' He cringed.

Oh, what a coward, thought Nick, after all that pre-combat steel in the car; his father had taken off his trilby and was squeezing it with both hands.

'Just want to sort it out peaceful an' all.'

'All right,' she said easily. She showed them to the round table in the middle of the kitchen, and they stood around it but did not sit.

'Why won't she come down?' their father said, looking at Melinda with sentimental eyes. Perhaps it had occurred to him

that someone did not like him. It seemed to defeat him momentarily. However, anger came smartly to his solace as soon as he
remembered she was wrong and he was right. 'Sod 'er then! Now
she can't bear to clap eyes on me? Do me a favour! She leaves me
on a Frid'y for a start and just buggers off without so much as a
word. She could have been dead on the road! I wasn't to know,
was I? She could have had a terrible accident, couldn't she? Been
in some 'ospital somewhere, all smashed up, and I wouldn't have
known. I mean, that ain't right, is it? To treat another *youman*
bein' like that.'

'Hell, I don't care what you are, Ken—human might be an
overstatement—but look, she's happy here. You know? She's
starting to get her head round the idea that women are not slaves.'
She leant back against a counter and, taking a tea towel, began to
wipe the clay off her hands.

'Ah, come on, Melinda.' Dave stepped forward. 'Be fair. I mean,
you've only heard her side of things.'

'I'm not inclined to be fair, Dave. I believe a woman should be
treated like a queen. Have you heard of a succubus?'

Dave and Nick exchanged looks. 'We got the car outside,' said
Dave.

'Well, watch out, the lot of you, is all I'll say.' She picked up an
open bottle of beer from the counter and took a swig. 'A pack of
chauvinists on a day trip. Wonderful.'

Dave licked his dry lips.

Ken carried on, alternating reasonable appeal with furious
glances up the stairs. 'Look, if it's to be goodbye between us, me
and the Queen of Sheba, I'll abide by her decision, course I will,
but can't she least come and tell me 'erself?'

'Maybe she's feeling guilty about nicking the cash,' said Dave.

'She can't look me in the face for what she's done to me. She's 'iding from me. Well, she can 'ide from me but she can't 'ide from the Big Man.'

'She's playing bingo online, actually, *Kin*. She got ten pounds free when she set up her account and since then she's been playing it round the clock. She's three hundred quid up. Bless her.'

'Gordon Bennett, don't she know the bank always wins? She'll blow all the money that way! She'll go through it like a dose of salts. Look sharp, Melinda, and go and get her to come down, please. We ain't driven all the way from Hastings to stand about 'ere while she plays bingo.'

'All right. Now look. She didn't want me to tell you this, but I told her I would do if you showed your face.' She went and closed the top of a stable door and shut out the sounds of *The Simpsons* theme tune. 'She's not been eating since she got here. Andy and I are pretty clear that she's starving herself to death, because of you. So, you have your little chat. But whatever you do, bear in mind her health. She's not as strong as she looks.'

And with that, Melinda took to the stairs, trudging up and calling out to June that it was 'just' her.

'*Kin*, she calls me. *Kin*. Funny old accent, ain't she? *Kin*. Like as in kith and kin. Like as in family.'

'That's not what she means, Dad.' Dave picked up an olive from a dish on the counter and popped it in his mouth. Then he picked up a carton and read it. 'Soya milk.'

Nick folded his arms over his chest and looked serious. 'We should all sit at that table when she comes down.'

Dave scanned the steel-lidded glass jars on the shelf next to him. There was a long row of them rather like an old-fashioned chemist's. 'Lentils. Sago. Quinoa . . . what's that then? Quinoa, acai berries, bulgur wheat . . . Vegetarians! They're bleedin' vegetarians, Dad. Take a look in the fridge, Nick.'

'No.'

'Go on. See if there's any bacon.'

Nick pulled on the door. The fridge was a laboratory, stacked with plastic containers, its uniformity floodlit. There were three huge round tubs on the middle shelf marked 'live yoghurt' and 'quark' and 'tofu'. Dave came over, barging into the round table in his eagerness. He pushed Nick aside and bent to look inside it, using his sober eye. 'Not a sausage.'

'June can't tolerate vegetables too well.' Ken spoke out of the side of his mouth. 'Sometimes one'll slip through, and she'll swell up with the wind in her sails. She'll say, 'Ere, Ken, there must have been something funny in that lasagne. And I'll say, What? Like a *tamada*? See, her constitution just can't handle 'em. None of 'em. No chance. Give her a bit of cauliflower cheese and it's who let Tommy out of prison.' On hearing the women at the top of the stairs, he dropped his voice to a whisper and said with heavy sarcasm, 'Look sharp, she's coming down now. The Queen of Sheba herself. Watch out.'

32

She came round the corner of the stairwell, slippers formerly of Bulverhythe, in a pale pink sweatsuit, her handbag over one arm. She came a step at a time, testing it with one foot, finding it, settling a moment before going on again. One hand wobbled on the banister, the other was in Melinda's grasp.

'That's it, now, remember you're unsteady because you're weak, June. That's why.'

About four steps from the ground, she stopped and wobbled, quite overcome to see Ken. She put her hands to her face and rocked in her slippers. Melinda redoubled her grip on her.

'Oh, those eyes. Oh, Kenneth. I didn't think you'd come. I'd never have thought it in a million years.'

Ken moved shakily towards the stairwell and peered, wrinkling his nose to see through his glasses. Melinda stood between them, one leg raised on a step, one below it; she looked like a shot-putter, paused after the throw. It made Nick uncomfortable to see a woman display the space between her legs that way, even in denim, even in crisis. The old man cleared his throat.

'June,' he began, with forbearance, 'June . . .'

She put her fingertips to her mouth.

'*Have . . . you . . . got . . . my . . . money?*' And he enunciated each word as though he were dealing with someone mentally ill and dangerous.

She drew her handbag in to her stomach. 'What money, Ken?'

'Don't come the—' He clenched his fists, but then recovered himself. 'The money what was under the mattress. Now, by rights, that's mine, June, you see.'

'Well, some of it,' said Nick, making an apologetic face as he stepped forward from the side of the fridge, ducking under the hanging light. 'The point is, until things are worked out it ought to be held in escrow, perhaps.'

'What things are worked out?' said June, her face falling, looking at him. It was clear from her expression that, if Nick was there, things weren't normal.

'Where's the money, June?'

'What? From the bingo?' she said with a nervous trill of laughter. 'Did you tell him about the bingo then?' she said to Melinda.

'Sod the bingo! The for'y grand, June! The for'y sodding grand! Under the mattress!'

'The forty . . . was it as much as that? No, I think it was thirty-eight thousand and fifty-six pounds, if I remember rightly.'

'You cunning bitch! Welsh! You can't help yourself, can you, you lot! Where is it?'

'Calm down, Dad.'

'Take it easy, Dad.'

'Well, Ken, now where do you think it is? What a fuss. I don't know!' She doubled her chin and displayed dimples. Her eyes shone as if the prince had come and the shoe fit. 'Now, you know me, Ken. What do you think I'd do with it? I put it in the bank.' She offered a glamourous smile to those gathered in the kitchen. 'I've said to him for donkey's years: better off in the bank. Well, you wouldn't want someone thieving it while I was away, would you? And with your comings and goings, I couldn't be sure when you'd be home. No, best way was to put it *in the bank*. Didn't you look at your bank account, Ken? Have you not taken your pension out this week? You must have took some money out for your fares.'

'We drove,' said Nick.

'Oh, well, you should have said, Ken!'

'I asked you on the phone, didn't I? You bin playing some sort of game with me!'

'Well, now you're here, won't you have a cup of tea?'

Melinda went over to the kettle and pressed its button. Then she opened the stable door. 'You can come out now, kiddiewinks, and see your, um, see who's here, if you want.'

They didn't.

'No chance of a beer, is there, Melinda?' Dave sidled up to her. 'Where is he then, your fella, Andy?' asked Dave.

'He's upstairs, working on his poems. He's doing an epic romance in sonnet form.' She put two spoonfuls of tea into a brown teapot. 'Do you want your tea with soya milk or just black, guys?'

'All of this nonsense at our age!' June let out a peal of laughter as she glided across the slate floor towards Ken, half his height.

Ken stood there, opening and closing his mouth and hands.

'Tea? Ken?' Melinda cried out, assuming he was struck deaf as well as dumb.

He turned, his mouth a firm tight line, and blinked at her. After a minute, he pulled his shoulders back.

'No, thank you,' he said, feeling his trilby. 'We're leaving.' He turned his back on them and went to the door. 'I won't be made a monkey of.'

33

As there was no such thing as a Happy Eater anymore and the Little Chef didn't have rooms, they stayed at a Premier Inn. They drove for an hour before they found it. In the pitch dark and silence of the empty roads, when Ken seemed to be sleeping, Dave put his head close to Nick and whispered to him.

'It's a terrible thing, though—divorce—innit, Nick? Terrible. I couldn't even think of it. To me, right, it's worse than dying. Worse, because you got to live through it, you got to live with the mess all around you. I mean, seeing what happened . . .' he lowered his voice further, 'with Mum and Dad. Christ alive, it was bloody awful, wasn't it? All my mates, right, they're all divorced now. We're the only ones, me and Marina, who're still together. See, Nick mate, we need women, don't we? We're nothing without them. My biggest fear, right . . .' (Nick looked sideways at his father; he looked like a cat concentrating on sleep.) 'My biggest fear,' Dave went on in a near hiss, 'is being alone, or not just being alone but being without Marina.' And he pronounced her name as if it were holy.

Nick made a small noise through his nose, so that Dave knew he'd heard him, so as not to wake his dad and because he had nothing to add. He knew what Dave meant. In the dark, in a strange place, on a lonely road, he missed Astrid sorely, as if she were his other half.

He was only himself, or the self he liked, when she was there. He was no longer his own invention; he was Astrid's. At the luggage belt in Gatwick, when they came home, he had been much amused by the chit-chat of the very elderly couple next to him. They worried over every single suitcase that passed. Tired and desperate, the little old man no higher than Nick's elbow made a panicking attempt to pull a suitcase from the belt now and again so that they could further investigate, but he never succeeded in removing one. It reminded Nick of the sword in the stone. This little old chap was clearly no Arthur, and Nick was about to offer his help, but his woman said, her voice thick with adoration, 'If you can't lift it, John, no one can.' And Nick had had to smile at the way in which, when it comes to each other, we see what we want.

But Ken wasn't asleep. He had his eyes closed so that he could focus, and with every mile he was becoming more and more determined. The years were weighing heavily on him, forming a diamond inside of him, a decision made.

In the morning, Nick settled the bill at reception and they ate breakfast together. Ken didn't respond to Nick's counsel to patch things up with June, 'If only for financial reasons.'

Dave sat glumly eating balls of cold green melon, because he said he felt obliged to, with it being on the buffet.

Nick reasoned, 'Look, Dad. You and June. You've been through a lot. You've got stability. And security. You're company for each other. And you've been together a long time now. . . .'

Ken slurped his tea. 'Couldn't agree more. You're dead right, son. It's over.'

When at last they quit the M25, and took the A21 in the direction of Hastings, Dave, back between the tombstones of their front seats, began to go through the events of the night, lionizing each of them in turn. 'And old Nick, right . . . and she, that Melinda, right . . . and I could have cacked myself when you, right, when you said, Dad, when you said, I won't be made a monkey of. And you should have seen their faces! *Ooh, for those eyes!*'

Ken took up the baton. 'And her standing there like that, smoking like a man and calling me *Kin*, and there's old Queen Elizabeth, upstairs on the bingo, and 'im—where was he, Dave, that Andy, the great big girl's blouse . . . ?' He passed it back to Dave.

'He was writing his poems, she said, an epic love song or something . . .'

'Epic! Not 'arf. What a carry-on!'

'And them thinking June was on hunger strike!' Nick joined in.

Dave blew a raspberry and they all fell about, their father telling him to stop being so vulgar, through squeaking laughter. Dave would not stop. He blew another one on his arm.

'Jesus Christ! Them vegetarians, they'll be able to run that place on wind power next.'

'Well, serve her right! Serve her right! She done it to get me to chase after her, didn't she? One thing she'd always wanted, that woman, was a man to chase after her. Fat chance,' he said. 'You can't fuss round a woman. They don't thank you for it.'

But it fell flat. As soon as he'd said it, he looked out of the window. The car was quiet. Women, Nick gathered, tried to get a man to say what they wanted to hear, or do what they wanted them to do without having to ask them directly. This was called romance.

'Nice touch, though, Dave—taking her in the car pack,' said Nick.

'Well, I couldn't leave her to them nuts and beans, could I?'

Dave had leapt out of the car in the few minutes before they left the house in Wales, and had taken in the carrier bag for June. He said he'd seen Andy come down the stairs and disappear back up them fast. 'Well, I sin his trouser-legs anyway.'

'What was in that bag you give her then, Dave?' Ken asked him.

'Some Polos, a big Twix, some Quavers—or did I eat them? Bacon Fries, Nobby's Nuts and a couple of cans of Harp. I should have taken them out, but I didn't think of it.'

'Well, that was very good of you, son.' Ken nodded gravely.

'It was,' said Nick. 'I mean, it was really, *really* good of you, Dave. I mean, I've never seen a settlement like it. Goodbye, darling, we're through, here's a bag of crisps. . . .'

'Yup,' said Ken sombrely. 'He's got a good 'eart, your brother.'

'He has.' Nick winked at Dave in the mirror.

'I always said to your mother, it don't matter he ain't the sharpest, he's got a good 'eart, that kid. Still, you've both been good boys to your old dad. I'm grateful. Don't know how much longer I've got, but you came right in the end, the pair of you, and I can die a happy man.'

Dave's hand was blasted away from his mouth first by the explosion of laughter. ''Ere, Dad,' he said, 'why don't you lay it on a bit thicker?'

The old man grunted. 'You two'll have plenty of time for laughing soon as you've left me on my tod in that shit'ole.'

Dave's throaty chuckles and high dry-roasted snort infected Nick and Nick's long wail at the end of each wave of laughter got Dave going again, and so they went on with the old man shaking his head and muttering, 'Pair of bleedin' numbskulls.'

'So. What are you going to do about June then, Dad? No, seriously,' Nick added quickly, hearing Dave start up, about to make some sort of joke. 'Have her back? Take some time apart? Relationship counselling? What do you think? Is it over?'

'Narrgh,' he said, pulling on his lapels, trying one of his expressions and then the other. 'Well . . .'

'Don't forget you're entitled to half her bingo winnings. . . .'

'Money's not everything, David. 'Ere, I know what it was I meant to say to you, Nick. I promised your mum you'd go and see her. That's the thing. I promised it to her. She made me give her my word. Lying there, she was, at death's door on the hospital ward when I saw her.'

'Really?'

David put his head between them. 'She's broke her leg, but she's back home now in a cast, Dad. I sin 'er last week. She's all right.'

'Poor cow. Abandoned there like yesterday's newspapers. You'll go round, won't you, son?' he said, and this time he put his hand on top of Nick's on the gearshift and patted it briefly.

They bypassed the town that once you could only drive

through, where they used to go to a pub with a fire for her birthday—it had been famous for its cherry pie and trout—and at the next village they drove across a crossroads with all of the local stores on either side closed apart from a Chinese takeaway. Then they went past an old haunt of his father's, a roadside pub, closed too, and he pointed out what used to be a lorry drivers' café in a lay-by, where he took the boys for egg and chips on the days they came to work with him.

'I used to bring you back 'ome filthy, them days. She'd holler and shout at me and have you in the bath.'

When they put their boys to bed, Ken and Pearl took turns to poke their heads in to get the last word, and the boys competed to keep them at the door, calling out after them all the brightest and best things they could wish for them all: 'It'll be a nice day', 'We'll have a cup of tea', 'The sun'll be shining!' Nick recalled this now, and looked at his father, and then at Dave. Sadness such as there was in their home wasn't all cruel—no, not at all—some of the sadness was nothing to do with cruelty, or even each other.

'She could remember every line of a poem she liked,' said Dave.

'That's where you got your brains from, Nick,' the old man said. 'From her, not from me.'

It occurred to him that in this case the old truism about the journey being more important than the destination was right, but he didn't say it, because it was lofty and he didn't want to set himself apart in any way from them. He wanted to be with them, and like them. He wanted to be in the car with his family. And he thought of how they came back from that cherry-pie pub on her birthday, mouths full with After Eight mints, his mother dispensing them from her handbag, fairly and squarely, and how he and his brother slept the sleep of angels in the back of the car, how sleep was never as good as that ever again, a rocking contentment, well fed, happy, with the rollicking of the car round the country lanes and the sound of his mother and father talking together, lurching in and out of his tubby little brother and ending up in their favourite arrangement, where he had his head on his brother's back and his brother had his head on his lap. They pretended to be asleep when the car door was opened just to have the luxury of being lifted.

'Aah. Look at them, Ken. My two little princes.'

'Little sods, more like. Come on, I know when you're having us on, you two.'

34

When he walked the dog, on Sunday, he found spring had thrown up its last but best: bluebells, little pink milkmaids, and the white greater stitchworts with their little yellow pincushions set amid white petals. Passing the empty larder of a bramble thicket, the spaniel poked his head in and out of the warren holes with the ghastly fake smile of someone enquiring through a serving hatch as to dinner's imminence. Elsewhere a rabbit ran for its life.

He gladdened his step, up the hill, out of the woods, coming up by chalet bungalow and terrace row, keen to find Astrid.

His father would be lonely now, he thought. He'd made sure they knew it when they dropped him at the bungalow in Bulver-hythe. Ken had stood on the pavement, hands in pockets, wind at his hair and coat, making sure that, should they look back, they'd see him like that.

'You'll enjoy the peace and quiet, Dad,' said Dave. 'You'll be a bachelor boy again.'

'Job's comfort, you are,' his father had retorted.

Outside, on the lane, the dog hunched, concertina'd on the cusp of next door's driveway, giving him an awkward look as if to say, Come on, be fair, look the other way. Then as a last gambit the dog scarpered on past the house. Nick called him back, whistled too, and praised him when he skidded to a halt and turned back, tongue like a scarf.

There was only one thing amiss at home, it seemed, and that was Laura. She seemed a different girl, withdrawn and diffident, who barely answered questions apart from with 'I don't know'. Sensing something was wrong the night before, he'd made cheese on toast. He was scraping the burnt edges off the toast, talking to her and the dog by turns, when out of the corner of his eye he saw her put her head on the table. Her arms hung either side of her and she simply turned her chin and let her cheek rest on the smooth surface, and a tear rolled down the cheek and onto the table.

Astrid had bustled in and busied the girl about getting her schoolwork together. She asked her daughter, sharply, what was wrong.

'It's just,' Laura said in a small voice, 'that I worry about him.'

'Who?'

'Dad.' Her throat tightened around the word.

In the beginning, in the early days, he'd complained to her about Laura, as if he could thwart that great love of theirs. 'She moans so much, don't you think?' He'd put his criticisms slyly, as if a question, as if it were a matter of education or improvement.

'She doesn't read much, does she?' 'She doesn't seem to have any curiosity . . . like we did as kids, our generation.'

Then he learnt, in loving Astrid, to emulate her, to speak only of the good things that Laura did. In fact he could beat her at it. He mentioned them first—how Laura had good manners, how she was a brave girl, how she came out with such funny old-fashioned things. . . . And this worked well. Astrid was happy, and it worked for him too; he looked for the good in the child and found it.

'She certainly dotes on Danny, doesn't she? But why is she coming back a touch hostile to us?' he'd asked Astrid.

'Well, every child wants its parents back together, deep down, don't you think?'

Nick had met Danny a number of times at station gates and, in exchanging plastic bags with him, found a slight man eager to please. For some reason, and he could not explain it, their eyes lit up when they saw each other, and smiles sprang to their faces. Perhaps it was that they hoped the other was decent and good and fair so very much. Perhaps it was because of Laura. He day-dreamed of standing with Astrid at Laura's graduation. He went to the lacrosse fixtures and flinched and ducked with the other dads, and he went to the school play early to secure them places at the front.

But it wasn't him that Laura wanted.

Astrid was standing in the stuffy heat of the conservatory, waiting, when he and Roy got back from their walk. He assumed a frown, keen for Astrid to see his readiness for tasks numberless, and to appreciate him anew.

'Shed door needs fixing. Dog took a shit on the neighbours'

drive again. And Dozie, Ed Crozier, called on the mobile, When are you coming to stay? I forgot I'd said we would. I don't fancy trekking up to bloody Oxfordshire, do you?'

'I don't mind.'

'It's always the same old stories, you know. But, you see, I did promise we'd go and stay, just the one night.'

'When?'

'Um. Next weekend. Laura's with her dad, right?'

She nodded.

'You're OK with that then, are you?'

She touched his face and he went to kiss her hand and saw that her eyes were red and that she'd been crying.

'What is it?'

Laura had started her period. He had to steady himself and pull himself together, so strong was his discomfort.

'She didn't want me to tell you,' Astrid said, her hands moving up and down either side of his arms. 'She was worried she wouldn't be a little girl anymore. That we won't love her anymore. I remember thinking that my father wouldn't love me anymore when I had my first period. I know it's silly.' She tendered him a little faithful smile.

'Tell her not to worry. It doesn't make her a woman, does it, Astrid? It's only that she's growing into one. She'll always be our little girl,' he added with conviction, and he surprised himself with the emotion he felt saying 'our'.

'I want Laura to feel she can do anything.'

'Of course.'

'Well, bloody Danny keeps on to Laura about how unhappy

and how unlucky he is. He says he might die. It's the booze and drugs but he doesn't tell her that. Did you know she writes letters to him?'

'No.'

'She sends him chocolate bars.' Astrid smiled thinly.

'More like a fiver he wants, isn't it?'

'Don't. That'll be next. Nick, I love her but I am going to have to let her go one day. And best if she's strong. Like your parents did, Nick. They made you strong and they let you go.'

'Well, I'm not sure that was the plan.'

And she sat with her daughter in the front room and introduced the young woman to the salve of chocolate, a soap opera on TV and a hot-water bottle, and they sat feet up, cuddling close. They could hear poor Nick, edgy, moving around the kitchen, putting the dishes away, something he'd not done before, and coming in and out of the front room, to ask where a bowl or a spatula went.

After a few minutes he came and sat next to them, yawning in his feigned way and turning down their offer of chocolate most politely. Then he went back out to the kitchen, and came back in with his plate of cheese and biscuits.

'I know it's a bit . . . well, you know . . . unfashionable, but in my book you can't beat a Jacob's Cream Cracker,' he'd said, sitting back alongside them, giving Astrid one of Roy's ingratiating looks and holding up an oatcake for reference.

'I'll get some,' said Astrid. 'Next time I'm at the shops.'

Laura made sure the blanket was extended to his knees too.

When he went up to kiss Laura goodnight, he saw on her bedside table arranged meticulously were the things she'd bought in

Boots with her mother: toe separators in pink foam, a small bottle of nail varnish, a soap in the shape of a strawberry, some hair slides still in the plastic, and a glitter lip gloss.

'Don't grow up too fast, darling,' he said to her. Stay a child in some part of you, he thought.

The seasons were changing every day, it seemed. The world was turning too fast, his hair was thinning, and it seemed that the end was coming for him too, after all, not just for the old man. And it was coming neither dramatically nor brutally, like the stage villain he'd anticipated, but unexpectedly fleet of foot, and with a woman's touch somehow.

35

'What are you thinking?' Astrid asked him, after they'd been sitting in silence on the motorway for half an hour. They were on their way to spend the weekend with Ed Crozier and family in Banbury. Nick narrowed his eyes as if scrutinizing each and every one of his motivations, behaviours and emotions to prise open his unconscious mind. 'I was just wondering whether the bad smell I keep getting a whiff of isn't my socks.'

They were side by side in the Range Rover, in their usual pose, her with hand in his lap. There were two cold stale coffees in cardboard cups in the cupholders from their last stop.

'I should have called my mother. I said I would. I must. She was strange, you know, compared to other people. And I'm so conventional. Funny.'

Astrid rubbed his leg.

'We're so greedy, these days. We get greedier. We must be the greediest generation of all, you know. The thing about her, Pearl, was that nothing was ever rubbish. Nothing was ever no good. Me, I'm all for ditching things and moving on. That would be sacrilege to her.'

He'd popped into the shed that morning to put away the loose trowel and watering can that had been roaming around the wind-swept hilltop garden since the autumn. Stepping round the lawn mower to put them against the wall, he took in the artefacts of his former self ranged out there: the abdominal press, a rowing machine, a wetsuit, his cricket bag, a motorbike helmet, an industrial espresso machine, and his skis propped against the wall like a pair of fingers crossed. A Paul Smith holdall. He'd asked Astrid to get rid of them.

As a boy, he sat in the car, visor down, while his mother delved through skips, hauling out a mangle or a pram. Brass matchboxes, mottoed jugs, framed photos of someone else's great-grandfather; these were the things she found that others had thrown away, and gave each one that unflinching eye of hers as she turned it to the light and granted it, for a while, a turn at the mantelpiece or her dressing table, or hearth. She directed them to find beauty in dirty places and commonplaces, everywhere. He felt once more the blow of Morwen's depiction of him as a snob.

'You know, the last thing anyone wants in a parent is for them to be enigmatic.'

Astrid tilted her head. 'I suppose so.'

'It's like we want cartoon characters, or cardboard cut-outs; we want to be able to sum them up in a sentence when people ask. Oh, a parent can be larger than life for the purpose of an anecdote, but they must never be bigger than us, you see. I could never sum up my mum if you asked me to.'

'Well, it's not surprising. You've only got memories to go on, since you haven't seen her for twenty years or whatever.'

'No.' He put his finger along his upper lip. 'No, we don't want them enigmatic or inscrutable or any of that malarkey because we are supposed to rise triumphant, aren't we? We're not supposed to have parents as complicated as us. We're supposed to be far more fucked up.'

When he accused her of not being like other mothers, it tickled her pink because he'd hit the nail on the head. She did not conform to convention. They'd fallen in behind their father to try to make the witch abjure her magic and do the dishes and shut her mouth. 'Sod you,' was her reply. If that's the way you want to play it, I'll stop being a woman.

The way to eternal life was sexlessness. Some were ready for it sooner than others. He felt Astrid's hand, nestling in his crotch.

Against his will, she had packed the Paul Smith holdall, dumping its former contents into a wet cardboard box in the shed.

'Leave the stupid bag there. It's too fey,' he said the last time she wanted it in the house. 'It belongs to the past.' Inside it were framed photos of his university drinking clubs, showing young men looking languid, feigning foppery as if they were born to it. The vivid colours of its stripes made it too conspicuously moneyed for his liking. He'd kicked it. 'Bloody thing.'

It amused her. 'I *like* that bag; it's so trendy!' she said every time he took it back out to the shed like a bad cat.

This time she'd got it in the boot before he could object. When he saw it there, he knew it was there as a rebuke, but he couldn't think what for. He used it last when he left Natasha and their flat in Wandsworth, four or more years back, and when he looked at it he could see himself swinging it down the stairs now, humming the tune from the bathroom radio, the Bryan Ferry track—'Come on, come on, let's stick together'—and when it came to him out on the pavement what the hell he was singing, he'd felt bad and doubled back down the side alley and checked on her through the kitchen windows. She was dialling a number and chewing on a corner of toast. When the phone answered, her face changed; she came alive in anger.

Astrid had scrupled over the packing. She went for a single colour and that colour was beige. It was irreproachable. It took her close to a week to get the contents of that bag to be both minimal and opulent, making amendments and changes here and there, slipping in extra thongs, adding accessories on day six. After seven days it was done. And she saw that it was good.

'There's barely any room,' she said to him, holding one of his shirts up with a critical expression.

'I only need the one I'm wearing.'

'That's true.'

He said he didn't want an extra pair of underpants but she put them in with ostentatious generosity, sighing and saying how she'd have to start again, that they'd fit but her palazzo pants might be creased as a result.

She had an A-line dress for dinner and a string of pearls, and a cashmere shawl-collared cardigan, vest and palazzo pants for the breakfast in the orangerie she imagined they'd have. She saw herself loafing elegantly like the models in the White Company catalogue. She would stand next to a piano, waiting for eggs Benedict, sipping on Buck's Fizz, possibly running a long nail along the keys, elegant and thin.

Her restless hands gave away her nerves when they came off the motorway.

'He's a complete big softie, Bunny. You'll love him.'

'Hmm.'

'He's a twat. But in a good way.'

'What's she like?'

'I don't really know her. Seems nice enough; I've only met her the once, at Johnno's wedding.'

'Oh, who did you take to that?'

He drew a breath and considered; no, he couldn't porky pie. 'Natasha.'

'Oh. So they've both met her then.'

'I've known Dozie for twenty years, love! Actually,' he wiggled in his seat, humour and vanity aglow in his eyes, 'he's always been a bit jealous of me. Used to have my cast-offs. So, you'd better watch yourself, Bunny.'

'Ha.'

When he felt for her knee, she moved her leg. Was he missing something? Over the last few nights, since he came back from Wales, she'd begun to go downstairs and sit with a book as soon as she thought he was drifting off. As he grew more contented, she became more discontented, and lately she sat brooding apart from him into the middle of the night.

Astrid was unhappy with his new docility, which was to her way of thinking a slur on her sexuality. Are we to shuffle into old age? she asked herself when she heard his snoring. Her parents had sustained the same lassitude over forty years and they called it a good thing, and people generally thought of it as a good thing, but she didn't. Is this it? she said to him from time to time, poking him in the ribs, but he was too thickly asleep to hear her. She sat downstairs with a book open, picking her nails, biting them, going gently crazy.

When she moaned over breakfast about putting on weight and getting old, Laura asked her a question.

'Will you still love Nick when he's bald and wrinkly and a fat-guts? Even worse than he is now?'

'Yes.'

'Mmm-hmm.' And Laura gave her trademark eye-roll to make her point clear.

Stay in bed and be cheerful, was the advice Nick gave Astrid when he joined her in the bathroom. She'd leant over the sink to brush her teeth and seen the shadow of her long eyelashes in the porcelain and been briefly happy. Then, straightening, she saw in the mirror the bags under her eyes that she knew nothing but a blepharoplasty could mend.

36

Ed Crozier's country pile was something of a surprise. It was a 1970s A-shaped home that narrowly avoided being a semi—by about three feet. It was at the end of a cul-de-sac in a suburban area outside Banbury. It was unbelievably modest for a lawyer of his income.

'Blimey.' Astrid's face fell. Her first thought was for her luggage. She'd not taken the label out of the cashmere cardigan; it would be going back on Monday!

There was a Swingball stuck into the small front lawn, the garage door was perched up above its opening unevenly, and under it was an old Volvo estate with a motto sticker in the back window. They parked up behind it and approached the house via crazy paving leading to a front door that bore a sign with an arrow pointing to the side door. The house number next to it was given in faux-brass adhesive lettering. Astrid felt a surge of nausea.

They passed round the side of the house, along the fence, taking in the smell of creosote and pine and bad bins. The lantern by the side door was missing its black hat and bulb and was full of dead wasps.

When Nick pushed the door, there came from the interior the smell of burning toast and the racket of children firing toy guns and shouting. He and Astrid put bright insincere faces into the door space. Two boys were kneeling on the kitchen floor, the *linoleum-covered* kitchen floor. One was hiding behind a multi-tiered plastic vegetable stand, which scattered dead onion leaves when the kid shook it. When he saw the two of them standing there, he leapt up and screamed 'Dah!' and both boys bolted into the hallway beyond.

'For Christ's sake, turn it down,' was the cry from upstairs.

Charlotte came downstairs in a bathrobe and bare feet. 'Oh hi, there! Good timing! I'm gagging for a drink!'

They handed Charlotte their two bottles of Veuve Clicquot, the bunch of white lilies, the Jo Malone gift box, and the truckle of organic Stilton, which she thanked them for and left on top of the microwave oven and didn't bother with further.

'Slush, we call it,' she said, taking a jug from the fridge along with two highball glasses from the dishwasher and filling them to the brim. She handed them one each. 'It's a secret recipe. So secret I can't remember what the hell's in it.' She poured herself one into a tumbler by the sink, touched their glasses with a 'Cheers', drank off a good gulp, then dragged herself upstairs, holding on to the rail and leaning and calling for Ed.

All they could deduce concerning the 'slush' was that it was red and contained gin.

'Not quite what I expected,' Astrid said to the side of her glass.

'No, nor me,' he replied. 'Bottoms up.'

Ed came down after a few minutes, shaking the rafters with his agitated jog. She had seen the drinking-club photo of him in their shed; his waistcoat struggled to hold him even then, but where he'd been perhaps florid, he was now full-on jowls and paunch. His wife followed. They both wore T-shirts, hers with his chambers' logo on them, his with a large Nike logo on it. He wore cords, she sweatpants.

Assembled as a four, leaning against kitchen counters, they polished off one pitcher of slush, and then another. Their conversation proceeded from one reliable convention to another, from Marmite to reminiscences along the lines of beef tea, junket and blancmange and on to the ha'penny in the Christmas pudding. There was a brief foray into figgy pudding, a detour made into the outrageous cost of dentistry, and on they went through the various agreeability of sedatives, the merits of laughing gas, some shared experience of helium, and thence to the subject where all middle-class middle-aged folk meet each other in drink—their former use of recreational drugs.

When they at last sat down at the pine table and ate the sloppy lasagne with huge glasses of warm white wine, they were half-cut and keen, and the two chaps recalled for Astrid's benefit their meeting.

'He was fiddling with that effing cafetière in the communal kitchen. He had these gold-rimmed dark green coffee cups. Sort of octagonal-shaped. Continental. By God, he'd come prepared. Then he meets a duffer like me, and I wouldn't know one end of "a press", as he called it, from another. And! And! There was an espresso machine the next year when we were in digs on Mill Road. If you please! Bloody thing. It dribbled out cold muck. And of course he smoked Marlboro Reds to impress the girls. Do you remember?' He clasped the side of his old pal's arm. 'Do you remember, matey boy, how we watched that bloody *Withnail and I* over and over again, didn't we? As if we'd ever end up so sodding arty-farty, or anything remotely close to romantic failures! Look at us. Utterly bloody predictable. Me barrister, you solicitor. What a surprise! Hey, remember old Timmy Taylor? "Hopeless Failure" we called him, right from the start, and that's the way it worked out. You had to be a complete moron to mess anything up when you'd come through the system like us. All roads lead to Rome. Yes, old Timmy was the only one who screwed up the bar exams, and only a complete twat fails them.'

He was becoming rather muscle-bound by his expletives, and the use of 'twat' seemed momentarily to cause him to seize up. His eyes bulged.

Charlotte had left the dirty plates on the table and barged from counter to counter in the kitchen. Astrid was astounded that she opened two cans of custard—*Tesco's own label!*—with a tin opener, right in front of them, shamelessly, and then *microwaved* the contents in a jug. Their three boys swooped to claim their portions of crumble and custard. They were clad in pyjama bottoms and hoodies and wellies. She served them each a portion in mismatching bowls.

There was no cheese course.

And when Dozie went for another bottle, Charlotte told him to bring the choccy and he did so, tossing it onto the table, and Charlotte broke off great triangles of Toblerone to offer them. As they sat there gnawing, she told them about some of the stranger goings-on at the residential home where she worked.

Some people become drunk in a moment, as if having a stroke, and of a sudden, Dozie's eyes lost expression and the lower half of his face lost purpose. His mouth carried on without him.

'Ah! The hangovers were legendary. We used to go and drink Bloodies in Browns on a Sunday. Course it was all new to us, the drinking thing. Pretty much everyone took to it, though. Apart from the Chinese. The damage we did! Remember sleeping on the bench in Parker's Piece? Setting off the fire alarm on J staircase? Pinning old Jockstrap to the lawn with croquet hoops? What a life. Crashing the John's ball. This one here put on a wetsuit and swam to it. I walked in the front door with a pair of maracas, claiming to be part of the band. And then there was going to the Joshua Wiley do and just going missing from life for three whole days.'

'If you couldn't pull at the Joshua Wiley, you were Vic the Virgin.'

'That's right.'

Charlotte began telling Astrid what a terrible job she'd had to reform Ed from his high table manners and Cambridge pretensions into a normal human being. God gave men and women two ears for different reasons: men used them for balance, but Astrid was listening to two conversations at once. She was paying due courtesy to Charlotte, but more crucially following what the boys were saying, listening out for women's names.

'Remember Hairy Mary, Nick . . .'

'Who was she?' Astrid intercepted.

'Oh, nobody.'

Dozie carried on, sentimental in the droop of his eyes, fervent in the roll of his rhetoric. 'What became of them anyway? What became of those cunts we so wanted to be like, the ones with their Eton socks and curls, the ones with their famous daddies and saddle-arsed mummies: accountants, bankers, management consultants? Lawyers. Like us. Well, bugger me. Was that really the pinnacle of achievement, or ambition, or desire? With all those advantages they had over us? Oh, I expect they've had a few more gang bangs, more five-star holidays, a sod sight more days at the races, maybe even one or two police cautions.' He stalled. He closed an eye. 'But have they got a cunning plan? Have they got a plan at all, mate? Ask yourself.'

'I don't know. Have they?'

'Have you?'

'How do you mean?'

'Everyone needs an exit strategy, chum.' Ed leant on his elbows, fixing Nick with all he had in the way of focus. 'We've got no mortgage, she and I, we've got no debt. Nothing. We've got savings. And I'm going to retire in five years, and spend time with her over there, that drunk there, my wife, yes her, doing whatever the fuck I like.' He risked a variance of facial expression and hit upon a smile. 'Or whatever *she* likes,' he corrected himself.

'Good for you, mate.'

'Because, because, *she* is my best friend. Her there. She is a man's best friend. Not a dog. No, not a dog. The dog's an animal. The woman's not an animal, is she? She's something else. She's something different. Different to us.'

'Mmm.'

'Quite, quite different.'

'That's true.'

Nick decided it was time for bed; Ed was exceeding himself, and things would only go further downhill. They did.

'And you, mate, you're my best friend. The best friend a man could have. And a man needs a friend. More than he does a dog. But not as much as he needs a woman.'

'No.'

No.

'No, but almost. You know.' Ed rested an arm around his shoulders. 'We go back. You and I. We go back. Loyalty, that's the thing.'

Nick yawned and stretched. Astrid looked over at him as he rose. 'Time for bed,' he said. 'I'm all done in. How about you, honey?'

They left the couple *à table* with a new bottle of wine opened, and took the stairs on all fours like mountain goats, and it was with his face to her backside, halfway up the stairs, that Nick decided to propose.

They made it to the spare room, after popping their heads in two others, and lay on the guest bed fully clothed, hand in hand. 'There's been a lot of talk of marriage of late . . .' he began.

'No, there hasn't.'

'There has. Certainly there has . . .'

'Who's been talking about marriage?'

'Downstairs.'

'Oh.'

'There comes a time in a man's life . . . I mean . . . let me make it clear first that, although I've had a lot to drink, I'm not drunk.' He rolled off the bed and hit the floor.

'Are you all right?'

He reappeared with his chin on the covers. 'That was intentional.'

'Nick, I feel a bit sick. I hope I'm not going to throw up. Do you think the bed will be clean?'

'I doubt it.'

'I hope it's not crispy. The bed.' She rolled to face him. They were nose to nose.

'Well, stay on top of the covers then.'

'I'm all for grubby—you know, good for her, and all that—but not when it comes to beds. She should get her roots done. Don't you think? Did you notice? There's no excuse for grey these days, none at all.'

'Astrid, I'm down here for a reason.'

She offered him her hands to help him up.

'Look, listen to me, just listen a minute. Astrid. I sort of think it might be time for us to get married. And anyway, why not? You know, what with the house and everything, it makes sense, and well, look, anyway, why not? We might as well. It might work out. It does for some people, and we're pretty steady sort of people, aren't we, nowadays? I mean, I'm not up for nightclubs and bars anymore and neither are you. We're past all that. We might as well get old together.'

She rolled away and lay back, head on pillow, feet crossed at the end of the bed, nose in the air.

'Well? Astrid?'

She put her hands behind her head. 'All right.'

'Is that it?'

'You've taken so long about it, Nick. You should have asked me ages ago. It would have been better if you'd done it in the beginning. More romantic. But still, I suppose you finally got there.'

'I was thinking how you, you're my best friend . . . we're best mates, you and I . . . we like the same things to eat, and we like the same programmes, don't we? *Relocation, Relocation,* and all that. We like that stuff and . . .'

'Oh, don't make it any worse, Nick.'

'Hey?'

'What you should say is—Christ, I can't believe I'm having to tell you this. You should ask me, shouldn't you? You should say—God, I can't believe I'm having to spell it out—Will you marry me?'

'OK.'

'Say it then.'

'I *will* marry you, Astrid.'

'You're a fucking idiot, you are. Oh, Nick,' she said, moving her head. 'It really pongs. The pillow.'

'Pongs! The old man used to say that: *Cor, dunnit pong in 'ere?*' he said thickly, lying down beside her, feeling for her hand. 'We'll just sleep on top of the covers. We've got love to keep us warm.'

'Arsehole.'

'Thank you.'

37

I should have turned the mobile off, was Nick's first thought that
Sunday morning.

'Where are you then?'

'What?'

The electric alarm clock with its red numbers hurt his eyes: 6.15.

'Where are you then?'

Astrid rolled towards him. 'Who is it?'

'Ken.'

'Oh God, no.' She rolled back the other way.

'What is it, Dad? Is something wrong?' he whispered.

'I don't feel right.'

'Are you ill?'

There was a pause, then, 'I'm lonely.'

'Can we talk about it in a couple of hours' time?'

'No, we can't.'

'Well, if it's just a matter of feeling a bit down, why do you have to call me at six in the morning?'

'Because I need you.'

He said nothing. Then came the old man's querulous voice, and in the background the cry of the seagull.

'You still there, Nick?'

'Yes.'

'Where are you then?'

'At a friend's in Oxfordshire. With Astrid.'

''Ave you called your mother?'

'I've been busy.'

'Busy? Busy?' Nick held the phone at a distance from his ear, recoiling from the noise. 'Too busy to call your own mother? What's wrong with ya? Time's not on my side, sunshine. Now, you listen to me, big'ead.'

'Don't start—'

'You call her and you call her now! She's your mother!'

'I'm not calling anyone at six in the morning.'

'You call her and you tell her you're coming to see 'er and you tell her we're all coming to see her, that's what I need you to do. Now, you give me your word you'll do it. You've been nothing but a disappointment. Not so much as a bleeding card on my birthd'y. You might think you're something, son, but I tell you what—'

He turned the phone off.

'Go back to sleep,' said Astrid. But he wouldn't sleep again now. This was the way a hangover always got him: guilt.

It was a matter of seconds before he said, 'I've got to give up drinking.' Normally he said it around midday. Astrid made no reply.

'I've got to start getting some exercise.'

Still she said nothing.

'We've got to stop all this.'

'All this what?'

'Fun.'

'Sleep . . .' she said greedily, 'sleep now.'

Maybe getting married will help, he thought, treading down the stairs gingerly.

He found Ed in the kitchen. Wearing a hotel-issue white bathrobe, he turned to Nick with the faintest smile and said, 'Just the man. Make the coffee, pal. Feel rough as guts.' He resumed his dinner seat, pushing the plates away from him. 'Can't bear to look at them now. I said to her, to the missus, Come on, let's do some shots. And she tricked me. I did mine but she passed out. So, who is it that calls you at six in the morning?'

'My father. Sorry.'

'Ah, Ken,' said Ed, ruminatively. 'Poor old Ken.' He picked at the corners of his eyes.

'To be honest, he's been a right thorn in my side lately.'

Nick brought over their coffees. With mugs warming their cold hands, they sat at the table side by side and squeamishly counted the bottles from last night on the table and on the counters.

'Eight. You?'

'Nine. There's a dead one in the sink. Two and a half each.'

'Shit.'

'The girls will have had one and a half each, which means we had three apiece.'

'Just like old times.'

'Hardly. This is high living. It was always spag bol and a two-litre bottle of red.'

'That's right. Mince fried in canned tomatoes. That was as far as our culinary skills stretched. God, I'd love to spark up a fag now, wouldn't you?' Ed sighed. 'How is your old man then?'

'I hadn't seen him in years, then he starts calling me out of the blue just before Christmas. Off his rocker. Silly old shit. First of all they're silent calls, then he starts abusing me, calling me all the names under the sun. Astrid didn't know what to make of it. I'd sort of avoided the subject of my family, you know. I'd just said to her we didn't get on, that was all. Anyway, Dave calls me and says the old man's at death's door, so I give in and agree to have a sort of family reunion, and we go to meet for lunch at Dave's and it turns out he's leaving everything to my brother—which is fine, by the way—but what's more, and this is how nutty he is, Ed, the old sod, he wants to divorce his second missus, and for me to do the paperwork. But then she does a runner, doesn't she? And he's on and on all the bloody time about going to meet his maker. This morning it was all, "I'm lonely, Nick." Honestly, Ed, it's like having a kid.'

'Poor old fucker.'

'And Astrid seems to think I'm a chip off the old block now.'

'Dear old Ken, we used to live high on the hog thanks to him. You'd get that cheque and we'd pop down to PizzaExpress and stuff ourselves with dough balls and Valpolicella and raise a glass to old Ken and his clients at the DHSS.'

'No, we didn't.'

'Many a time.'

'I never got any money from Ken.'

'Don't be an arse! We used to whoop when the envelope came through the door. We used to do a jig.'

'Bollocks.'

'Course we did. Memory's a selective thing, matey, I can tell you. There are plenty of things I'd prefer to forget.'

'I don't remember it at all.'

'He used to send a hundred here, a couple of hundred there, and I used to say, Christ, you're a lucky sod.'

'I used to work at that champagne bar . . .'

'Oh yes, you did, but not for long. You got fired. You were nervous of opening the bottles, you big jessie.'

'I'd forgotten about that. Kettner's, it was called.'

'Well,' said Ed, breaking off a piece of the Toblerone that was left, 'I expect you remember things about me I don't.' He popped it in his mouth.

'Not really.'

'Hmm.' Dozie chewed.

'I wasn't much interested in your goings-on.'

'I didn't have much in the way *of* goings-on.'

'There was the fat bird.'

'Yes.' He nodded, then swallowed the mouthful. 'Your poor, poor, poor old mum,' he went on theatrically. 'Pearl. I knew who she was, of course, because you're the spit.'

'When did you meet her?'

'When she came up.'

'She didn't come up.'

'We were at McKenzie Road, and one day she just turned up, rang the bell and I went to the door and I knew it was her right away. So I called you and you came down; you were having a lie-in, or more like a love-in. . . .' he said, his eyes vacant as a butler's, looking but not seeing. 'We'd had a bit of a night in The Prince, and you got your end away with that girl from the poly, and you came downstairs and I kept saying, Ask your mum in for a cup of tea, Nick. And she said, *Ni-ick?* I remember it well. You gave her short shrift. Said you were tired, it was too early and why hadn't she called, and so on. She'd come all that way, hadn't she? And I did take you to task over it and we fell out, and you moved in with that girl for a while. What was her name?'

'I can't remember any of that! Was I even there?'

'Mandy? I think it was,' said Dozie, breaking off another lump. 'Want a piece?'

Nick shook his head. 'Jesus Christ.'

'You wanted so much to be the angry young man.'

They sat there in the morning light, their feet sticking to the lino, surrounded by dirty dishes and empty bottles, the pine table stained, place mats encrusted, the nauseating sweet vinegar of wine in their mouths no matter the coffee they sipped.

'You had your good points too. You were quite fun on occasion. Well, if you were shit-faced you could be rather amusing. You were ambitious of course, what I'd call a real eighties man, though of course the eighties had just ended. Callow youth. That's the phrase.'

'Cheers.' He peeled one sole, then the other, from the floor and felt for the crumbs, which he rubbed off. 'So, I let my mother stand at the door after she'd been a couple of hours on the train.'

'It must have been more like four, what with changing stations in London. I can see her now. She was a country mouse, quivering on the doorstep. And all that way she'd have been thinking she'd soon be in the warm embrace of her favourite son.'

'All right! No need to lay it on. I was only eighteen.'

'Twenty.'

'Well, there must have been a good reason.'

'Yes. That girl, Mandy, she was upstairs. You were giving her one. That was it. Embarrassing, the utterances from that room of a Friday night. You know they don't mean it when they go on like that.'

'What made her come anyway?'

'Who? Your mother? To see you.' He raised his eyebrows and took a swig from his mug. 'I'd imagine.'

'Well, trust her not to ring in advance or write or anything.'

'Yes. That was really shit of her. Really deplorable,' said Ed, popping a finger into his back teeth. 'Still, she must have learnt her lesson because she didn't come again. More coffee?' He got up and shuffled over to the kettle. 'Sometimes, mate, sometimes, well, take old Tim Taylor—he's happily married with four super kids—sometimes failure, as they say, can be as good for one as success.' He measured out two spoons of coffee into their mugs. 'In any case, the thing is to take from this hoo-hah with your dad what you can or what you need. I mean, you know what you *want*, Nick, more than anyone else I've ever known, you've always had the next thing in your sights and got it.' He doused first one, then the other, with boiling water, then slapped the spoon against the sides of the mug. 'But you've never known what you need.'

'I just asked Astrid to marry me.'

Ed sat down so heavily on the bench that it lifted at Nick's end. 'No!'

'Yes.'

With his mouth open, Ed undid the top of the port bottle and poured an amount into each of last night's smeared tumblers. 'Bugger me,' he said. 'Are you sure?'

'Yes.' Nick found that he could drink it quite easily. And, accepting another glass, said to Ed, 'Seriously, mate, I've changed. Since I met Astrid, since I moved back home . . .' It was the hangover; it made everything feel like it mattered. 'I sort of think maybe it's time to pick up the pieces with my family.'

'That's good, mate. Well, you know, as two quite obvious heterosexuals, I don't think an arm around the shoulders could be misconstrued.' He clasped Nick and shook him. 'Had my doubts about you of course in that department, but this proposal thing has cleared them up. It was that George Michael rough-shaven look you sported, that's what made us wonder. And all the exercise. And that fad diet you went on.'

'What fad diet?'

'Few years back.'

'I stopped drinking for a couple of weeks one January.'

'That's the one.'

38

Laura sat in the back of the car on the way home from the station, taking it in, their news. She seemed pensive. After a while she said, 'Is there a drug that makes you see things in different colours and makes you happy?'

He took the day off on Monday to go down to Hastings. He got up at six and sat on the toilet. It was the best seat in the house, affording views across the valley. The oak tree had sprouted ginger leaves and in this secret early hour cast a golden aura. Horses hung their heads in the long wet grass. A red post van crept down the far hill, turning off its lights halfway down, acknowledging the day just come. It occurred to him that it might be one of the first days of summer.

He wanted to share it with her. He made tea then coffee in an attempt to stall her, but Astrid was not to be delayed. She was going to work.

She applied a number of different creams in a regimented order, make-up followed, hair somewhere in between, and she begrudged his presence, moaning as he passed behind her, trying to get sight of what she was about.

She was humourless about these procedures, terrified he'd see her back-of-thigh cellulite in a bad light—or, worse, a good light—or of being caught confounded by a thong and having to go at it two or three times, having bunting left and bunting right and something like parcel string up the middle. The bathroom door with its scraping drawl was a noise that put fear in her and, sure enough, she'd hear it the minute she began to daub fake tan on her lower legs and was arsehole to the air.

'Will you just sod off, please!' she screamed. There was no audience participation when it came to beauty, everyone knew that, but Nick seemed intent on getting onstage.

Downstairs, Nick and Roy got in each other's way, waiting for the bride-to-be—for Astrid emerged wedding-day-ready daily, beauty being her business—and she came down the stairs radiant of smile, magnanimous in her evasions, thin-skinned and irritable.

'Can he not spend a minute outside, that mutt?' she said, clasping her pale skirt.

And with his almost human understanding, Roy sheathed his tongue, turned round and pushed the conservatory door with his head to let himself out. And then he'd invariably turn round again in that room, poke at the door with his head once more and reappear with tongue out and a great grin as if they'd not recognize him as Roy, the brown and white dog.

The pair bothered her on her way out, Roy with his spittle

loose and free and Nick with the same line of questioning he'd pursued all the way home from the Croziers'.

'Blood means something, Astrid. Doesn't it?' he said.

Grumpy because of the bags under her eyes that the eye cream was no use for, she had imperfections top of her mind only and was dwelling on the vision of that great clod Katie, dusting off her shoes with the hair-colour wheel, and of Sally, the new girl with the perma-cold hands as idle as her brain.

'Doesn't it, Astrid? I have to do it, don't I? I have to make it right again. I can do that. It's within my power.'

They'd been through it on the M40. She'd been enjoying her own train of thought: Oyster silk? Champagne silk? Décolletage? Low back? Online or Selfridges? Or why not just go the whole hog! White? But he'd kept interrupting, harping on, just like his father in the car when they went to Dave's for lunch.

And there they were now on the threshold of the conservatory with him grabbing at her and importuning her. So she agreed thoroughly, conclusively, and left him there, mulling it over in his socks and underpants.

By the end of the lane, in her mind she was already in Rye and taking big Katie aside and giving her a speech. You either got beauty or you didn't. It was an illusion that used a smidgen of science, a dollop of magic and a shedload of willpower. And money. Katie, have you ever been hungry? For days. Katie, have you ever been bothered by the ridges on your nails? Katie, have you ever thought—surgery? Katie, beauty is not brassy; it's steely.

Big Katie was a big mess. Nice girl, bad skin.

Then she was thinking of Sally with her flawless skin and her gormless gob. No matter what the punter said, with Sally the reply was a limp '*Brill-i-anne*'. No 't'. She had a rota of two customer-friendly questions: 'Is that pressure OK for you?' or, 'Been on holiday this year?' And she delivered these in a sing-song nasal voice thick with insincerity. But she was sincere. Sally was the most boring girl Astrid had ever met. She was the perfect cipher, the sort of girl women wanted sloughing their hard skin.

As Astrid sped past the beautiful small doll's houses of Beckley, amid the chestnut trees with their candelabra alight, she thought how they'd woken that morning in each other's arms and it came to her, out of nowhere it seemed, Maybe, just maybe, he loves me, as he says he does, regardless of 'beauty'.

She'd tried so hard for so long to be perfect. Just like Linda, only what her mother took as a standard for home furnishings, Astrid applied to her body. Nothing can be perfect; only misery.

She would have to call her parents and tell them their news. She knew how they'd respond. Her mother would be tight-lipped and ask her if she was sure and she'd add '*this time*' with her customary loading.

How do you know he loves you? Astrid guessed her mother might well ask her. One day she'd ask Laura the same thing.

Pulling into the car park with that thought uppermost, she looked in the driving mirror and saw she looked clean, straight and clear-headed, and the lovely silver car responded with all of its power, just as she wanted it to, and just for a moment, it came to her that she was the woman she always wanted to be. The woman she'd imagined she'd be when she was a kid. She'd achieved what she set out to do. She'd done it all.

She got out of the car and swung her bag over her shoulder, clicked the key button.

Because he can't leave me alone. I can't be five minutes alone when he's at home. He hovers at doors or comes right in and I have to jettison the razor, legs half-shaved. He can't leave me alone. He wants my secrets. He wants all of me; that's how I know. He's lost without me. He needs me.

And, walking into the spa, she left the door open and let in Nick and Laura and Roy and their home and she dumped her bag and coat on reception, something scruffy she'd never done before. Then she went back out and up to Jempson's café and bought thirty doughnuts, and she came back and made a full jug of coffee. She assembled them, all the staff, notwithstanding the ladies with cricks in their necks waiting to have shampoo washed out, notwithstanding the poor woman on her knees with her eyes screwed shut, holding the paper knickers up her crack in the waxing room, ready for part two of the Brazilian.

She told them she was getting married.

'Aw. Brillianne,' said Sally.

And the others were more fulsome than truth could possibly allow for, being indentured to her really, and they set to billing and cooing and pandering to her with talk of hair extensions for the big day.

She wanted to tell them, There's more to life than beauty. But they were young, and there was a time for everything. For now all she said was, Help yourselves.

Downstairs in the plasterboard-partitioned treatment rooms, on towel-clad gurneys, women lay pending beauty. Immobile, cotton pads on eyelids with lashes tinting, fingers splayed with varnish drying, face masks congealing, they lay still as still, breathing slow.

39

They were not the only ones eating doughnuts that morning; Nick and his old man sat down at a picnic table in the funfair in the Old Town, with a bag of six. Roy was soon done with the sea. He tore down the pebbles, took a shit by the sign forbidding it, then raced full tilt at the sea. When it chased him back, he flew back up the beach, sought Nick's legs and stayed there, panting.

They were sitting opposite the bumper cars.

'Daft little sod, innie?' said Ken fondly, patting the dog's head.

Inscrutable, with the hot dough occupying their mouths and their thoughts to themselves, the three of them—Ken, Nick and Roy—looked into various distances, considering their prospects: marriage, death and seagulls.

The Polish woman on the token-sales kiosk stared out of her booth with equal melancholy. The rides played old glory tunes, and the Polish boy on the bumper cars helped himself to a slow turn, standing on the back holding the pole, leaning with a love-lorn look on his face. Three children were hoisted skywards on the ride nearby and given a bone-shaking a couple of metres into the air to loosen any change or sweets from pockets, and when their heads were well banged against the vinyl, they were released in jolts back to the ground. The blonde who pressed the button of the ride wore an expression of great disappointment.

They washed down the doughnuts with weak coffee. Nick caught Ken giving a spiteful look to the man who took a seat beside them. The chap sat a toddler girl upon the picnic table; he could not stop himself stroking her head, over and over again, as he jollied her along with endearments.

'Nervous wreck, innie?' said Ken, his lips pursed.

Nick cracked a grin and Roy followed suit.

Ken sipped his coffee. 'P'raps I oughta have been more like that old-timer,' he said, wiping his chin and gesturing with his thumb at the sixty-year-old, who was exclaiming and chortling now that the girl rummaged through his wallet.

'How do you mean?'

'Well . . .' he said in his habitually inconclusive way, asking you to join the dots.

'Spent more time at funfairs?'

'In a way. In a manner of speaking. I didn't have much to do with Dave's nippers and that was my fault. They're nice kids, you know, but they don't *know* me. And I don't suppose you'll ever get round to having kids. So that's it. I could have been down 'ere, you know, like that old geezer. I mean, look at him. But he still manages to get himself down here to give the kid a good time.' The child started crying and Ken flinched. 'Coo dear! Noise! Come on, let's walk down the fish 'uts.'

He steadied himself with a hand on Nick's near shoulder. Nick went slowly, feeling the wobble of his father's body through the shaking hand.

The dream he'd had that morning surfaced as they walked. It had happened so close to his waking state, it seemed real. In it he'd been gagging, bent double, aware of something in his throat, a thick phlegm he couldn't shift, choking him, and he'd been in their conservatory, grasping at furniture, his vision upside down. It had come to him: My God, I can't die like this, not like this. He'd wanted help. But he couldn't get anyone's attention. He couldn't call out. And yet the word he wanted to pronounce, the word that stuck in his gullet, that he was trying with all his might to force through the phlegm was: '*Mum.*'

He looked down at the winkle-picker shoes his old man wore, and smiled to think this was the man his mother fell in love with.

'Tell me again what your mother said, will ya?'

'She asked us all over for tea, next Sunday. All of us. Dave and Marina and the kids, me and Astrid and Laura—I told her I was living with someone—and she said, Tell David to bring Ken.'

'So, she only wanted me on me own, like, then. She didn't ask after June.'

'She seemed to know you were on your own.'

'She must of asked Dave,' he said. He nodded, grim as a secret agent, hands in mac, stooping, examining his shoes. 'Mustn't she?'

'I don't know.'

———

Nick had had great difficulty bringing himself to speak when she answered, and the first word was hardest of all.

'Mum?'

'Who is it?' she'd said harshly.

'Mum. It's me, Nick.'

There had been a silence, like a pit.

'How are you getting on?' he'd gone on, heart sinking.

There was a silence, then after a moment she said, 'Hello, darling.'

And he could have wept to hear her voice soften that way. *'Hello, darling.'* A capsizing. After all the years. *'Hello, darling.'* He fell right back into his childhood. No one had ever said that word 'darling' the way she did. She didn't use it casually the way other women did; she reserved it for him. Goodnight, darling, she used to say when she put him to sleep with a kiss.

He let himself into his father's house that morning. The door was ajar and he'd had to bite off his own grin at the eavesdropped sound of his father, singing, 'I believe in angels . . .'

His father was in the living room with cardboard boxes, packing up June's belongings to send to her. His old man didn't say hello when Nick came in, he merely continued a conversation he must have started some other time.

'A waste of the years, when I look at all of this.' He showed Nick a Whimsie piece, a King Charles Cavalier. 'What a load of tosh.' He proffered the box; in it were handfuls of Wade Whimsies. 'That's not even counting the bleeding toby jugs.' He gestured to the other boxes stacked by the window. 'Or the shepherdesses. Your mother would never have given this lot 'ouse room.'

He was wearing pyjama bottoms and a vest. He stood in the middle of the room, in bare feet, and faced his son. He slapped his chest with his hand, hard. On his face was excruciation.

'It 'urts, Nick. It 'urts 'ere.' And Ken's face, usually tight with spite, collapsed and his mouth seemed to burst and gape with pain. Nick put his arms around him and his father wept.

Then they finished the packing; more or less everything in the house, he said, belonged to June and he could not help exclaiming over every item, sometimes in high spirits, sometimes angrily. 'A toothpaste squeezer! Coo dear, what next? And you should see under the bed, what I found there. She was a dark 'orse, I can tell you.'

Nick recalled Natasha finding his porn magazines under the bed when packing for his departure.

'Waders! A pair of brand-new waders! I told her not to get 'em!'

With Nick about to tape up the last box, Ken suddenly cried out for him to stop. He took off into the kitchen and came back with a frozen pizza. 'Look at it, son. Meatfeast. She'll be glad of that.'

And so they put that on top and closed the box, with Ken getting his fingers in the way of the tape and remonstrating with Nick for being 'cack-'anded.'

They bought a tub of jellied eels at the stand next to Rock-a-Nore and stood leaning with their backs against the counter, looking over at the fishermen's huts, with Nick dropping the occasional chunk for Roy's delectation.

'Funny,' said Ken.

'What is?'

'How one day you can see everything clear and the day before you don't.'

'Yes.'

'That June. She didn't have what you call breeding. Not to my mind. She was common as muck. She was very money-minded. In a greedy sort o' way.'

'Was she?'

'Oh yes. Look at all that stuff! A hoarder. Told me they was investments. My arse. She can have the lot. And I shall send her her 'alf the money too, by the way. I'll follow your advice on that. Just to be fair and square and done with it. To wash my 'ands of it all.'

'Well, that should be acceptable to her. That's fair, Dad.'

'Course I got a lot more than that she don't know about,' he whispered, nudging Nick and causing him to drop another chunk of eel for Roy's panicked gobbling.

'Never marry a foreigner! You can't understand each other proper. Oh, it seems fancy at first. But it don't work. Your mother, she weren't anything but 'erself. Didn't give a shit what people thought of her. And the best thing about her was—'

'Her integrity?'

'Well, yes, son, you're right. I grant you that and that's a nice word for it. But what I was going to say was she was tight-fisted, and I like that in a woman. She didn't like to spend money; she used her loaf more.' He pointed to his temple, then startled and stiffened. 'Blimey!' Nick followed his eyes. He was looking at a couple peering into the windows of a fish seller opposite. 'Now, there's a woman! That's my Audrey, that is! Audrey Bury. Beautiful gel. A proper angel.'

Nick looked at the near-obese middle-aged woman holding hands with a grossly overweight middle-aged man.

'She's a sweetheart. That woman there, she done something for me no one else could ever do, Nick. She got me to face reality. Do you know what I mean?'

'Did she?' Nick tipped the polystyrene tub and dropped the remaining jellied eels down to Roy.

'She runs the funeral parlour what did your Auntie Pat's do. She got me to face things I never could of done before. And she taught me something about 'ow *strong* a good woman is.' He winced so heavily as he said this, it was as if he were watching a woman pulling a lorry along with a strap between her teeth before them. '*Strong*. I spent a lot of time with her.'

'Did you?'

'Listen, *if* anyfing, well, what I mean to say is *when* it 'appens, you know, when I get my call-up papers, I want you to make sure it's 'er who's called, right away. No one else. Just 'er. First thing you do. Before the doc and that. I told Dave the same thing.'

'OK.'

'You listen to your old man and do one thing right by him.'

'All right. So, what reality did she introduce you to, Dad?'

The couple strolled off, hand in hand, down the pebble alley and onto the beach, where they disappeared behind boats and nets.

'Well . . .' he said, evasively. Roy jumped up and took the last chunk of jellied eel from Ken's cocktail stick. 'The little perisher.' He put the tub back onto the counter. 'Among other things,' his father looked uneasy, 'among other things, she made me realize, son, that I'm too old to be of any real use to a woman. Know what I mean?'

Nick grinned.

'Never mind laughing, you'll be in my shoes one day.' He pulled on his lapels. He smiled down at the dog, who sat looking up at them in adoration. 'Nice little boy, innie? Nice little thing.'

40

On the news the top story is that the World Health Organization has raised the pandemic warning to level five. This is what Audrey has prepared for, what Audrey has warned others about, and what her business is singularly ready to meet. And yet Audrey's not going into work today, neither did she go in yesterday.

'Funny,' Audrey says to him. It's all come at the same time: love and disaster, Roger and a pandemic. She doesn't dare move.

They spent the afternoon, yesterday, in bed in a guesthouse. This is something they could never have expected and so they lay in hiding. Outside, at the window, the weather changed for the worse and the seagulls, like joyriders on the coming storm, wheeled and moaned and whooped and jeered. And the two of them lay together and watched the gulls mix the paint of sky and cloud with their claws.

Today they are holidaying in their hometown. The noise of it is new to them, it crawls up their ankles and makes them tread with a tingle: the crunching of the pebbles on the beach, the chiming of the fruit machines, the chit-chat at coffee tables, the murmur of tipsy pensioners singing at a pub table. Down to the beach for lunch they go and in their carrier bags they have tins of beer and cockles and mackerel and bread. He carries in one hand a large portion of chips. They sit on stones and watch the frothy palaver of the sea skittering on shingle. Roger begins by throwing chips one at a time up into the sky, and then he chucks the lot sky-high and the seagulls scream in from all quarters of the earth and pluck the chips from thin air so that in seconds only an empty bag settles on the beach.

'Don't the gulls look like old men, all puffed up, ready to give someone a telling off?' Roger says. 'Look like your friend Ken.'

'You've come on all talkative.'

He smiles ruefully. They kiss, and the gulls turn the world again with their claws, pedalling the globe, faster, faster, and the wind comes up with the night, bringing more bad news, more deaths.

Filling in for them at work, Andy is more than obliging, ready to take up the call, ready for Christ's victory, ready to be the last man standing, shepherding them through the valley of the shadow of death to the green and pleasant land, while the two undertakers do their loving.

That night she startles and finds him. 'Roger, tell me I'm not dead.'

'You're not dead.'

A man of few words, he has just enough to save her.

41

Dave creeps upstairs with the tray, his broad feet taking the strain as he goes up the groaning stairs. He goes carefully, mouth cracked. He pauses midway to let the trembling knife settle on the plate. On his tray is a midnight feast of breakfast sundries. They are either way ahead of the game or way behind it, he thinks to himself as he pads along the hallway, passing by the children's rooms soft of foot.

'Marmite for me, marmalade for Marina,' he sings in a Louis Armstrong voice, kicking the door open with his toes. He sets the tray down on the bench at the end of the bed. His dressing gown opens and his tackle sways free. He completes his burlesque with a hip thrust, sending his sack south circular, and she tells him to put it away. But he doesn't, not until he gets a laugh from her.

Slipping in bed with their plates, he takes his slice and she takes hers and they savour them in quiet for a few minutes until the plates bear nothing but crumbs and he takes hers from her and puts both on the night table next to him. Marmalade meets Marmite when they kiss. 'I love you,' he says and Marina shifts a little bit beside him. It is her sign and he knows it well. He rolls onto his side, kisses her again and then moves on top of her. She can see stubble, the thinnest of horizons on the side of his face, and she places her hands on each of his shoulder blades. This is not new. They have been here a thousand times before. It doesn't need to be new.

Afterwards, holding hands, they float on a raft into dreams of a velvet quality, action-packed, of derring-do and yet familiar too. Their eyelids flicker. He lies on his side and she lies behind him, nose to his back, then she turns over onto her other side and he turns and lies behind her, nose to her back, and so they follow each other on the path of the moon.

They grew up in the same village until they were eight and then his family moved away. Both of their mothers picked fruit in the fields—blackcurrants, strawberries, raspberries, apples. When they first met it might have been at school, but she likes to think it was when she was sitting on her big frilly bum in her pram and the boy pushed a strawberry into her mouth. Or it might have been that they walked the length of a strawberry field on a warm day in June or July with red pulp, dirt and straw on their knees from where they'd knelt to take the smallest tastiest fruit from under the leaves.

Then they were greedy and dirty and happy and their mothers weren't far away, busty and coarse, laying into each other roundly and raucously, and enjoying most of all slandering and deriding

their men. Suddenly a mum would stand upright and call out a
name and they'd both run back, hell for leather.

Marina's mother, Lynn, was in a nursing home. She went to
see her the week before, and spent an hour with her, the old girl
in her armchair from home, sitting in the sunny part of the room,
in wool hat and anorak, looking at the light and shadow on the
wall. From her old mother's bifocals came a glinting light, draw-
ing from the open window to give a message in semaphore: I am
nearly gone, goodbye, goodbye, farewell. . . .

Marina wakes and sleeps and wakes, turns and finds sleep at
last in a small space on the right of the pillow, just an inch square,
and she passes through the gap in the hedge into the fields again
and finds Davie already there, filthy. No one else is there, not even
their children exist in that place. They spend the rest of the night
there together.

Matt hates waiting for them to rise. He yearns. He yearns particularly on Sunday mornings and finds no solace in television
or computer games. He wanders the house disconsolately, sitting
in the cold kitchen looking at the mess his dad left behind the
night before: breadboard sticky, crumbs underfoot, jars unlidded.
He kicks the kitchen table and scowls at the clock, and goes back
upstairs to fire up his computer and gets to work on his project for
his granddad. 'Project Death', as he likes to call it, and he checks
his MySpace messages from people all over the world, but mostly
from the USA.

It seems there is a form of arsenic that is easy to take and can
be purchased online, so he prints out the information. And it's as

the printer whirrs at seven in the morning, shuddering and clattering, that his father comes in, disgruntled, his eyes barely open, and he puts a hand on Matt's chair and leans forward to squint at the computer screen. Matt can't shut it down in time.

'*DIY Death*? You what, Matt?'

So Matt has to tell him how Ken asked him to help him out of the world.

'You what?' says Dave again, coming to. And Matt's unsure whether his father is slow, or whether he's tired, or whether he's in disbelief, so the only thing he can do is put it simply.

'He wants to die.'

'You what?'

'He doesn't want to go into a home.'

'I tell you what, M-M-Matt, this is absolutely beyond belief, isn't it? M-m-my old man's having my son buy him poison, lethal poison, online on the flaming Internet? What do you think you're doing, killing your grandfather?'

Marina comes in. 'What's going on in here?'

'He,' says Dave, pointing at the son behind the fringe, 'is only helping his grandfather top 'imself.'

The mother looks her son in the eyes as if to absorb the entire story in one look, so as to go ahead and protect him from his father's anger; she steps between them. 'It's just the Internet, Dave.'

'I could . . . I could . . . I mean . . . you couldn't . . .'

'Calm down. It's just kids. Just a game. Isn't it, Matt? They *all* do this sort of thing these days, Dave,' she says with warm condescension. 'It's just . . . role play,' she says, finding a term she's heard on the television. 'It's because of the Internet. They all do it. They all look up these things. Kids *do*.'

'What—killing your grandfather?'

'He asked me to.'

'Things are going to change round here. The-the-that thing, that computer, right, that's finished, done with, gone! And we're going to get your hair cut!'

'Oh fine. Sure! What's that going to do? God, Dad, you're so illogical.'

'Turn that thing off. Right now!'

'It's not *evil*.'

'That thing is bringing you up to be some sort of weirdo, some sort of . . . I don't know. He sounds American, don' 'e, Marina? I said to you, he sounds American. We need to get him a part-time job delivering the papers, or something. On a bicycle. So he can see a bit of the real world.'

Matt closes his eyes: Zen, think Zen. His MySpace name is 'Zendudehastings'. The first part of it is massively hard to live up to at times.

'OK. Let me explain it to you both. Granddad is scared of going into a home. He's seen what you did to Granny Lynn and he's worried about it. I don't blame him. He'd rather die than go in one of those places.'

'Granny Lynn is off her rocker!'

'Well, you say the same about him.'

'Only as a joke! Fuck me, this is like having some sort of double agent living in your own home.'

'I believe in individual liberties,' he stammers, borrowing something from school.

'Oh shit me, Marina. Do you hear this? It's Che Flaming Guevara now!'

'Look. Someone's got to stand up for him, for his human rights.' Matt catches sight of his father's expression, and his mother stepping back, and he folds. 'I was going to tell you about it at some point. I was just doing the research.'

'See-ee,' says Marina quickly, using the 'e's in the word to sound 'peace'. 'He was going to tell us about it!'

It's clear that Che has left the room. Matt's knees collide as he uses the chair's pedestal, swaying left and right. 'I said to him, They'll find you somewhere nice. Mum and Dad will.' He lifts his long-lashed eyes to them and throws his fringe back, and Marina's heart lurches at the sight of his beautiful freckled face and perfect nose; its innocence decries the would-be goth and death-monger. 'And we looked some up but, Dad, honestly they're really the pits . . .' He checks the American inflection. 'They're *shitholes*, Dad. But even if they weren't, it's not what he wants and why should he have to go into one? He doesn't want to die in a home or hospital; he just wants to go naturally. He wants to die his way. What's wrong with that? Is it so much to ask?'

'No, Matt,' Marina moves forward to touch him. 'No, of course it's not but, love, you shouldn't be looking up lethal poison on the Internet. Anyway. Anyway.' She turns to flash fierce eyes at Dave. 'It's Ken who's to blame, not Matt. It's like what they call grooming. He shouldn't have asked a *child* to do this.'

'He's daft in the head. Matt's not.'

'See! See! That's what I mean!'

Having stood with a hand up at his head to shield her from his vision, Dave drops his hands and catches sight of Marina's look now, and grunts. 'I don't mean he should be locked up or done away with, do I? He's just old, Matt. And nutty. Gordon Bennett.'

'Well. Is he even ill? Is Ken dying?' Marina asks him sharply.

'I don't know, I don't know. Could be. It makes sense of a lot of stuff.' Dave turns round and presents his back to them, both hands on his head. They see his back rise and fall. When he turns back, he's thin-lipped. 'All right, Matt. All right, son. Leave it with me.'

We're too soft on that boy, he thinks as he goes off to the shower. But he doesn't know what to do about it. What Matt's done, it's just the kind of thing his brother would do, all high ideals and no common sense.

Over lunch, he snuck a look at his son and when his son snuck a look back, Dave gave him a wan smile of recognition and of love.

Dave couldn't bear to have bad feeling in the air. It hurt him to punish his kids. It ate him up.

He offered Matt his crackling. He winked at Emily and told Marina she looked nice.

'That a new top, love?'

'No, it's old as the hills.'

'So, Matt mate, maybe we could get tickets to go and see your, um, Chemical Romance people,' he said, catching the drop off the spout of the gravy jug and making sure Marina saw him do it. 'Just in time. Don't wanna spoil the cloth.'

The best thing about Dave, as they all knew, was that he had not much in the way of pride. He didn't want to be alone and he never would be.

42

'Why is she crying?'

On the Friday night, Laura cried from eight thirty to nine thirty. She couldn't explain it, she said, she didn't know why. 'It's just all so sad.'

The girl sat on her legs on the sofa in her yellow fluffy dressing gown; she looked like a canary with ruffled feathers.

Nick was standing by with eyebrows to attention. He took Astrid aside when she went to make tea. 'Is it the, um, the—er, time of the month?'

Astrid gave him a scathing look.

Ah, but it smelt like a good home! They'd had Mrs Watson's cracked pepper sausages and mash for supper with onion gravy. He'd stopped in at the butcher's on the way home: E. F. Watson and Sons. It was like going back in time, when you were your trade, when your living was your family's and your family was your living. One went in through the stable door, lifting the latch and teasing apart the steel strings, and entered into 1935—a clean humble place where everybody was addressed by their surname. Mrs Watson sat in there at the desk, feet splayed, hip on the mend, cushion in the small of her back, back to the window, preferring for a view the sight of her boys at work. Her vision of happiness was seeing fifty-year-old boys with meat cleavers hammering offal on wooden blocks, and each one coming with a smile to the counter, proud of the cut, and then the joke-fighting and shoving for a turn at the scales. And just behind them was the cold room with the biggest handle in the world, and beyond that was the back door, invariably open onto an English garden where Mr Watson's ghost tended to the marigold borders.

'Three pounds seventy-three, please, Mrs Watson!' called out one son. And Nick left a few pence for the Lifeboats box and earned Mrs Watson's warm approval.

He daydreamed on the way home, about him and Astrid having a butcher's shop together. But things were not happy when he got in. If boys gained something at puberty, then it seemed that girls lost something. Laura was gloomy and distant. She went off after supper and Astrid went after her. They were like the hands on a clock, he thought, one always after the other. Sometimes he was jealous when he saw how they clove to each other, on the sofa or in bed. They could lie quietly, thought in thought; they wore each other at times.

He felt lonely. Roy was determined to sleep; even the rapport of the cracked pepper and pig fat, sent up from Nick's stomach and out via the bellows of his cheeks, failed to stir the dog, who was head in paws, frowning.

Astrid wasn't reaching Laura that evening.

'You're a hard person,' she accused her mother. 'You were hard on my dad. I know you were!' And when Astrid disputed it, Laura said in the most piteous voice, 'See! You're cross with *me* now!'

The noise of this conflict caused Roy to prick up his ears. Nick slurped his wine shamefacedly and the dog went for a second fly-by licking of his bowl.

Glass empty, bowl clean, the man and dog exchanged looks, regretful of their consolations with all this noise and pain.

'I'm *not* bloody cross, Laura!'

The dog panted with hopeful idiocy. In mimicry, Nick put his own tongue out. The dog put his tongue away and stood back as if in review of his opinion of the man.

Nick topped up his glass.

Astrid came downstairs, her face thunderous. She went straight to the computer. Ten minutes later, she had all she needed and by way of evidence showed Nick the email Danny had sent Laura. He put his reading glasses on slowly since his wineglass was balancing on his tummy.

'Oh, don't bother then,' she said.

'Now, just a minute, Astrid, now don't get pissy with me—'

She ripped the page away from him.

The dog shrank back in retreat and Nick heard the conservatory door shutting softly in his wake.

'Astrid. Let me read it, please, and calm down.'

She sat, perching again, biting her fingernails while he reviewed it. When he paused to take another sip of his wine, she bristled and was about to remove the paper from him again until he stopped her.

'Well,' he said, in conclusion, setting it aside.

'That's it! She's not going to him anymore!'

'Astrid.'

'Did you *read* it?'

'Yes. I must say that in circumstances where—'

'Oh, Nick! Don't give me the solicitor bollocks, just be bloody
Ken, will you?'

He twitched his nose, took another sip, put the wineglass down,
took a moment before swallowing. 'Well,' he said, in a different
way, allowing time for ill will to develop, as Ken might, 'he's an
arsehole, isn't he?'

'Thank you! What are we going to do about it all?'

'I'm going to go and see him.'

'What are you going to say?'

'I'll tell him to lay off all of this.' He read out the offending
sentences. ' "The doctor says that I'm very ill, Laura. This is just
between us, and don't tell Mummy as she won't understand. She's
a very hard person. It means the world to me to see you, Laura.
Life is pretty empty without you. Remember our song, I teach it
to all the birds that pass my window. . . ." ' He changed voice here.
'Talk about overegging the pudding! How did you get tangled up
with this joker anyway? "Tell Laura I love her . . ." ' he warbled
with great pathos.

'Don't! She'll hear you. I don't want her to know about this.
She's supposed to have a "private correspondence", as she puts it.'
Astrid was vibrating with anger. Such passion, so close to the surface; she and Danny were now both in love with the same person,
he thought. They'd gone from lovers to competitors.

'Maybe she's too young for anything private, Bunny,' he said, folding his glasses. 'She's not as grown-up as you think. This is a big burden to carry. I mean, for God's sake let the kid have a life. . . . "Tell Laura I nee-eed her." He's making some sort of girlfriend out of her, isn't he? If only people *would not* make lovers out of their kids. Dear me. Or if they love them, can't they do it a bit quietly, a bit privately, and keep it under their hats, so to speak? That's how it used to be. A bit more indifference would go a long way.'

There came from upstairs an elongated sob.

'I'll go,' he said.

'Don't say anything!' she hissed.

Nick got up and went out of the room and, passing by him, gave the dog a look, raising his eyebrows at him. The dog returned a bloodshot look as it put its nose up its tail. 'Coward,' said Nick.

He went upstairs to find Laura poring over a picture book of fairy tales her father had given her, wiping the tears from her chin with the back of her nightie sleeve.

'It's a sad story, this one, Nick, isn't it? "The Little Match Girl".'

'Yes, baby, but why do you keep reading it then?'

'I don't know.'

'Does it help in some way?'

'Yes.'

'I see. Does it help you feel sad, and you want to feel sad— or you feel you ought to?' He was a little pie-eyed for this stuff, admittedly, but catching a glimpse of himself in the mirror, he thought he looked rather good.

'Yes.'

'Hmmm.' He forgot where he was going, thrown off course by the effects of the third glass of wine and catching sight of the photo-booth pictures of Laura's mother and father canoodling and, in the last one, Astrid with her tongue out.

Laura followed his eyes. 'Sorry, Nick,' she said.

'Oh no, no,' he said in his solicitor's voice, 'don't be. Don't be.'

She put a small hand on his. 'You're always a bit left out, aren't you?'

'Now, don't start worrying about me! I'm a big boy!' He sat tall, wobbling. 'Look, baby, if you're feeling sad about your daddy—'

'I am!' she said with vehemence, pressing his hand.

'Then why don't I take you to see him tomorrow?'

'It's not his weekend!'

'It doesn't matter, this once. Mummy won't mind.'

'She'll be angry.'

'No, she won't. Look, you sleep tight, sweetie-pie, and I'll arrange it all and drive you up there tomorrow morning.'

'OK then.'

She slipped down into her covers and gave him a grateful look. He put the covers close around her chin.

'All right, petal. Now, sleep tight. And by the way, that Match Girl thing, it's just a story some twisted horrible stepfather invented to make his stepdaughter be a good girl.'

'Oh,' she said, and gave him a look that was right out of her mother's collection. 'Night, Nick. Don't get too drunk.'

43

Closeted in the bathroom before bed, he found himself talking to the mirror, just to speak with another man. 'It really is like two steps forward, three steps back, this whole business, of relationships.'

'These women are 'ard work, mate,' he heard his father say. 'And can't they talk!'

When he looked in the mirror, in the keen light, he stood a moment, looking at the nose they shared, he and his father.

And then he remembered a very strange thing, how one Christmas Eve, just before the old man left home, Ken had insisted on walking over the fields, in the dark, over to the church for midnight Mass. They'd never done it before, they'd never do it again. Dave hadn't gone, nor had his mum, it was just the two of them. Coming home afterwards, in the near pitch-darkness of the lanes, they'd trudged over the field and at the high point, underneath

the moon and stars, his father had faced him and said that he had
to tell him something. He had to tell him that there was no such
thing as death, that his own father had come back to him to tell
him so, and that one day he'd be with his old dad again, just as
Nick would be with him.

'And your mum,' he'd put in for the sake of fairness. 'You'll be
starting out on your own life soon, son, and I want you to know this
because it's something that means a lot to me. He came to me to
tell me it one night. It weren't a dream. It was him, I promise you.
I'm not daft. I know he was there because I could smell him. . . .'

He could remember standing there, listening with bated breath,
excited by the apprehension that this was something important,
vital, memorable and secret.

And he did believe him, for a child will trust his parent long
after he pretends not to.

'He smelt good. I could smell the way his jacket smelt from the
boozer and from the rain, tweed it was. Right in my nose it was.
There ain't no death, son. That's what he said to me and now I'm
telling it to you. I'm handing it on. He was there beside me like
I'm standing 'ere with you now. Now, you remember that. You
remember what your dad told you one Christmas Day.'

Ken called just as they were dropping off to sleep.

'How am I to get to Pearl's Sund'y? Dave ain't got the space in
'is car.'

'Yes, he does.'

''Oooh?'

'Dave. Dave does.'

'Dave? I'll be dead before I get there if I have to go with 'im. Naargh.'

'You'll be OK.'

''Oooh?'

'You'll be OK.'

'Yes. That's right. You'll have to fetch me, son. See you at nine sharp.'

'What? Look, that's too early. We don't have to be there until lunchtime.'

'Listen, son, I feel a bit down, to tell you the truth. I think I'll check into an 'otel for the night tomorrow. Can't bear it 'ere. I'm rattlin' around in 'ere like old bones. Nothing on the telly. It's giving me the willies. Anything to have a bit of *youman* comp'ny.'

Astrid opened an eye and murmured, 'Let him come and stay with us for Saturday night. I'll go and get him tomorrow when you take Laura to London.'

Nick put his hand over the receiver and looked at her. 'Are you sure?'

'Why not?'

After he hung up, he said, 'Shit.'

'What?'

'We've got dinner with your parents tomorrow night.'

'He'll have to come too.'

'That will be bad.'

'They have to meet at some point.'

'Why?'

She sighed.

Getting up first thing, Nick watched the sunrise, from his throne. The firmament was swollen, it was black and blue like a great bruise. The dark was in retreat and on the rim of the hill there was a rim of gold, the promise of a fair day. The noise from down below the window and across the valley was a hubbub of birds, some in tune, some tuning up, the noise one hears in a theatre before the curtains open: a buzz and mutter, some discordant notes, a few bars of real harmony emerging, the hum of anticipation.

A pale saintly Laura was up and at the cereal at first light. He and Laura were both washed, dressed and breakfasted by nine, and earnest and scrubbed when they went up the garden path to the car. Astrid watched them duck in and out of the elderflower trees, then she heard the engine start and the gravel snap. And when next she looked, the parking space was bare and the elderflower was nodding and reaching to shake hands with the cow parsley, bobbing in the car's wake.

Inside, with Roy sitting on her feet, Astrid called Danny to tell him Laura would be with him at midday. Evidently she woke him. He sounded put out. He said he had plans and would have to cancel them. Tersely, she told him that Laura was worried about him.

'Why?'

'I don't know. Do you?'

'No-o . . .' he said, but he let the 'o' sound too long.

'Well, she's on her way to see that you're still in one piece. It's a lot for a little girl to handle, this kind of worry.'

As Nick observed, once parted, parents were locked in combat to claim their children's hearts. There was a silly notion knocking about that love was like a bar of soap—not so good shared. Short of anything else, they resorted to cant about 'values'. With parents together, 'values' were unnecessary; no child ever knew they had any, until his parents divorced, then he must have them coming at him from every quarter, day and night.

'No one ever *wants* a stepparent,' Nick said to Laura as they came into Dulwich. 'And that's something that a stepparent just has to accept. But I hope you can think of me as a good friend, Laura.'

She shrugged and sucked noisily on the stripy straw to evacuate the remaining vanilla from the two-pint milkshake cup, then she rummaged through the fries to find the little cartoon character that groaned when you pressed its stomach and said in an American accent: 'Oh boy, I got gas.' She pressed it once or twice and nibbled the batter off a cold chicken nugget.

Divorces were OK. Everyone knew there was an upside. It was called shopping. Stepparents were OK. Everyone knew there was an upside. It was called McDonald's.

44

Ken would not go in the house, no matter how she entreated him. The best she could do was take him out a chair from the kitchen. He sat outside, training his eyes on the movements of a robin redbreast while ruffling Roy's head. In the distance, a muffled gunshot went off every fifteen minutes in the cherry orchard to scare the birds off the new fruit. Ken jumped every time, but that was the only movement he appeared to make. Astrid brought him out a cup of tea. Her small talk in the car had amounted to nothing; it had been a one-way exercise, more to reassure herself than him.

When she gave him the cup of tea, a meek smile came to his face as if seeing her for the first time.

Nick called her from his mobile later in the afternoon. He'd dropped Laura off and been introduced to a scrawny woman, keen to demonstrate her intimate knowledge of the place and her rights to it by asking him in and making the coffee in her nightie. Laura had rolled her sleeves up and gone to clear the sink, and Danny had stood, gauche as a boy, allowing Nick to talk traffic and miles per gallon and the congestion charge and agreeing with almost anything he said. He asked what time he should pick Laura up and Danny had looked so open to suggestion as to imply now would be a good time. And when Laura, mid-ashtray-emptying, had looked round at her father and said, 'Aren't I staying the night?' the woman had reminded Danny they were going to a party, and when Laura had said, 'Cool,' Danny decided to be the grown-up and tell her it wasn't the sort of thing a little girl could go to.

Nick took a stroll through the park and returned for Laura after an hour, finding her more than ready to go.

On the way home, she commented on her father liking really skinny women. 'Like boys, I mean,' she chattered on candidly. 'Dad will never be fat. Thank *God*,' she said, scoffing at the very idea of it. 'I mean, I hope I take after him. I've been dieting since I was born. It's *so* hard, though.'

Nick had a feeling at times she played games with him, as if she were going through her fancy-dress trunk, trying on different people.

'He's very cool, my dad, Nick.'

'Yup.'

'No offence.'

'None taken.'

'I mean, his clothes and everything. He listens to, like, um, drum and bass and stuff.' She was using an American inflection, he noticed. 'He has the coolest decks.' But here she ran out of anything else to say and he saw that she folded her hands and sat as primly as a little old woman at the front of the bus, and she fell silent until they reached their village.

'He doesn't need me,' she said when they turned off the main road into their lane.

'Well, it's good he has someone in his life to look after him,' Astrid said, pressing her advantage when they had a cup of tea together.

The old man was outside. The clouds had come over and still he sat there. Nick greeted him and touched his shoulder when he came home, and Ken touched his son's hand with a small pat but sat there stiff-backed as if on sentry duty.

'Who's he expecting to come up that hill anyway?' Astrid peeped out at him through the kitchen window.

Phone under her chin as she rang the babysitter, she looked at her hands as she chopped vegetables for Laura's supper and saw those of an old woman. They were rippled when laid flat, as if a stone had been dropped into a pool. She was taken aback. There was no way of stopping it then: getting older.

She felt her daughter's head on her back and her hands around her waist. 'You're home now,' she said, turning round to enfold her. 'We're all home together,' she said, seeing Ken come in. He came in as far as the kitchen table and stood in front of them all and, after a moment, yawned.

Laura and Astrid exchanged smiles. Laura took charge. She invited Ken up to 'settle in' to his room. 'Perhaps you'd like to freshen up?'

When she got up to the spare room, she went back halfway to see where he was. He was very slow coming up the stairs.

'This is the guest room. You can put your things in the drawer,' she said, when he got there at last. He appeared to have nothing with him. This was a disappointment. 'Oh, well. You can take your coat off.'

But he declined.

'There is an en suite,' Laura said in the manner of her grandmother, Linda, 'and there are some little bottles in there Nick has stolen from hotels, which you can just help yourself to. It's a shame there aren't tea- and coffee-making facilities,' she said. 'Isn't it?' She checked his face.

'It's very nice, thank you.'

'Well, we'll watch some television now, shall we?' she said with the authority of a matron.

She sat next to him on the sofa downstairs, not too close, checking his face for vital signs every time a joke was made on the television.

'He's very silly,' she said hurriedly about the TV host, seeing Ken's blank face. 'Perhaps you'd like Noel Edmonds better?'

''Oooh?'

'Noel Edmonds. Or there's an old programme on you might like. Morecambe and Wise.'

'When he says "who",' Laura observed to Astrid in the kitchen, 'it's as if he's pulled a sock inside out. It's all the wrong way round. The "w" is at the end, not the front.'

She took him in a small plate with three biscuits.

'Help yourself.'

'No, ta.'

'You can put your feet up, if you want,' said Laura.

'On the table?'

'Yes, we all do.'

'No, ta.'

'Shall I help you put them up?' And she began lifting them one at a time, squatting down to do it, with him wheezing with laughter and telling her to leave off and calling out to Nick, ''Elp me, son, 'elp me, 'ere, Nick! Nicholas! This young lady's roughing me up in 'ere, an old chap like me. . . .' His voice was high and loony.

'You'll be much more comfortable with your legs up.'

Laura had another patient. And the Little Match Girl, the daft old sod, the bighead and the beautician all sat side by side on the sofa, watching TV, with Roy making occasional attempts to mount Ken's leg.

When there was a close-up of a young girl on the television, Astrid said, just as the thought came to her, without censoring herself first, 'She's beautiful.'

'Not as good-looking as either of you two gels,' said Ken, shaking off Roy, who was straining to get to the biscuits. 'Cor, get 'im off me, will you, dear? 'E's trying to have it off with me leg.'

'Would you like a blanket?' Laura asked him.

'We've got the babysitter coming any minute, Laura,' said Astrid.

'Lovely being 'ere, innit?' Ken said, giving the mantelpiece a dusting with his melancholy eyes. There was no photo of him there. 'What a nice home it is,' he said sadly.

'Don't get too used to it, Dad,' said Nick, and he got an elbow in the ribs from Astrid.

'Well,' he said to her when they were upstairs, changing, 'corny old sod, buttering you up with all that rubbish.'

She sprayed her collarbone profusely with the scent of Mimosa and he squirted a mean drop of his aftershave on his own neck and, on patting each place dry, removed the scent to his palms. Then, wiping his hands on his trousers, he pronounced himself ready.

'Like father, like son,' she said, looking down at his slightly pointed new shoes.

45

There was nothing that Astrid's parents, Linda and Malcolm, liked more than eating out. They'd been into it since the late sixties. They'd introduced Astrid to the meal out in 1976 with a small cut glass of German wine on her sixth birthday. (Steady! said Malcolm.) They were careful when it came to the larger things such as cars and lavish when it came to the smaller things, such as hand cream, and as it seemed to fall between the two they went to 'a meal out' in both trepidation and titillation. It could be deemed a pure waste of money if it was something Linda could cook herself and the place was empty, or it could be their finest hour if there were 'people' there—people who would see that they too knew the difference between a foam and a coulis.

They got there early. Linda had a cream clutch bag that matched her heels, and fine good ankles on show, bronzed. Her hair was forked and fluffed and sprayed and, since her eyelashes were sparse, she'd decided to have a go with some false ones. Brown so as not to be too silly. It was a high-risk strategy and she'd have to be careful not to blink. She never winked under any circumstances. A woman of her age couldn't get away with it. A woman of her age could get away with navy and white, a nautical look, and good jewellery. Malcolm wore his safe jacket, tweed in winter, linen in summer and spring, and chinos. A little anchor emblazoned into the cuff of his sock struck up a repartee with his wife's theme. He wore a white polo shirt. They both wore wedding rings. Hers had extensions, two up, two down, in diamonds, given on anniversaries coinciding with boom times.

They were early. It gave them time to look over their bifocals at the clientele and through them at the prices. They would choose something middle of the road, no matter who was paying.

Linda checked the room. If she spied people who squirmed and salivated and were all excitement and clung to their glass and gobbled and craned their neck to see the desserts or keep track of where the cheese trolley was going, she gave Malcolm the tip-off, with a discreet sideways tilt of the head, saving him from extending any untoward friendliness in that direction.

Nevertheless, she was on the edge of her seat and had to swallow once or twice at the mention of bacon and at the term 'pan-fried'.

They rose when the other couple came in, she in a half-curtsy with cramp in her right leg, he going the whole hog, with both hands clasping his would-be son-in-law at the forearm. They exchanged partners for the continental double-kiss, which came to England in 1986 along with the eponymous breakfast. Congratulations were said and Malcolm brushed off Nick's apology for not having asked him before proposing to Astrid.

'No, no, not at all. We're not people for all that sort of fuss and pomp and ceremony, are we, Linda? No, no, no,' he said pleasantly, dragging the thing out to the point that they all felt they'd been standing a long time. 'Not at all! Nick.' And he pronounced his name with the relief of one finding safe footing at last.

Astrid smelt on her mother the terribly strong perfume she'd worn for over twenty years; it reeked of credit-card activity in House of Fraser. When she looked at her, she saw only the signs of struggle—the pink powder pressed upon upper lip hair and stubble alike, the grey frizz at centre parting that no hair colour could long subdue, and the sagging skin just before her ears. Astrid felt sad, and it occurred to her why for some time she'd preferred to speak to her on the phone rather than see her mother. The voice was more *her*, as she liked to think of her, than the sight of her was.

As they sat down, a sharp look passed from Linda to Malcolm and was stowed somewhere between his bottom lip and the bread roll, its meaning private. Nick pottered across to speak to the small lady who waited tables, explaining they'd need a fifth chair.

In came Ken at last; he'd stopped to get his breath and told them to carry on ahead. 'I'll get there. I'll get there.'

He came in like a desperate man, clasping the door handle and shoving the structure back into its frame, making quite a noise. It was as if he'd been wandering the souks of Northern Africa for many months, shoeless, before finding the British Embassy.

It was as if he came with news of the enemy at the city gates. All eyes were upon him.

'All right,' he said.

He resisted the removal of his mac by the waitress.

Ken's ideas about a 'meal out' were at variance to Linda and Malcolm's by about fifteen years. He was born before the war.

He sat in his chair in his coat and took the menu Nick gave him, shaking it open. 'All right,' he said again with a nod to the table. He looked alternately aggrieved and disgusted as he studied the menu. He cleared his throat every few seconds as though about to say something, thus shooting holes in their fledgling conversation.

The ladies fluttered in and out of topics mooted deliberately by Linda to be exclusionary—dealing, as they did, with people only *they* knew, and cryptically.

'So, I saw Jane Deakin the other day.'

'Poor woman.'

'She's let herself go.'

Ken slapped the closed menu down onto the table. 'All too dear,' he said, tight-lipped and final.

Nick's professional experience in dealing with difficult people in challenging circumstances persuaded him to coax the old boy.

'It's actually very reasonable, Dad. A nice, elegant menu, not too pretentious. If you tot it up, it works out quite a good deal if each of us takes the prix fixe.'

But he wasn't speaking Ken's language. 'Too dear,' Ken reiterated.

'There's liver and bacon, Dad, on at fifteen. You like liver and bacon, don't you? That's right up your street.'

'Do me a favour! Fifteen nicker for a bit of offal. They sin you coming, sunshine.' Ken made a bid for the other couple's opinion. 'What d'you think, Malcolm? Dear, innit?'

Nick leant back in his chair, putting his mouth close to his father's ear, to escape the audible range of their table.

'Just fucking order something, all right?'

Ken closed his eyes.

'Have you got an engagement ring yet?' Linda asked her daughter.

'Not yet.'

'Not yet? I know that with Danny you didn't bother: We don't do conventions, Mummy. I'll say! But at your age I would have thought you'd have been traditional. The ring is the man's pledge to support you. It's a symbol of his troth. It's not nothing.' She turned to her husband.

Malcolm was still poring over the menu. 'Mutton. You don't see a lot of that anymore,' he said, taking off his glasses and smiling warmly at Linda as he closed the menu.

Ken cleared his throat. 'I'll have the *tamada* soup.'

'The . . . what's that? I can't see that on the menu. . . .' said Linda, with murderous eloquence.

'There's always a *tamada* soup on the menu.'

Malcolm tried to look wry and debonair, both old-fashioned and modern, with one side of his face doing the 1950s and the other lost in space.

'Tomato soup.' Astrid came to the rescue. 'As in Heinz.'

'That's the job,' said Ken.

'He doesn't get out much,' said Nick to the waitress.

'And tap water, please,' said Ken. 'From the tap, please, miss. Yes. Thank you. And I'll have some bread with my soup, ta. I don't drink much, do you, Linda? Don't feel the need.'

The bottle of red that Nick ordered was opened by the waitress under Ken's disapproving noises, measured out under his unforgiving eyes, sipped to the sucking in of his breath and, under such scrutiny, it completely failed to inebriate.

'People seem to need to drink to have a good time these days.' Ken shook his head.

'It doesn't always follow,' said Nick, knocking back his glass and pouring himself another.

After some talk of the wedding and putative dates ventured during the main course, some careful, none-too-enthusiastic chat, and one or two poor laughs supplied by elements proposed by Linda that they would not be including—such as a disco—Ken started to grind his teeth. He was bored. If a conversation were started by either of Astrid's parents, he'd start talking over it to Nick, or torpedo it with a sullen remark.

''Ot in 'ere, innit?'

'Take your coat off then.'

When Malcolm began an amusing anecdote about the prime minister, Ken nudged Nick, nodding at his steak rind. 'You leavin' that?'

'Do you want it?'

'Naargh. Raw. Fancy servin' it like that.'

Malcolm gave up.

Nobody seemed to want a dessert and so they went straight to coffee and Ken deigned to have a milky one. He drank it down, then sat and fiddled with his coat sleeves and cleared his throat a number of times.

'I know I shouldn't go white with the dress, but I am tempted since it does feel like a new beginning,' began Astrid, broaching the subject most likely to meet her mother's disapproval and thus best dealt with here and now.

Ken cut in. 'Do you believe in Jesus, Linda?'

'I'm not much of a churchgoer, I'm afraid.' And she began to serve her signature cold starter on the subject. 'When you see the suffering in the world, and what has been done in the name of religion——'

'I was like you once, Linda.' He put his elbows on the table. 'I was *ignorant*.' He patted her hand. His touch caused her to startle; an eyelash came loose and she tried to blink it back.

'It makes you nervy to talk of it, dunnit? I can see that. It did me an' all. But when 'e comes into your life and you don't say no to 'im, everything changes.' He squeezed her hand. 'That's all right, dear. At our age, things 'appen to you all of a sudden, and good job, because time ain't exactly on our side no more. See, if you start crying at nothing, if you start shivering for no rea-son, and if you feel *sorry*, if you regret *fings*,' he used his other hand as a fist to smite his breast, 'if you start to finkin' about what other people are going through, and 'ow some people are kind-'earted by nature, not greedy and graspin', and you fink, Bli-mey, I've 'ad it easy, a'n' I? Then you know He's close by.' His voice rose.

'Steady!' said Malcolm with a splash of a grin.

'If you feel sure that your life's been a failure, that you've been a miserable excuse for a *youman* bein',' and here he cleared his throat, for it was thick with emotion, 'then 'e's with ya.'

'Thanks for that, Dad.' Nick turned in his chair to find the lady there like a good nurse. 'Can we have the bill, please?' Linda excused herself.

Ken threw a backward nod. 'She 'eard me. No mistake. What about you, Malcolm? You believe?'

Her father caught Astrid's eye. 'Absolutely,' he lied, and the three of them broke into smiles of relief and pleasure.

'That was a quick conversion, Dad.'

'Good man,' said Ken gravely. 'I tell you something, mate. Once you say it, you're almost there. You're almost 'ome.'

'Talking of which,' said Nick, putting his code into the machine proffered by the lady.

With the bill settled, Linda rejoined them underneath the bright lights of the restaurant and, ready to double-kiss, they took turns with each other's forearms rather like the little dancing couples on *Trumpton*, turning and spinning, but Ken hung back and gave them a nod. 'Ta-da.'

When, at last, Linda and Malcolm passed by the restaurant window outside and braved a flash of a smile and a parting wave, he fixed Linda with a pointed finger.

'Nice couple,' he said as Nick held the door open. He stood for a moment on the kerb, looking up at the stars and taking a deep breath. 'Nice evening, wannit?'

Nick put his arm around Astrid as they walked down the hill.

'Dear old Lord! Could they tuck it away! Still. As long as you're 'appy, Nick, you two, that's the thing. The thing is, well, you look 'appy, don't you? And I tell you something, I'm pleased. I couldn't wish for more.' And he put a hand on his son's shoulder. 'Good boy,' he said.

Astrid linked arms with both of them as they stepped down on the uneven concrete into the car park. 'Well, I think that went well,' she said.

'Steady!' cried Malcolm as their car shot forward onto the high street under Linda's hasty release of the clutch.

They'd gotten away lightly, though they didn't know it. They hadn't met his mother yet. Neither had Astrid.

46

The sun was pestered by clouds, and every time it gave them the slip they found it again. Outside, Ken was in the garden in his mac, sitting on the same chair, fixated on the place on the fence where the robin had been the day before. Astrid asked him if he wanted a cold drink. He shook his head. He was waiting to go to Pearl's. He would have to wait four more hours.

The sun flexed its muscles and Astrid was impressed. She got the fold-out sunloungers from the shed and put them both up, then she went upstairs and changed into a dress and feeling her legs with her hands, she went to the shower and used the hand-held shower mixer to wet them and shave them, not too well. Her shinbones were orange and sore afterwards. She salved them with cream. She put her hair up in a clip, found the magazine section she was after among the Sunday papers, poured herself a glass of water with a dash of lemon juice, took her sunglasses out of her bag and went outside. The clouds had moved and it was cold.

She went back inside, took one of Nick's sweaters off the hook on the door and put it on, went back outside and sat down. The phone rang and, with relief to get out of the cold, she went inside.

Ken sat all the while in the same place, stiff-legged, bearing down upon the uncomfortable chair, buffeted more by memory than weather.

It was Big Katie saying she was ill and wouldn't be in to work the next day. Astrid went and got her diary to see who else was on. She noticed she had scrawled a big 'P' next to tomorrow. She had felt bloated for a couple of days and, wondering when she'd be having a period next month, she started to look back through the diary to check the interval in days and then plan forward.

Ken came in. 'Where's Laura?'

Still counting, Astrid put a finger in the air to pause him.

'Where's Nick?'

'Twenty-seven, twenty-eight . . . Well, now, hang on a minute! I don't need to do that, do I!'

'What's that then?'

'Counting the days of my menstrual cycle, Ken.'

His top lip snagged.

'But, as it happens, I needn't bother.' She closed the book.

'Jolly good,' he said. He'd never heard a woman speak of it in such a way, not in his whole life, as if it were a thing of interest, or for public conversation. Pat kept it quiet; you wouldn't have known she had them. Pearl glowered, and you only knew because she was particularly angry, but otherwise there was no talk of it. June used to turn over when an ad came on the TV and they poured the blue water onto the sanitary towel. 'Don't want you put off your cheese,' she'd said.

But this young woman was barefaced about it!

'Because, it's incredible really, because my monthly period falls, and has fallen for more than six months as far as I can see, on the day of the month when there's a full moon. It's in the calendar marked with a little circle, you see. And every month that's when I start. Amazing, isn't it? All the while, without even knowing it, I'm being ruled by the moon.'

'Nick about?' he said, edging in a cowardly way to the stairs and craning his neck. 'Nick? You up there?'

'Full moon, blood flows. Incredible.'

'Nick? Laura?' he called plaintively into the vacuum.

'So, can I make you some breakfast, Ken?'

'No, ta.'

'Maybe some toast and jam? No? Well, I'll make us some tea then.' And Astrid went, in a bustle, to the kettle. She was wearing a 1950s dress, tight at the waist and big over the hips. Her tummy was round and tight as a drum with the period coming. She turned on the tap and the water went in noisily.

Ken stood there with his hands in his pockets, wretchedly awkward.

'You know, I sometimes think that in the story of the oppression of women,' she flicked the kettle switch, and put her hands to the small of her back, 'beauty and being young and being thin are just the latest chapter.'

'You could say that,' he said, rooted to the spot. He looked from door to door.

'But the problem is, we've always been willing to do each other down, us women; it's been about elbowing each other out of the way to end up with the man. That's the problem.' The way she stood there, facing him, the way she was talking, it all seemed to point to one culprit.

'I daresay,' he said.

'A bunch of turncoats. At least you men stick together.'

Ken rubbed his chin. 'I've come to have a lot of respect for women lately. Because of Audrey, see. The undertaker lady. I've known her fifteen years or more, knew her parents too. I used to call on their services, see. When I had a tenant kick the bucket, they'd come right round and sort it out and never a complaint. You know, all hours. Well, you'd never expect to have a woman show up, would you? I wasn't 'alf surprised when Audrey come by. We had this one old geezer in one of our places and, well, it turned your stomach. But she came in and, well . . . how do you put it . . . ?' He squirmed. 'She was tender. Like he was someone once. Anyway, I bin working for her for a while now, 'elpin' out. The things you see 'er do. Just takes it in 'er stride. An 'eart big as an 'ouse.' He sat down at the table. Astrid poured the hot water into the teapot. 'I *thought* that women was whiners, you know, not much chop. I thought that of Pearl too but it turns out, 'cording to Dave, that she's done all right on her own without me.'

Astrid set the teacup before him with the bowl of sugar. 'Help yourself, Ken.'

'I don't like being alone, Astrid. You wouldn't want to be on your own, wouldya? Young woman like you?'

'Well, I'd prefer to be alone than to be with someone I didn't like.' She went to the pantry and took out a pack of biscuits and opened it and put those before him too. She touched his back as she set them down. 'Have one of those to dip in your tea. You see, the thing is, if a man marries a woman he thinks is stupid and grumpy, it's amazing how quickly she becomes it. But luckily,' she said, sliding a biscuit from the pack and biting it, 'there's a cure.'

She sat down next to him in a big flump. 'I was alone before I met Nick for a while. And,' she bit into a biscuit and chewed ruminatively, 'we *are* happy. It's just that I worry about things I didn't have to worry about before.'

Ken took a long slug of the tea in shaky gulps. 'Pardon me,' was all he said, and his eyes remained on the cup, and it seemed like she'd lost his interest since he sat, arms folded, looking at the steaming cup with cold eyes as if cooling it by will. Then after a while, he said, 'It's sufferin' what makes a person strong.'

She sipped her tea.

'I don't remember me own mother really, but it was my sister, Pat, what brought me up and she was a good woman but, well, she was me older sister, weren't she? See what I mean? But with Pearl, she looked to me, see. And Pearl, she was always *crying*. Nick'll tell you that. She couldn't 'elp it, I daresay. But the slightest thing set 'er off. When the film started, she'd start with the crying and when it ended, she'd start again and all the way through and I just didn't pay it no 'eed. But I couldn't,' he shook his head, 'I couldn't work it out, you know, the crying.' He looked her in the eyes.

'People cry, Ken, because they're sad,' she said, but he didn't seem to hear her; he was being absorbed rapidly back into the past again. He was in another kitchen, standing behind Pearl, looking over her shoulder into the mixing bowl of flour, sugar, margarine and tears, which were falling into the bowl off her chin, and her hands were working it all together, her wedding ring caked with dough.

47

Down in the dell where the beech trees jostle to see in the stream which is prettier, Ken follows Laura through the ragged blue-bells, in and out of pockets of midges, clearing twig and leaf from his nearsight.

Suddenly he hears her cry out, and in the dappled sunshine he sees her flying through the sky like a forest fairy. She has taken to the air on a rope swing and is dipping in and out of shadow and light, with her feet touching the top of a gorse bush and her hair trailing behind her in the leaves and brush of the bank. The great beech tree seems to bend at the knees to take the strain.

He stands open-mouthed, watching her.

'Come on! Try it!' she calls out and in a second she's on the woodland floor on all fours, then she stands to brush herself off.

He nearly trips down the bank, totters across the shallow stream, then goes to great effort to heave himself up the bank, using the tree roots as banisters; it's a miracle that he makes it at all. The smell of wild garlic wrinkles his nose. He's out of puff when he gets to the beech tree.

Merciless, she shows him the short plank that is the swing seat. She taps it.

One thing he has become afraid of as he's gotten older is being unsteady on his feet, not to mention being uncertain at all, and this is precarious.

'No, ta.'

But she cajoles him and exhorts him. 'It'll change your life, Ken. I promise.'

'Don't be daft.'

She shows the seat to him and shakes it. He manages to slide the plank between his trouser legs. He stands a minute, while she arranges his mac via its back slit, to divide it to either side of the plank. She pronounces him ready.

'No,' he says, stock-still. He is not ready.

'There's nothing to be scared of!' she says with incredulity. 'Of course you can do it! Anyone can do it! Go on!'

He lifts his heels, tests the notion, then drops them. 'No.'

'Shall I give you a push?'

'No,' he says. 'Don't you do that. You stand back.'

'Oh, come on!'

And suddenly he's aloft and falling and rising. He doesn't know what possessed him. As soon as his feet lift, he feels joy. Fear to joy, fear to joy; he can hear a whirling sound in his ears as he travels over the earth. He's hanging on to the rope with both hands. His vision swoons from leaves and sky to earth and nettles and back, and in his nose is the smell of soil and the fragrance of the bluebells, and the world is rushing fast at him and away from him and for music there is the laughter of the girl. He closes his eyes and bobs, hanging limp in the hands of gravity.

'You did it!' she says when his heels strike earth and he comes to a standstill. 'I told you it was easy! Now you won't be scared to do it again, will you?'

He slides the plank from between his legs and, staggering backwards, remembers the painful feeling of being articulated to stand on the earth. He wishes to lie down; it is only lying down that he's at ease.

'I shan't never do it again,' he says severely.

They walk back up the hill, where the forget-me-nots and the hogweed are out in the hedgerow, and she stops to pick a posy and to lament the passing of the primroses, with their demure mob caps, in favour of the flashy satin buttercups.

'I love the primroses,' she says. 'I love the smell of them. I wish they didn't have to go away.'

'Them primroses'll be back, Laura,' he pants. 'Their roots, see, they're just 'iding, see, beneath the ground. You can't see 'em, but they'll be back,' he says, barely finding the breath to say the words.

They are at the iron gate and, drawn to it, he staggers over and leans on it to recover, standing where his son has stood many a time.

'Nice view from 'ere.'

'Ken?'

'Yes.'

'Does God exist?'

'Course 'e does.'

'You know you ask people whether there's a God or not and they never give you a straight answer, do they?'

'That's right. You're right there, mate.'

'So, how do you know He does?'

'How do I know? Because 'e's inside of me, innie? I can hear 'im, and I can feel 'im. And 'e gives me a bloomin' great shove, now an' again. Like 'e did down there on that swing.'

Laura is pleased someone has finally cleared up the matter for her.

48

The gamekeeper's cottage smells of mildew and apples stored over winter. It is damp, with thin windows knocking in their frames. It was never meant nor made to welcome guests. It was not conceived for 'entertaining'. It was made to provide recourse from extremes of weather, but not the basic cold which is the birthright of the Englishman and certainly the due of a gamekeeper. It was built proud and pretty enough to make coming home across the fields an agreeable end to the day. Its grandfatherly Victorian exterior with its gabled eyebrows and finger-to-lips front door seems to say: Come in, eat and go quietly to bed.

Its construction didn't reckon on any untoward physical activity. The floorboards resent agitated footsteps. Under Pearl's regime, with its thin curtains and carpet, its pine furniture and its piles of precarious bric-a-brac, it is not the sort of house that could brook much jumping about.

They never had friends come and stay when they were kids. Even now, there are no guests, there are only trespassers. The dog sees off those who stray from its brick pathways. Pearl doesn't admit anyone to the interior. Today, the most they each get is a peek into the living room, over the stable door at the kitchen. Heading them off, the great mongrel bouncer swings saliva in a sort of rope chain. They drag their feet, crane their necks for glimpses, like paying visitors to a country home keen to see 'where the family live', until Pearl pulls the upper half of the door to and gets them to do as she asked, which is to carry the trays into the garden.

She seems eager to get it over with. She greeted them with no more than nods. On her crutches, with a lower leg in plaster, she still manages to keep a hand on the dog's collar, holding it back, and scolding the mutt with such colourful rage as to make the three children hang back in trepidation.

'Stay back, sod you!'

Whatever social manners Pearl might have had have been left long ago in built-up places.

'Mad,' whispers Matt with a note of reverence.

On the long drive up the unmade track to the house, which is now almost entirely grown over with chestnut trees and rhodo-dendrons, Laura pointed out dolls hanging from the trees.

Nick braked. 'Decoration?' he offered uncertainly.

As the Range Rover moved forward again, the four of them looked through Astrid's window, safari-faced. From every other tree there were plastic baby dolls, suspended by a leg, or upside down, or more often squashed into the crook of a branch, one eye stuck closed. Naked, they were ghastly in a way, green-haired from the weather or bald and threadbare. Made originally for the delight of maternally minded little girls, their once cooing expressions seemed creepy here in the woods; they were like vulgar harpies jeering at the traffic.

'Grim,' said Astrid.

In the middle of the back lawn, on a trestle table covered with a lace-edged tablecloth, there is an assortment of plates of cakes and scones. There are a few odd glasses and there's an enamel jug. The chairs are ranged about the table on the lawn uneasily, some upholstered, some wicker, and at the head of the table is a broad oak dining chair with a patchwork cushion in its seat.

The garden is tropical today, wet and lush and redolent of honeysuckle. The wisteria weeps. The roses are pressing for the birth of their blossoms. In dank gutter-grates, toads hunker down, waiting for frightful things to pass them by.

Pearl takes the oak chair and is the first to serve herself. She does so generously, slathering her scone with margarine before passing anything to anyone else. She chews, only half listening to Ken's fawning words. The others help themselves one by one to seats, then scones.

Marina pours the tea.

With his high-pitched noises, Ken goes between simpleton and naughty schoolboy, whimpering and simpering, complimenting the garden, complimenting the spread, thanking her and commending her.

'She's a wonderful woman, your mother, i'n' she? Always was.'

At the far end of the table, Laura stands to pour squash into cups. The children taste the drink and show each other their tongues. 'What is it anyway?' Emily whispers.

'LSD or something,' says Matt, then with all eyes on him, looks dashed.

'This garden 'ere's a paradise, Pearl. I don't know how you keep it up,' says Ken.

'You never did know anything about gardening.'

Dave does the best he can. 'Well, Dad used to help a bit, didn't he? I remember we all did a bit. I used to get a penny a dog turd, didn't I? Well, I got a ha'penny actually, after I'd given Nick his share.'

''Oooh?' barks Ken. Under his breath Matt mimics the crazy sound and Emily shows the yellow crumbs in her brace.

'*Nick*,' says Pearl harshly. 'Nick, he said.'

Her eyes fall on her elder son for a moment, as he slices his scone open and tries to make sense of the butter that's hard as cheese. Having crumbed the stick of butter and left the scone unscathed, he catches her eye in his moment of failing—just as when he was a child. But she passes no comment. Her face is obscured by weather and age now, like the bricks of the house; her cheeks are no longer coral but ruddy and her face is crowded by unkempt hair and large glasses.

When Emily upsets her glass, Pearl sighs heavily and lifts herself up with difficulty, hoisting herself onto her crutches, going in to get a cloth, ignoring the protests of both her sons. The two couples and the three children dare to look at each other. This is no picnic, much less a tea party.

'I could murder a drink,' says Dave.

Nick rises and follows his mother out to the kitchen where the dog is getting the rough side of her tongue for having ventured out of its bed again.

'Didn't I tell you to stay there? I don't want your sodding hair all over the place. . . .' The more the dog cowers, the more her voice rises. And outside, with clouds gathering overhead, her family sit, shoulders hunched and uncomfortable.

'Mum,' Nick says.

'I'm bringing the cloth now!'

'Never mind the cloth, Mum, it's only a drop she's spilt. Why don't you come and sit down and enjoy yourself?'

'It'll spoil the table.'

'Mum.'

'What is it now?'

'Mum. I am so sorry.'

Her back rounds over the crutches, her head dips. 'What are you sorry for,' she says, not turning, 'you got nothing to be sorry for, you done nothing to be ashamed of, have you?'

He comes behind her, and looks at the hands on the counter and the strong short fingers that grip all the time now, with arthritis in them. Those hands were his first toys, followed by her feet, on winter's evenings when he'd call the hands crabs and the feet lobsters and invent seaside stories with her cackling at the tickling. She'd flinch and jerk and hoot and it would end in her getting him by the ribs and poking him savagely, making him scream and threaten to wee himself.

'Mum. I am so sorry for everything.'

When she turns round, her mouth is loose and her eyes are briny and she says to him, 'Why shouldn't I just carry on living without you?'

'Because I'm sorry.' His lips blurt, 'I'm so sorry, Mum.' His eyes are hot and tears come and he puts his arms around her and kisses the crown of her head. 'I'm so sorry.'

He wants to say sorry again and again to relieve the pain but she is holding him fiercely and saying into his shirt, 'No, no, don't say it. I'm proud of you. It was what I wanted. I wanted you to do well. I'm proud of you.'

They are gripping each other tight when Dave pokes his head in the kitchen.

'Everything all right?'

Nick releases her and turns round and his mother hides her face with her sleeve, wiping it. Dave is standing at the back door with big anxious eyes, not daring to come in.

'Come in, Davie,' she says, sniffling. 'Where is that bleeding cloth? Will you please go in your bed, dog!'

'Sorry to interrupt.' Dave evades Nick's eyes as he ducks in under the door frame. 'Shall I take the cloth out for you, Mum, and wipe it up?'

'Yes, you do that, thank you, Davie,' she says and hands him a grey string cloth.

Dave gives Nick a look, then retreats.

'The prodigal son, you are,' she says with a short laugh, wiping her glasses.

'Something like that.'

'Any chance of a cup of tea, Mother?' comes Ken's voice from the garden. This was his catchphrase back in the old days, and the request that was most likely to get Pearl into a lather. The response was reliable: 'Do it yourself, fuck you.'

But now Pearl says, 'Ask the daft old shit if he still has sugar.'

'Two sugars, Mother!' comes the voice, and there's laughter from the table. 'If you don't mind!'

Pearl takes the dirty teaspoon from inside the sugar jar and measures a level teaspoon of sugar into the cup. 'One's enough for him,' she says.

49

Hopping behind Ken's chair, crutches wobbling under her elbows, she pulls the half-scone off Ken's plate.

'Come on, that's enough!'

He shoves what's in his fingers into his mouth posthaste, shoulders high in alarm. She puts a slice of bread onto his plate and reaches round him for his knife; she plunges it into the jam jar she's holding and spreads something dark, thickly.

'Taste that.'

They all look.

'Go on, taste it.'

He brings it to his nose, sniffs first. A smile starts on his mouth before he bites into it. He chews with obvious pleasure.

'I never thought I'd taste that again in my life.'

'You won't. That's your lot. Too good for you,' she says with a sideways grin, and Nick and Dave laugh.

'Don't be like that, Pearl,' says the old man. 'I'n' she awful to me? She always was 'orrible to me, you know,' he confides across the table to Matt.

'What is it then, Dad?' asks Dave.

'It's what my old mum used to make. Elderb'ry jam.'

Pearl puts a forefinger where the knife went and tastes it herself. 'Too much sugar, but it's a devil to set without it.'

'You're being spoilt, Dad,' says Dave eagerly.

Pearl sits back in her place. 'Help yourself to cake, girls. And you, Matt.'

'It's a lovely tea, Mrs Goodyew,' says Laura.

'Yes, it's all worked out all right in the end, hasn't it?' says Pearl. When she smiles, she's a different person. She looks young. 'I was worried about the scones, but they're not bad.' Her big cheeks rise and she helps herself to another of her scones. When Nick looks at her, he sees winter setting in too, as with his father. They are being run down by nature and time, the white in her hair taking over from autumn colours, yet their eyes are lights, they flicker and crackle; it was these lights that set alight most of the other lights around this table, that set certain eyes seeing.

He swallows. He looks around the table and sees Dave's eyes on Emily, Astrid's on Laura's. He swallows again; there is nothing he has lit. Catching his eye, Astrid gives him a full happy smile.

After tea, the children go off to explore the orchard that's now full-grown, with Laura asking Matt about bands and websites. While they are dubbing this rapper cool and that girl band uncool, Emily suggests they play hide and seek. And though Matt pooh-poohs the idea at first, when Laura agrees he says that Emily should do the seeking. They go into the chestnut wood and Laura finds a bower that she dubs an igloo, and the two of them squat inside it and tell each other the most outlandish stories they've heard, forgetting all about Emily. After a while Emily discovers them and, standing outside, knees level with their eyes, she says several times with increasing hostility, 'I could hear you. I could *so* hear you.' But they have forgotten the game. She stands awhile with her arms folded and her chest rising and falling, hurt to hear their laughter and be outside of it.

When she gets back to the table, it's just the four of them sitting there: her dad, her grandfather, her grandmother and Uncle Nick. Her mother and Astrid have wandered off to see the magnolias. She goes to the car and gets her recorder. When she comes back, she offers them a tune. Nobody seems keen. She begins earnestly piping, going from one of the five notes she has to the other, giving each one all of her puff, and roughly conveying 'Lord of All Hopefulness,' and though they clap and praise her and thank her after every chorus, she makes sure they get the full song.

As a final flourish, she makes a shape in the air with the butt of the recorder.

'That's the one, that is!' says her grandfather, and he slaps the table. 'That's the one I was after! That's the one I'll 'ave,' Ken says, fixing her with a squint as if he's seen something important in her, '. . . "'oose presence is balm".'

'For your funeral, I suppose,' says Dave, rolling his eyes.

'That's right. Got it all planned, a'n' I?'

'Got your rig out, have you? Got it on the bed waiting?'

'Naargh. Nothing wrong with this suit, is there?'

'You've come oven-ready then, have you, Dad?'

'I'm always ready.' He throws a meaningful look up at the sky.

'Come on and I'll show you something, Ken,' Pearl says to him. Dave jumps up to help and misses the chance. The pair of them go in under their own steam.

''Ere, Nick, right, you don't think they're going to rekindle any of the old magic, do you?'

'He told me himself those days are gone.'

'Thank Christ for that. I thought he was going to proposition that undertaker woman.'

'Did I tell you I'd proposed to Astrid?'

'No, mate, no, you didn't. Bloody hell.' He runs his hand over his head. 'Seriously, mate, that's great news. She seems like a nice girl.'

'She's not.'

'Even better. Listen, mate—seriously, though.' Dave moves forward and speaks out of one side of his mouth. 'Best tell you while I can. Dad's only had Matt looking up how to top yourself on the Internet. I think he's a bit doolally. That, or he's ill, or something. He said anything to you?'

'No, nothing. He does bang on about it all, the grand finale and that, but no, I don't think he's going to end it himself when he can get it for free.'

'True.'

'Christ, he's not going, not while he's in the limelight. No, listen, Dave, it's just a way of getting attention.'

'But he shouldn't be getting a kid to sort him out with arsenic on the Internet, should he?'

'Arsenic?'

'He got him researching death drugs. It's not right, getting a kid to do that. I could kill 'im.'

'Problem solved.'

'Yeah. There is that.'

'It's not working, him living on his own.'

'I know. He's on the blower all the time. He still calling you?'

'All the bloody time. He's being nice as pie, though.'

'Christ, he must have seen the Angel of Death.'

When the women come up from the garden, they see the two brothers at the table in cahoots; Dave is up close to his brother, his hand gripping a spindle on the back of his brother's chair. 'Right, Nick? Right?'

50

'Shoes off.'

Ken sits at the bottom of the stairs and removes them with effort, wincing and exclaiming.

Abandoning her crutches, Pearl goes up the stairs backwards, hoisting herself with her arms and taking a step at a time. He comes up frontwards, using his hands, moaning under his breath but stopping himself from complaining about the tiny 'bleeding' stairs like he used to.

Look at the pair of us now, he thinks. People used to say we was a handsome couple. We used to chase each other down on the beach. We used to go to dances on the pier. We was at it like knives in the old days.

In the bedroom, things are just as they were. It's like stepping back in time, not that things could stand much rearranging in such a small room—no en suite here, no master this and that, no dressing room. There's space for a wardrobe, a bed and a dressing table and that's it. The bed with its faded pink-buttoned velvet headboard fills the room.

Hiding the fireplace is the pine dressing table she fixed up, with its carved mirror and modest drawers. On a white lace cloth, like an altar cloth, arranged devotionally are photo frames; the larger to the rear are of her parents and the smaller ones to the front of her children and animals. And in the middle, just as he remembers, in a 1930s Odeon-style frame, there's the picture of him and his old mum, taken when he was three years old. She's behind him, with a hat on, her coat done up, and he's there in socks and shorts and a sleeveless Fair Isle sweater.

He shuffles round between the side of the bed and the dressing table. He sits down on the bed and his greedy fingers reach for it.

Standing to the side of him, she feeds his hands.

His neck buckles under the weight of feeling, and his chin hits his throat. After a minute or two, he wipes his nose with the back of his hand.

'I'll leave you with her then,' says Pearl, going out and pulling the door to.

She stands there a minute, looking over the view across the fields to the orchard and remembers the day the gamekeeper's granddaughter stood facing the house. She has stood there many times, seeing eye to eye with that woman, long gone. She hears the bed creaking and the headboard tapping the wall. She looks through the crack of the door and sees Ken settled onto the bed, feet crossed, contemplating the photo of him as a three-year-old boy, with his mother, nearly seventy-seven years ago.

51

Downstairs, Pearl produces the greatest of all her curios, a bottle of brandy kept for many years under the sink, and in the garden Dave and Nick sip it from mugs and it warms Dave up to telling stories about Pearl's father, their grandfather.

'He was a funny one.'

'People were funny in those days.'

'For his twenty-first birthday, right, he asked his dad for a grandfather clock, dinnie, Mum?'

'He did. It's in the dining room. Still going. I wind it once a week.'

'I mean, you couldn't see Matt asking us for one for his twenty-first, could you, eh, Marina? Eh?'

'No.'

''Ere. Listen to this, girls, right. Mum, Mum, he come round 'ere, didn't he? One Christmas when Gran died. And he sat and never spoke all day and when Dad asked him what was up with him, he said, I never bin the same, Ken, since that Indian doctor stuck his finger up my arsehole.'

'That's right,' says Pearl, spitting crumbs and reddening and chortling and wiping her face with her hand. 'He did.'

'D'you remember, Nick?'

'No.'

'Come on, you must.'

'Was I here? Maybe it was after I left?'

'Course it wasn't. He died when I was thirteen, you were fifteen. Don't you remember?'

Nick looks at Astrid. 'I can't even remember the funeral,' he says.

'Neither can I,' puts in Dave. 'Think it was just something up the crem. He was a character, though, wasn't he, Mum? Your dad.'

But he's lost her; her eyes are unfocused, her face twitches.

'Wann'e, Mum? Old Albert?'

'Better check on your father,' she says, coming to. 'He's been up there ages.'

'I'll go,' says Nick.

'I'll come,' Dave adds, swigging his brandy. 'Just finish this. Won't get a chance to enjoy it when Holy Joe comes downstairs.'

Pearl looks them over as if inspecting them for dirty faces. 'Go on then. He's been in there long enough. But come right back the pair of you, please. Don't *dawdle*.'

'He's probably on the toilet,' says Dave, keen for more easy laughter.

The dog shudders and startles when Nick pushes at the stable door; he sniffs at the garden romantically but dares not move even though Nick's left the back door open for Dave.

The temperature drops by about ten degrees as you round the stairs that divide sitting room from dining room, where the game-keeper's little girl died. Nick looks at the window and thinks of the brothers and sisters arrayed, waving her goodbye. He glances at the sitting room where they all once sat. It's such a small space. He's surprised. With its sofa and armchair (where once there was another sofa) those sitting would be in such proximity as to touch knees or smell breath. The sofa is capacious and slovenly. The throw cushions look like they've been punched, and littered on the sofa is a newspaper, a ransacked box of chocolates and another unlidded chocolate box full of pencils and ballpoint pens. Down the side of the armchair cushion is a torn envelope, and on the back of the envelope is a list in her handwriting, a sort of cop-perplate. In the fireplace there is a wood-burning stove with a mantelpiece above it, crowded and cramped with ornaments and photo frames. There is nothing under fifty years old and no photo-graph under twenty years old. Time stood still here, when they left. Like a brute intruder, there is a great hulking old-fashioned television on a wooden box in the alcove to the left of the fire-place. In the right-hand alcove is a modest set of pine shelves stacked with books on Tudor and Elizabethan times, written in the twenties and thirties, and D. G. Hessayon's complete library of *Expert* guides to hampering, outwitting and killing everything that bedevils the good gardener.

It is truly lovely, he thinks. He looks at the sofa and longs to sit on it, to bring his knees up, as he did as a boy, to stuff his feet into the corner of it, to let his head rest on the arm of it. To smell it. To listen to the hum and snare and buzz and roll of the TV, to have the night lick the windowpanes, and the rain and wind threaten and gasp, and to hunker down further into that smell, that lesser-washed smell, the faint fug of home, of apples, damp and Mum.

Up the stairs he climbs, a hand on the single banister, encouraged by the stalwart ticking of the grandfather clock that reverberates on the parquet floor of the dining room. The landing creaks under his weight. He pauses at the middle window with its view onto the orchard field, remembering when he and Dave cut across there, their long trousers wet to the knees by the time they reached the main road. Dave used to stop and fiddle about, trying to roll his trousers up, and Nick would leave him behind and make his way ahead, heedless of his brother's calls.

He pushes the door to what was his parents' room.

'Dad.'

Ken's lying on the bed, feet up, head on the pillow.

'You're missing it all in here, you know.'

Nick smiles to see him there, mouth open, arms at his sides, and on his chest a photo frame, picture down.

'Dad,' he says again, softly. He catches sight of the dressing table and goes round the end of the bed, and sits. He picks up a small photo frame, its brass stand too weak to hold it well, and sees a teenage photo of himself, sulking, with his head half down, his fringe hiding his eyes. He has the miserly look of Ken, he thinks. He glances over at his father.

Let him have his nap, he thinks. It's so calm and good in here. It's like the nave of a church. And he closes his eyes a moment too and there come to him the smell and feel of the rubbing of a dock leaf on his knee, over the little nettle bumps, the hoot of the wood pigeon, then the sound of his father's car coming up the last of the track, the crackling and splitting noise of gravel and stone and brick and mud, an ominous feeling in his chest, the sharp call of his mother, he and Davie running; running to be first to get to their dad.

This is where I come from, he says to himself. This is who I am.

When they left the house that afternoon to come here, shutting Roy in behind the gate, Ken said, 'That dog of yours, that spaniel, he don't chase rabbits, does he?'

'No, he's only interested in birds.'

'You see, son, you can't change what you are overnight.'

Nick goes to the bedroom window and looks out at the garden. Roy, a spaniel, chases birds. A rabbit can thumb his nose right at him and Roy will run right by him into the bracken, looking for tail feathers. Generations of breeding have made him so. And he and his brother, like Ken, were sons of this land, this corner of England. This land made them, it made the people who made them, and gave them certain interests and manners that you couldn't change in one lifetime.

'Come on then, Dad,' he says, turning round. I suppose this is how he'll look when he's dead, he thinks. 'Come on, Dad.'

The clouds move and the sunlight withdraws. It will soon be evening.

Nick goes over to his father and shakes Ken's arm a little, then more, and brusquely. The arm falls away and hangs over the side of the bed. The expression on the old man's face doesn't change. Then it comes to him: My God, he's not sleeping; he's dead.

5^2

From his early intensive studies, Dave has come to know Nick's every expression and what it means. He meets his brother's eyes and puts his mug down.

Pearl's pouring some of the brandy into her own mug. 'Congratulations!' She raises her mug at her elder son as he comes across the lawn.

The whole scene seems to expand and vacillate like a bubble. The sky stares. The ground gives. He's having déjà vu. He knew it would be like this. He's seen this before. They've always been arranged like that, waiting for him to come and say this. The children are giving the dog a drink from the hosepipe and, yes, that's part of it too. It is all as it should be.

'Something's not right with Dad,' he says, and the bubble pops.

Dave makes his way round the table and comes across the lawn to him. Nick steps backwards into the kitchen to receive him, hidden. He whispers, 'I think he's dead, mate. I thought he was sleeping but he didn't answer and I tried to wake him, but he didn't stir. Then I looked at him and he looked totally different; dead, you know.'

The dog stirs. The top of the stable door squeals and bangs the wall, the latch rattles, the floor receives three thudding steps. The stairs brace and sigh as he comes aboard; Dave goes up them two at a time and the floorboards on the landing protest at the extra-ordinary fuss. Dave shoves the bedroom door farther and harder than it's ever been shoved and it smacks the wall. He falls down on his knees by the side of the bed, in the crack of space along-side the wall. He puts a hand on his father's face, a thumb on his cheek and fingers on his brow. 'Dad,' he says, 'Dad, time to get up now, mate.'

He gives him a little shake by the shoulders with both hands. He picks up the loose wrist that's hanging over the side of the bed, and feels for a pulse with his fingertips. He leans over his father and puts his ear against his chest. He sits back, in a crouch.

'Dad,' he says and puts the pad of his thumb to his father's eye. Just as he's about to pull back the hood of his father's right eye, he hears the snap of glass; he has put his elbow on the photo frame. He picks it up. The glass has a break across it. He looks at the pic-ture, then shows it to Nick. His eyes fall.

'This is how he wanted it, Nick. This was what he wanted,' he says. He takes the loose hand and kisses the back of it. 'This was all he wanted, to be back here.'

Nick goes back over to the window and looks again at the field and brings to mind the path that once ran through it, up the hill in long grass—the way out. He never looked back when he took that short cut. Even though he knew she was standing here, watching them go. And he and his father stood on the brow of the hill on Christmas Day 1986, in the first hour of that day, twenty-two years ago, on their way back to church, and swapped confidences. It was a goodbye and a farewell; they knew each other well enough to know they'd soon be going their own ways. They knew each off by heart. He half expects to see the old man standing there now.

53

Downstairs in the cold dining room, Dave uses his mobile to call Audrey Bury. 'He said, First thing you do is call that Audrey. She'll know what to do.'

The grandfather clock ticks; the dog's nose nudges the stable door. Nick feels inside of him a low growl: Your father is dead. Then Dave begins to speak.

'If you can,' he says.

'We appreciate it,' he says.

'Thanks so much,' he says.

It's in his nature: kindness. Even at a time like this, he's thinking of the other person, Nick marvels.

'No rush, I s'pose, is there? Not being funny.' He closes his phone, runs his hand over his chin. 'Right. That's done, mate. They're on their way. It was a chap. Said he'd call Dad's doctor for us.'

'Well done, mate.'

'The tricky part is going to be telling Mum, Nick. She's not that stable, is she? I mean, who knows how she'll take it.'

'Do you want me to do it?'

'No, no, I'd best do it.'

'Sure?'

'Sure. Come with me, though.'

When they turn to step across into the sitting room, they see their mother is sitting on the sofa there and is bound to have heard them.

'You give Ken an inch and he takes a mile.' She gives Davie a half-smile. He puts out a hand to touch her shoulder, but she looks away and sighs. 'Best bring the others in, duckie. No point in them standing out there worrying.'

The dog counts them in with his wet nose, marking the hand of each as they go through. Pearl sits and looks at the black screen on the television and watches it fill with the reflections of her family as they come in. So many evenings Pearl has sat there without noise or life other than that given to her by the TV, and now this.

The two grandchildren sit on the tiles in front of the fireplace, backs to the wood-burning stove. Dave's over at the window, Nick's by the stairs, and Marina's beside Pearl on the two-seater. Pearl's leg in its cast is stuck out straight into the rug like a tea-spoon on a saucer. Astrid takes Laura on her lap on the armchair.

Dave does the talking, and they each use the cover of it for their own thoughts. Astrid is wondering whether the wedding plans will go ahead. Marina's thinking about June, and that Dave should call her. She's thinking too how her husband was always the elder brother in reality. She looks at Nick and thinks how a face can be handsome and mean nothing to you too. She's thinking how she dislikes him in proportion to how much Dave loves him.

Feeling her eyes upon him, Nick gives her a small perfunctory smile and she returns it because she was brought up to hide her feelings and not be caught out, and also because Dave is her world. But Nick sees the smile die too soon to have been real and looks down at his feet. Shoes. They were never allowed to wear shoes in there. He sees that Dave's in his socks. When did he find time to slip off his shoes? It must have been force of habit. Next to him, at the foot of the stairs, are their Dad's winkle-pickers, a slight brogue effect, highly shined, and the shape of his toe knuckles in the worn leather.

Laura gets up and goes and sits with the other kids on the hearth. 'Have you ever seen anyone dead before?' she asks them quietly.

'No,' says Emily, her face making space for fear.

'I want to see him,' says Matt.

'Everyone's to just stay down here, please,' Dave says, his fat hands bobbing as if to keep evil spirits from rising.

Matt lets his fringe fall over an eye. He wants to see what a dead man looks like. He looks at Laura and thinks she's pretty. He looks at his mother and wonders whether she loves him. He looks at his father and thinks he'll never be like him. They're all fakers, he thinks, adults. Reality is upstairs.

'In a way, though,' Dave's saying, 'I mean, I know it's a funny thing to say, but it's what he'd have wanted . . . right, Nick?'

Nick meets Matt's eyes and thinks about him using the Internet. Marina's son, he thinks, is secretive and sly like his mother.

Marina seized upon his brother, so open and good-natured, and in her, his brother thinks he found a more ordinary mother. For himself, he'd take the rough ways and honest talk of Pearl any day over all that is not said.

He puts a hand on Astrid's shoulder; light and fair and good was how she first appeared to him. Now he knows there's more, and there's dark. She loves him. She'll fight for him. She needs him and he needs her. These are the only things he has to know.

He looks at the stable door where his father stumbled and hit his head and he hit it back, his father—he punched it with his fist. And Nick said, 'It's the truth!' As if the truth were anything real, or anything at all.

'I mean, he more or less said so to us, didn't he, Nick? When we was in Wales. I mean,' Dave looks at Pearl, 'he was just desperate to see you, Mum, and for all of us to be together again. If you think about it, he brought us together, didn't he? He made this happen. He knew he didn't have long.'

Matt lets a tear slide down his far cheek where no one can see it. He shifts on the cold tiles and glances at the ceiling. He'll probably not get to see him at all, ever again. He could ask, but he won't. They'll think he's weird. Emily turns her head sideways and looks at Laura, who's holding her shins with her head on her knees too, as if they're in assembly.

'I couldn't live with him. I couldn't live without him,' Pearl says. 'That's what they say. We loved each other, we hated each other, we could have killed each other. I feel numb, as a matter of fact. I've done my grieving, you see.' She pulls a handkerchief from under the sofa cushion. 'The truth is,' she says, 'I've been happy on my own. The time's gone slower. I've enjoyed it. I've done what I wanted when I wanted. Every day's been magical in its way. I've been free, which I could never have been with him.'

Marina crosses her knee away from Pearl.

Dave winces. 'All right, Mum.'

Astrid does not know what kind of grief there is here. Of all of them in that room, she suspects her Nick is the one in the most trouble. She can feel his hand on her shoulder, his fingertips around the clavicle.

He wants her help, but he can't ask for it. When she leans forward to pull her shoe back onto her heel, his fingers slip and he looks in alarm at her back as if a boat were slipping out of its docks.

'I used to shake when I saw him,' Pearl goes on. She blows her nose. 'But I don't know now if that's what you'd call love.'

She gets up and goes out to the kitchen, closing the stable door, top and bottom. Privy to her next actions in their imaginations only, Dave sees her at the sink, leaning on it, looking out down the garden path as she used to when Ken was due home. Nick sees her kneeling on the floor with the dog, burying her face in the long soft hair at its neck, like a girl. Marina sees her making tea, and Astrid sees her going out to the garden to fetch the brandy bottle and taking a good long draught of it to burn away any love left.

Astrid believes that Pearl loved Ken the way she loves Nick, that Pearl never really thought Ken would go and Ken never really thought he was gone. Nick has never impressed her. He has moved her to compassion, and maternally so; there's some condescension in it. The passion in it has come from the chance to make one another new, from inside out, to swap pieces. Done too fast, it could run to destruction. Pearl and Ken were impatient; Astrid and Nick are patient.

She turns her face into Nick's hand, and kisses his palm. She kisses it hard, for Pearl's sake and for Ken's sake, for each and every love is also our own.

54

'He knew it was his time, Rodge. It was like some sort of animal instinct. This is the place he chose,' Audrey says as they turn up the unmarked track. 'Where are we then, Roger? Where are we now?'

He gives her a shrinking look and colours; he knows from her tone that the punchline is coming.

'Glassenbury?'

'No, Roger. This is his first wife's home. The mother of his children. See? It's like an animal going back to its den.'

This unmade road, all ditches and rocks, is going to give the hearse a lot of gyp, he thinks. We won't take the van, she'd told him. The family's all there; it's got to be the hearse. 'Decorum' was what Ken wanted.

They have slowed down to a creeping pace.

'Christ,' she says, nodding at the suspended wax effigies turning in the headlights. 'It's like voodoo or something.'

'Dolls,' he says.

She touches the hair on the back of his neck. 'Had they called a doctor, did they say, Rodge?'

'No.'

'Oh. So you did, I assume?'

'Assume nothing, you always say.' He gives her an apologetic smile.

She shakes her head and takes out her mobile phone. 'It's like *The Shining* out here, Rodge,' she says, texting and flinching as a Cabbage Patch doll swings into the side mirror, leering at them with a one-toothed idiot grin, his fat fabric gut green with moss. The hearse lurches from side to side and wobbles up the slight incline towards the cottage. She sends the message. 'Ken would have been very pleased with this for an ending.'

Where the track ends, Roger extinguishes the engine. They're in the full rig. They've even got gloves on. After all, as she said to Roger when they got dressed, it's not like she didn't know what the customer wanted.

'This is one of those rare occasions, Roger, in which your customer *is* the deceased, and that makes it special. All of this can be done just as he'd have liked. And paid up in full.' She'd placed one shoe, then the other, on the bed and wiped the toes over with a face flannel. 'There's nothing better than things working out as you planned them. Nothing.'

He'd been doing his tie in the rolling mirror, one knee up against it to stop it rolling.

'Did you see things working out this way?'

'No,' he said and tucked the tie inside his jacket.

She grabbed his lapels when he turned, and kissed him. 'What did you foresee, Roger?'

'Booze.'

She swayed against him. 'And are you happy? Do you feel like you've come home after a long time away? Do you feel loved?'

'Yes,' he said and, because it seemed to be a special occasion for which he had no card, added, 'thank you very much.'

He'd stood before her with his hands in his pockets, lifting his trouser bottoms from his shoes, waiting for his orders. And now he stands doing the same at the back door to the cottage.

'Jesus Bleeding Christ, dog, if I've told you to stay in your bloody bed once, I've told you a hundred times!'

The door opens.

Pearl addresses them curtly, as if they've come to read the meter, 'Come on, come in. He's upstairs.'

Audrey puts her head on one side. 'I'm so sorry for your loss.' Pearl nods.

'He was a lovely man.'

'You didn't know him well then.'

'Yes,' Audrey counters, taken aback, 'I did know him quite well; he was a friend and we did business together, but I knew him latterly when his sister died—'

'Pat.'

'Yes.'

'Will you bloody *be-have*!' Pearl screams, pulling on the choke chain as the dog uses its paw to scratch its collar. 'She was a saint, that woman.'

'She was.'

'If you like that sort of thing. She couldn't 'alf make your life miserable, if she wanted to. Still, we've all got our failings. Talking of which, you'll find him upstairs.'

'Sorry for your loss,' mumbles Roger, passing by.

'That's all right, sunshine,' she says.

Cap clasped to his chest, Roger bobs his head at the company assembled in the front room. Audrey asks if anyone's called the doctor. They shake their heads and look at each other.

'He said to call you first. He thought a lot of you, Mrs Bury,' says the bald son, David, coming forward to offer his hand. 'We're his sons.'

Nick extends his.

'He was a lovely man, your father,' Audrey says again.

'There weren't many like him,' says Dave.

'Thank Christ,' says Pearl. She looks unsteady and flushed. Audrey steps back out of the woman's breath.

'Mum, have you been drinking?' Dave asks her.

Their mother's never been able to hold drink.

'I might have had a little something to settle me!' she says, with a crazy movie-star smile which she directs at the three children on the hearth. Marina suggests the kids all go outside for a while until everything's sorted out.

'That's right, that's right,' says Pearl, 'give this lot some space to bring the old goat down.'

'Is he upstairs?' Audrey asks Dave, touching his arm.

'Oh yes, yes, he is. Just up the stairs and to the right. Help yourself.'

The couple in black go up the stairs, her first with her case, and then the chap with gloves, holding on to the banister as if there's a gale blowing.

Dave turns to look at Nick. 'Christ, did you hear what I just said?'

'Don't. We've got enough trouble here.' Nick nods in their mother's direction.

Pearl's sitting on the arm of the chair, above Astrid, looking over her glasses and trying to fix her eyes on Astrid's, but it's like trying to pin a tail on a donkey. 'I suppose you think he loves you,' she says eventually. 'I thought *he* loved me,' she throws her head to the ceiling. 'More fool me.'

'I know Nick loves me.'

Pearl gives a bitter laugh.

It was the third day Astrid had not put on more than a touch of mascara. She'd not done more than brush her hair, nor worn anything new, and he'd not said a thing. It had occurred to her that morning that it wasn't necessarily that he didn't notice but that it didn't matter. It was possible that when he looked at her, he saw the woman of his imagining just as she saw the man of her dreams. The rest was mere detail.

55

When their three faces pop up at the window, Marina waves the kids off with a brisk wrist. She is standing alongside Dave in the dining room. Because they resist, she taps on the window.

Pearl is leaning against Astrid, staring at her hands and smoothing over the recessed pale band of skin that persists on her wedding finger. 'Somewhere in those woods the ring is.'

Her weight has Astrid pinned.

'You won't find it now.'

'Don't want to find it. That's why I threw it away. I chucked it as far as I could.'

Coming back to sit on the sofa, Marina turns her head emphatically away from Pearl's boast and scans the mantelpiece and counts two photos of Dave and three of Nick. Pearl seems to think women can speak their minds. She never had a mother to teach her; Pearl's mother died from TB and she was brought up by her

father, a smallholder. He was a hothead, by all accounts, an opinionated widower. Pearl had been made in his image. She behaved
like a man, and upset people.

'No, I wasn't afraid to live on my own,' she says, running on
machismo boosted by the brandy. 'I know some people are. *Some*
people can't bear to go five minutes on their own. Some women
latch on to men and that's it. Not you, Astrid.'

'All right, Mum, give it a rest,' says Dave, glancing at Marina.

'I'll speak as I find.'

'Yes, but Mum, we've got our dad up there *dead*, haven't we?
It's not a good time.'

'I've had plenty of time to be quiet. I've had twenty years or
more. I don't know what I was punished for but I was punished
all right. I don't think you've asked me over to your place more
than a handful of times. Not that I'd have gone. No, I'm a bloody
nuisance, I am.'

'Oh, Pearl!' says Marina.

'You don't like me!'

'That's not true. It's just too much gets said. I don't know why
we have to have it. I didn't grow up with that sort of thing. It
upsets me.'

'Upsets you!' Pearl says scornfully. 'You're terrified you'll end
up like me, you are. You think, Let the old witch stay put. You're
afraid of being me.'

Nobody says a word. Pearl may speak her mind, but no one else
will. And it's a mercy, Astrid thinks, because minds change.

She looks behind Pearl's glasses. The glasses magnify her eyes,
but behind them, the eyes are little frightened blinking things.
Women, because they love, she thinks, have to be able to go back

on things, so as not to lose what they love. No matter how Dave wants to dress it up, Ken has died alone.

The stairs shudder and Roger's coming down backwards, as if from a tree house. He stands before them with his mouth open. He remembers to close it. He clears his throat.

'Your father. He's not dead, only sleeping.'

'Thank you,' says Nick, with a formal nod.

'Yes, thank you,' says Dave. 'Do you need a hand to bring the body down now? Because I doubt that my mother is going to want to give the old man a bed for the night, if you catch my drift, and we'd best be moving things along now.'

'He's not dead, your father, only sleeping.'

'All right, mate, that's smashing. Very comforting, thanks, but it's getting dark and we'd best think about getting the kids home. Come on, Nick, let's go and see if we can bring him down between us.'

On the landing Dave turns, with eyebrows raised, to say to Nick, 'Talk about gormless.'

They're at the bedroom door, and tentative, when they hear Audrey saying, 'I think I'll need my aneurism hook.'

Dave throws open the door. The lampshade swings, light ranges around the room, swooning up and down the walls. The funeral director's holding on to their father by his ears, shaking his head.

'What's going on in here?' cries Dave.

The lamp steadies and the room comes to a standstill. Ken blinks and licks his lips. 'All right, boys?'

56

When it turned out that Ken wasn't dead, the undertakers enquired with Astrid for directions to the Michelin-starred restaurant in the village. She took them to the door and hesitated over its proper name for the purpose of directory enquiries. She glanced back at the sitting room, and decided against asking around the room. It was a quiet night, they'd just give it a whirl without a reservation, the undertakers said.

'So, he's not dead at all then,' said Matt, coming into the kitchen, jerking his thumb at the departing undertakers.

'No, love, no. It turns out he was only having a nap.' She raised her eyebrows. With the interval evidently over, the three children resumed their places on the hearth, knees clasped for the rest of the show.

'All right?' said Ken from the sofa, when they came into the front room. 'I tell you what, I feel a bit rough. I dunno whether I didn't have a stroke, or something, up there. I dunno. I can't say.'

'It turns out he's just been having a kip up there!' Dave shouted at the kids as if they were in on it somehow.

'For'y winks; it can't 'ave bin more, son.'

Dave was hopping around like a hobgoblin, going from one foot to the other, while the old man sat on the sofa, mystified and enraptured, kept shaking his head and blowing out.

'Rip Van Bleeding Winkle he is,' said Pearl to the kids, nodding at Ken.

'For'y winks it was,' Ken insisted. 'Thass whaddit felt like anyway.'

'You old sod!' Dave was dark red.

'I come over all funny, di'n' I? Couldn't 'elp it.'

'My arse,' said Pearl, lifting one side of her bottom and poking it with a finger to make it clear to the children what she meant.

''Ere, Astrid,' the old man said with a chortle, reaching across to the armchair and picking at her sleeve, ''ere, Astrid, I bet when Jesus come to life ag'in, he di'n' get this sort of stick, did 'e?'

'Even the dead don't wan' 'im!' Dave was losing it. 'He only had me crying.'

'Thass more than anyone else did,' said Ken. 'I 'spect.'

'You were bloody listening, weren't you?' Dave slapped his own head. 'I tell you what . . . I mean, you just couldn't make it up, could you!'

Marina told him not to hit himself. He said it helped; he said it was helping him think straight.

'You'll give yourself a headache,' she said. 'Try and keep it together, Dave.'

'I'm sick of keeping it together! All I ever done was keep it together when there weren't nothink to keep together.'

'Well, I'm not dead, am I?' said Ken, looking pleased. 'I mean, there is that.'

Dave slapped his forehead again.

Marina told the kids to get their things.

'There's her there!' Dave pointed the sniper of his arm at his mother first. 'Not so much as a kiss 'allo, shouting bloody blue murder at the bloody dog. I mean, that ain't no sort of welcome, is it? And then she's cuddling up with old Golden Boy there, and not seen him in twenty years. And telling us off for not having her round more! I mean, Christ! When she did come round it was all moan, moan, moan, the kids this and that, don't they get on your nerves, and why do we fuss over 'em so much, and weren't they ugly babies, and don't expect too much of them school-wise. . . . Meanwhile I've been subbing her to keep this sodding fantasy of hers running. Self-sufficient! What a joke!' He mimicked putting a phone to his ear. ''Ere, Dave, you wouldn't believe what this plumber fella wants. You couldn't send someone, could you? 'Ere, Dave, this council tax is a shocker. You couldn't pay it, could you? Only it's cheaper when *you* pay it!'

Just back from the dead, Ken was loving every minute of it. He was grinning from ear to ear, and when Dave seemed to hit a high note, he'd whoop, and stamp his feet like he was at a barn dance or a spiritualist church. 'Go on, son, you let it all out! You get it off your chest. You tell 'em!'

'Nothing nice ever comes out of her mouth. But that's a family trait, innit? Apart from when it comes to me. I mean, I've had to keep it buttoned, 'a'n' I? I remember standing here, in the exact same spot I'm standing now, when I was fifteen, saying nothing, not a peep, while they brought the whole pack of cards down, the three of them—'

'Dave,' Nick intervened.

'No, Nick! No. Nick! Nick? Who are you anyway? The prodigal son, she said, didn't she? More like Walter Fucking Mitty. You weren't off eating peapods or husks or whatever, were you? No, mate, you were living it up, and never a second glance behind, while *me*, this here great dope,' he slapped his forehead again, 'the butt of all your jokes since I was born, was giving her a bit of cash and takin' orders from flaming Lazarus 'ere. Yes, you were *so* busy, weren't you! Shagging Eastern Europeans! And him, Lazarus, he's been like a torment to me, he 'as!'

He pointed out their father, who smiled and nodded and shook his head, all modest delight, as if he were hearing an after-dinner speech in his honour.

'The miserable old shit! What's wrong with magnolia, David? No one ever complains about magnolia! Oy, that ain't level, son. You'll have to take that down and start again. And the old chestnut: Nick's done well, innie? D'y'ever 'ear from him then? Wass 'e say then? Where is 'e now then? Yes, too big to call any of us. And us,' he pointed out his wife, 'we've had to take it, we've had to put up with it and, I tell you what, she's even said to me, her, she's said to me, Wouldn't life be easier, Dave, if we could just move away, start up again, someplace . . . ? I nearly broke my back keeping it all together, and for peanuts, out of duty really, and I never did what other blokes do, I never went on benders, I never went with other women, nothing. Take this bin out, Davie. Change that handle, will you, Davie? Why don't we go on holidays, Dad? When I hear my name said, my heart sinks, it does. Honest. Because it's never going to be good, it's not going to be anything *good*. I should have changed my flamin' name an' all. You know, call me sodding Mike, or something.'

Laura mouthed 'Mike' at the other two and made a face and the three of them had to put their hands over their mouths to stop themselves laughing.

He was standing holding his forearms. He let a finger point like a pistol, which he waved at all of them, back and forth.

'Well, I've got some news for you lot. 'Ere, Matt, you can look me up some flights on the Internet next. I want to go on a holiday. I want a break from you lot. A long one. Might not even come back.'

There was not a sound in the room, until Ken leant over onto one side of his body and cracked a knee joint. 'Stiff now,' he said. 'You get stiff after sitting awhile.'

'Dave,' Marina said.

Dave was staring at his sports socks. He made a face. 'You can come with me, if you want,' he said, shrugging and subsiding but not looking at anyone. 'The kids can come an' all. But none of this Dad that and Dad the other. I've had a guts full.'

'I tell you what, i'n' this good, eh? Here we are all together again,' Ken said, rubbing his hands together and smiling around the room. 'Here we are.'

And he turned to Pearl and patted her knee. Then, spotting something, he peered in at her face and, using his knuckle, so softly, he staunched the tear on her cheek and let it wet the back of his hand, and she looked at him as he did, and for a moment their expressions were the same.

57

Astrid was 'taking family time'. She had Katie take over on the front desk at the spa. Ken had come to stay on what, Nick assured her, was a temporary basis for the sake of his health, mental and physical, so she said to Nick she'd take the time off to mind him and plan the wedding at the same time. She ran Ken back and forth from Pearl's on a daily basis, leaving him there after school drop-off and picking him up before she went to get Laura. The arrangement suited; she got Ken off her hands, Pearl got garden help, and Ken was much obliged to the ladies all round, a condition he seemed to have become accustomed to quickly and happily.

'I tell you what, Astrid, I tell you what, I'm a kept man, I am,' he trilled several times a day. 'A'n' I?'

'Yes,' she said, every time.

'A kept man!'

Astrid took to her new role with gusto. She dispensed with the cleaning lady and thereby scuppered that woman's plan for a breast enlargement. She wiped the dust off the furniture with a pair of Nick's underpants. She had a whimsical circulatory system for laundry; it began with Nick's socks found next to the laundry basket, where he left them, which morphed into a single sock on the stairwell, and another behind the washing machine, which would become later a loose sock stuffed in a bag for the charity shop and another in the drawer. She did the ironing in the evening, hanging garments from the wall lamps around the room, while listening to Laura struggle through her homework, or Ken's belligerence on the subject of licensing hours. The impact of an extra inhabitant was far-reaching. It seemed that subconsciously the others were fouling the house to help him feel at home. She took the plates and mugs which they left just next to the dishwasher, but not inside it, and stowed them herself with merely an intake of breath. She picked up snack wrappers from sofas. Lids were left off. Cushions were used for comfort, not decoration, and she had to rescue them from the floor after they'd served their purpose. She would have liked to bring the speed and conviction of the emergency services to all the messes, spills and upsets but she couldn't get to them in time. The fridge shelves were sticky. The clothes in the drawers were creased. The kettle had crumbs in the creases of its spout. There were unassimilated items on floors and tables and the kitchen dresser. And inside bowls, which were for display only, were left combs or screwdrivers (Ken), hairclips (Laura), a Vicks inhaler (Nick), as well as a rusty key, a duff light bulb and a store voucher. So this is how it was: family life.

'I like it messy,' Nick said with a frisson when he came in one night, as if it were something really kinky.

'Because it's like your mother's house.'

'No,' he said, guardedly, 'not because of that.'

She dreaded their help.

To the polite enquiry: 'Can I help you?' came her murmured rejoinder: 'That's the last thing I need.'

When Ken brought his smalls downstairs shyly and demanded the right to wash them in the sink, she denied it to him, so he insisted he place them in the washing machine himself. After that, there were plastic carrier bags, knotted and left in the corner of his room.

He kept himself from under her feet in a very ostentatious way, pacing up and down clearing his throat, or sitting in the front room and coughing out of boredom. It was better when Laura was home. They played cards.

He was intrigued with Laura's comings and goings and doings to the point that he commented incessantly upon them.

''Ere, Astrid, the kid, she's laying daan outside with 'er ear to the ground. Funny, innit? Funny thing to do. Listening to the ground! Wish I could!'

When they went to Pearl's at the weekend, Laura had permission to skip off to the shed and tinker with the wire and beads in there to make earrings, all the while listening on a battery cassette player to Pearl's collection of musicals. Laura favoured *Evita*.

Every time Astrid drove Ken up the track to Pearl's house, she'd slow to gaze at the babes in the wood. Something about their plastic melancholy struck her as metaphorical; little girls petrified in plastic, never to become women. They made her think about the spa. Ken didn't say much on the way up there; he went quiet on the approach. From his side he had a view of the field of high grass. He was spruce and clean with a gift on his lap.

They'd stop on the way over at the farm shop for him to choose his gift. She waited in the car park. The first time, he came back with a box of Maltesers. She shook her head. 'Try again,' she said. He went back in and came back with a box of After Eights and some yellow flowers.

'After Eights?'

'She used to like 'em when we went out,' he said defensively. 'Used to give them to the boys.'

He was a slow learner when it came to romance, but death had much improved him. When she collected him on her way to pick up Laura from school, she'd quiz him on the events of the day.

'Then 'er mood just seemed to change,' he said, crestfallen one evening as they pulled into Laura's school. So Astrid ran through things said and done to try to pinpoint the problem.

'Should I just tell 'er then?' he interrupted irritably.

'Tell her what?'

'You know.'

'That you love her?'

'Don't be daft,' he said and looked out of the window, across the school lawns, a muscle in his cheek going. 'Too old for that caper.'

58

The summer came, as rain and rose petals fell to the ground in big sorry clumps like wet loo roll.

Dave had already called Nick a couple of times from Spain; they were having a good time, he said, but he was keen to get back.

'Because it's not all it's cracked up to be, this luxury holiday lark, right, mate? Right?'

'Just enjoy it, Dave, while you're there. Just relax, mate.'

'Yeah.' He didn't sound comforted. 'You all right?'

'Yup.'

'Dad?'

'He's fine.'

'Mum?'

'Yup.'

'Right.'

'Right.'

'No news then.'

'Nope.'

There was a silence. 'Nick?'

'Yup?'

'We all right, you and me?'

'Yup.'

'After what I said.'

'We're all right, Dave.'

'Right then.'

'Right.'

'Can't wait to get home. Could murder a roast pork. Bye then.'

'Bye.'

Nick hung up. 'Idiot,' he said, shaking his head and going back to the papers on his desk pertaining to Ken's divorce.

'You're under that Astrid's thumb, you are,' his father said to him that evening, when Nick was peeling the potatoes for supper.

'I say, Astrid, women's work, innit?' he called out after her, delighted with his own temerity, and Astrid came in and used the teacloth to whip at his backside and ordered him to get peeling too.

'She's beatin' me up, son!' he said, elbowing Nick, and the old fool broke into his 1950s routine minus the ukulele, shining and wheezing with excitement. 'Oy, Mother, any chance of a cup of tea for the workers? I bin slaving away all day, I 'ave.'

He had been working hard, that was true. Pearl had shown Astrid the fruits of their labours that morning when she dropped off the work detail. Ken had helped her bury the wire fence for the chicken coop in the ground. Her pact with the Devil was not working out. For many months she had served dinner at seven for the foxes and they came from far and wide, males and females, to dine on the lawn on off-cuts Pearl claimed from the butcher's, and in return they'd let her chickens alone. But a week ago, one of her ladies, as she called them, had gone missing. She and Ken had spent the week securing the premises.

They'd stood there, the three of them, by the coop, watching the old biddies pick about, making their tremulous quibbling noises, feathers fluffed up and prudish, and Ken was proud to reel off the name of each one.

'And that's old Edna.'

She was the blind chicken whom the deaf cock liked to give a regular seeing to, Pearl explained, adding with her customary cynicism, 'That's what you call a blessed union.'

Then Pearl bent over to pick up the little blind chicken and put it to her face, put her cheek to its yellow feathers and cradled it under her chin, stroking it and making comforting noises, and she smiled and swayed, like a girl. It was the most stunning transformation, and with the dust clouds of gnats and the haze of the early sunshine and the thick smell of the horse manure on the vegetable compost, Astrid felt quite overcome.

She looked back in the driving mirror at the pair of them, when she drove off. There they were, Pearl and Ken, standing again on the kitchen path some thirty years after they first stood there, in a less than blessed union. Now they stood there, an old man and an old woman, like doting parents, with the blind chicken between them.

59

The tulips had already loosened their stays and now they went right ahead and dropped their drawers, and the garden ran riot in an excitement of colour. The breeze was wet and creamy with the scent of its blooms, and the perfume of the tiny daphne, which Pearl brought as a sprig to Ken to smell, was so beguiling that he kept it in his pocket. When Pearl was out of sight, he sniffed it and said, 'Beau'iful that is, *really* beau'iful.'

They had their mid-afternoon cuppa in the kitchen after Ken had wheelbarrowed the compost to the vegetable garden and spread it with the pitchfork.

'They set a date?' Pearl asked him.

''Oooh?'

'Nick and Astrid. Have they set a date for the nuptials?'

'Well . . .' He prevaricated, as he did when searching his memory for things that were of no immediate concern to him, hoping he'd find a small note someone else had left behind. 'I don't think so. No, tell a lie, I 'eard 'em last night saying they was going to get on with it and do it sharpish. Might as well.' He sniffed, giving half of his biscuit to the dog. He dipped the other half in his tea. 'Reminds me of me and you, you know, how we was once.'

'Get back in your bleeding basket, will you!' Pearl growled at the dog. 'Do you have to bring your filthy ways into my house? Just eat the bloody thing. I don't want a load of mush in the bottom of the cup to wash out, do I? For Christ's sake. You must be making a right nuisance of yourself round their place.'

'They don't mind,' he said faintly.

She let out uproarious laughter.

'They don't!'

She shook her head and sipped her coffee.

'Mind you, it dun 'alf creak, that floor upstairs.'

'Have you ever once in your life stopped to think about other people?' She was judge and jury. 'You haven't, have you? Not once.' He looked discomfited, but didn't deny it.

'Well, I've thought it all through,' she said, wiping the stain underneath his mug. 'You'd best move in here.'

He blinked.

'You might as well be useful somewhere. On a trial basis. In the spare room. We're too old for bunking up.'

'I'll be a nuisance to you, Pearl. I'm not in good 'ealth. I'll be a drain on your ree-sources,' he waffled. 'I'll get on your nerves. I'm no use to anyone.'

'You can carry on helping me round the garden. Can't you?'

The dog looked up at him, his amber eyes full of appeal.

'It's like this.' She tapped the palm of her hand with a pointed finger. 'I'm not doing any cleaning or tidying. Unless I feel like it. That's none of your business. I'll cook when I want and you can have some. You can give me your pension to pay the bills with. You're not to wander off when there's work to be done. I don't want shirking or skiving. I won't have it. I'll do your washing, but don't change your clothes more than once a week. You can take a shower every day, though—I don't want you round here smelling like shit. And don't use all the milk up when you make your tea. Is that agreed?'

'Your rules, Pearl. That's good enough. It's very kind of ya. I'm much obliged, thank you. Just bein' 'ere and bein' with you, that's all I want, Pearl.'

They turned away from each other quickly, she to berate the dog, he to adjust the cuffs of his cardigan.

'Get in your basket, sod you! Do I have to keep telling you? You're driving your mum crazy!'

The dog lifted its nose and gave its 'mum' a woeful look, then donned a noble expression, seeing on the window ledge the cat blinking at his disgrace, and slumped. When he felt her hand caress his head, the dog put his nose in his tail.

60

'What are you doing, Pearl? Pearl, you all right in there?' Ken said, in a querulous voice, outside the downstairs toilet in his vest and underpants, squinting through the crack of the door to the light inside. 'You been in there ages.'

'I'm counting my dwarf beans, if you must know,' came the reply.

'Can't sleep.'

'Well, there's nothing I can do about it!'

'Just felt a bit lonely di'n' I. . . .'

There was the sound of the flush.

She came out of the toilet in her long nightdress with a stern look on her face. 'I told you,' she said, 'how it was going to be. Don't you think you can come here and start upsetting things or changing the rules. A dog has one master.'

'I was wondering if we could watch a bit o' telly, or something.'

He stepped backwards to allow her regal procession. She had in each hand, like orb and sceptre, a colander and the cardboard inner of a loo roll.

'At ten thirty?'

'There'll be something on, Pearl. They have it on all hours these days.'

They went through to the living room. The dog made a break for it, but the hound's black nose was squashed thoroughly back into the kitchen through the last inch of the closing stable door. Pearl switched on the side lamp and brought a humble light to the corner of the room. She sat down on the sofa and thumbed through the Sunday supplement with the TV listings. He perched himself at the other end of the sofa. The grandfather clock ticked. She took her time, now and again licking the edge of her thumb to use it to turn the page.

In their day's work, when they stopped to take a cuppa, they'd have a laugh often as not, the pair of them, at the expense of their boys, just like they used to: D'you 'ear Davie? Still trying to win brownie points with his brother, innie? D'you 'ear the way Nick carries on? Tsar Nicholas! Always was like a member of the royal family, weren't he? Used to ask if he was adopted, dinnie!

He looked at her now in the soft glow from the lamp. He could see the girl she was, the girl who sat in Jepson's acting big, all a-twitch and flutter, with a clever turn of phrase, a right big mouth, and hurt at the slightest offence. And now he was an old man who longed for hot tea and warm wishes in that cold house, who'd got only the day he was standing up in.

But he was done with dying for good.

He told her it today, when he was doing the rhodies for her.

"Ere, Pearl,' he said, putting down the hedge clippers, 'I think I'm finished with that dying business.'

'You keep going till you've got that done,' was all she'd said to that, as she would to any other remarks she might consider senti-mental or clever.

'This looks good,' she said conclusively, prodding the maga-zine, fat of mouth and not to be gainsaid.

'Go on then, Pearl,' he said with girlish encouragement.

She used the remote control, arm like a thunderbolt, just dar-ing the TV not to work. There was a bounce of noise and light that shocked the night. 'I've always wanted to know who took it and who gave it.'

'How do you mean, Pearl?' he asked, sidling across to her, ten-dering the chocolate box that had been on the arm of the sofa. He passed it over for her perusal.

Her fingers wandered over the chocolate box, bouncing and alighting as she felt the chocolates' surfaces, smooth or crenellated.

'You ain't diabetic no more then, Pearl,' he said.

Her shoulders set, her index finger and thumb stopped in a pincer poised over the central chocolate. Then her cheeks bal-looned and her glasses rose on her nose and she gave a small snort which he thought might have been laughter caught short.

'Them gays,' was all she said, popping the chocolate into her mouth.

And Ken was obliged to watch an hour-long American docu-mentary on the subject of homosexual intercourse, sucking on Pearl's cast-offs—for, every few minutes, she'd take one out of her mouth and pass it his way, with an expression of displeasure, announcing 'strawberry' or 'orange' by way of explanation.

"'Cause you don't like the soft'uns, do you, Pearl?' he said, ingratiatingly, now right beside her, close enough to smell her sweet breath.

'I only like the nuts,' she said, her brow grim, eyes narrowing to focus on the collection of rubber sex toys belonging to two Texan men.

On the window ledge, looking in, sat Pearl's black cat, blinking at the curiously variable light of the television, which made the two beings inside appear both solid and immaterial, otherworldly and ethereal, like ghosts or gods.

ACKNOWLEDGMENTS

With thanks to Johanna Leahy Marstrand, my kindest reader, and also to Rebecca Bell, Nita Carder, Niki Handover, Colin Miller of Towners Funeral Directors, John Pearce, Chris Parker and Jo Prescott of Abbey Funeral Directors, Les Shaw, John Weir of NAFD, and Le Meridien Dahab.

Bless you, ladies—Cara Jones and Jenny Lord, Gill Coleridge, and particularly my wonderful editors, Juliet Annan and Rebecca Saletan—for abiding with me!

Friends, thank you.

Marcus, my love, thank you too.

This book is for the family; it's for Jules, Cass and Elsa, for John, for Bette and Iris, for Rob, for Jim and for Denise, and it's dedicated to my mother and father, the two people I've trusted with my life since they gave it to me.

ABOUT THE AUTHOR

Louise Dean is the author of three previous novels: *Becoming Strangers*, which was awarded the Betty Trask Prize in 2004 and was longlisted for the Man Booker Prize for Fiction and the *Guardian* First Book Award, *This Human Season* and *The Idea of Love*. She lives in Kent and has three children.